This Little Girl Had A Little Curl

Written by S. G. Lee

SB

An imprint of *Shillelagh Books*

London, Ontario, Canada

Acknowledgments:

Sincere thanks to Jodi and Sydney, without your constant support and encouragement, this book would not be possible. You are the best friends a writer could have. I dedicate this book to my daughters, my granddaughter, my son-in law and my husband; who have supported my writing endeavours with encouragement and love. Special thanks to my beloved mother in heaven, who taught me dreams, can come true with hard work, perseverance and patience.

Table of Contents

Preface:

This story centres around a little girl who had a little curl and may or may not be rotten or horrid as Wadsworth wrote. Here's is the rhyme From Henry Wadsworth Longfellow himself below. Please read the book and judge for yourself. Frankly I think it wasn't fair in this poem that the little girl was punished for behaving as boys did and the boys were able to behave that way and not be punished. However, the reader may find the little girl in the story is very rotten… or not, let the reader judge.

"There was a little girl,

Who had a little curl,

Right in the middle of her forehead.

When she was good,

2

This Little Girl Had a Little Curl
By S. G. Lee

She was very, very good,

And when she was bad, she was horrid.

One day she went upstairs,

When her parents, unawares,

In the kitchen were occupied with meals,

And she stood upon her head,

In her little trundle-bed,

And then began hooraying with her heels.

Her mother heard the noise,

And she thought it was the boys

A-playing at a combat in the attic;

But when she climbed the stair,

And found Jemima there,

She took and she did spank her most
emphatic.~ **HENRY WADSWORTH**
LONGFELLOW

Chapter 1 - Bad News

Lily awoke happy. She hadn't

sleepwalked last night; she had no disjointed dreams that she couldn't remember. She hadn't felt this way since she was a child. What a wonderful way to wake –up. She stretched and bumped into an arm. Emmett, of course Emmett was there; that is why she'd slept so well. She snuggled into his arms that reached for her, cuddling her close to him.

Closing her eyes again, Lily thought another hour in Emmett's arms sleeping would be wonderful; unfortunately, all that was interrupted when a cell phone rang. She reached for her cell phone, as it rang and she realized she'd missed it yet again, because it had stopped ringing. She looked over at her ancient alarm clock.

Good grief, it was almost noon hour. How could she be waking up so late? The alarm didn't go off. What about Rose and Caleb? Caleb was at Dafydd's she remembered and wasn't coming home until tomorrow. Rose had stayed overnight, at Grandma Katha's and Grandpa Terrence's. Grandma Katha, Grandpa Terrence and Rose had said yesterday, that would be taking a driving trip to celebrate the start of summer by the calendar. They'd be gone for the day until at least suppertime. Rose had a half-day, because she was supposed to be studying for exams next week; but Rose was prepared so that shouldn't be a problem.

In fact, one of her teachers said that Rose would probably be exempted in most of her exams and they'd let Rose know by the end of the week. They'd probably visit some roadside farmer stalls and

bring back some delicious pies and cakes
and of course some fresh food and
vegetables.

Lily blushed at the memory of the real
reason why, she was waking up so late.
The phone rang again and she realized it
wasn't her phone, but Emmett's home
phone; she'd been ignoring.

"Emmett your phone is ringing," Lily said
prodding him and handing him the phone
from the bedside table.

Emmett sleepily answered, "Hello?"

"Will you accept a collect call from…,"
Emmett heard the operator say and then a
small child's voice said, "Dianna's
daughter, Deirdre."

Emmett overwhelmed with emotion
shook his head in disbelief and Lily

wondered if this was a crank call. Dianna was missing, presumed dead, wasn't she?

Emmett quickly declared, "Yes, I will accept a collect call from Diana's daughter, Deirdre."

"Unca Emwettt? This is Deirdre. We need you. You hafta come here to me!" The little voice demanded and then she said, "Hush brudder, the bad man will hear you."

Emmett then heard a baby cry in the background.

"Deirdre, your name is Deirdre? What bad man? Where are you?" asked Emmett hoping he was hearing right; but also scared that he this situation wasn't good. He realized that he was dealing with a child possibly very young. This wasn't a crank call.

"Where's mommy, can you put her on the phone?"

This Little Girl Had a Little Curl
By S. G. Lee

"Unca Emwettt, you have to come, mommy's hurt. The bad mens come and they shot fadder and then they shot mommy like that deer that fadder… shot last fall," Deirdre stated her voice laden with tears.

"Where are you?" asked Emmett

"Silly, we live in the province of British Columbia that's in the country of Canada, mommy says."

"Do you know exactly where you are?"

"I is in the closet with brudder," Deirdre answered.

"Brudder?" Emmett asked trying to understand.

"My brudder, Jacob."

"Are the bad men still in the house?" asked Emmett

"I don't want to look they might shoot us too." Deirdre said.

This Little Girl Had a Little Curl
By S. G. Lee

"Could you wait on the phone for a second Deirdre?" Emmett asked.

"You won't go away?"

"No, pumpkin, I'll be here. I'm just getting you some help."

"Okay, but don't hang –up. I'm so scared."

"Did you hear any of that Lily? She called me her uncle. The little girl said she's Dianna's daughter, Deirdre," Emmett said amazed.

"Are you sure someone is not tricking you?"

"No, it's real, I know the difference. Maybe I'll find my sister again, too."

"What should I do?"

"Call 911 and tell them that Deirdre says she's in British Columbia. I'll try to find out where exactly in British Columbia. We can get her some help, and maybe I can save Dianna too," Emmett whispered, covering the phone so Deirdre didn't hear.

"Are youse still there Unca Emwett? I'm really scared," Deirdre asked.

"I'm here, Deirdre. How big is the closet?" asked Emmett

"The closet is really big, Unca Emwett. We are hidin' in the secret room at the back. I don't think they will find us. Mommy said hide there, it's safe." "Mommy should have hidden with us. Do you think Mommy's okay?"

"I hope so. We will get mommy some help too."

"Mommy said if I was really scared use the phone she put in here and call the op…er…operator. She said nobody but her knows about this phone. Ask the person… to make a long distance collect call to Emmett Rogers, Happy Valley, Ontarreeo. I did and you'll help now, right?" Deirdre begged.

This Little Girl Had a Little Curl
By S. G. Lee

"I'll help Deirdre. Where are you? What city? Do you know?" Emmett demanded.

"Mommy said repeat after me. We live in Heavenly, British Columbia 15679 Fern Road. It a camp there, small home, third one on left, near da woods. See, I memered all of it," Deirdre parroted proudly.

"That's really good, honey," Emmett said and then repeated the address to Lily.

"Yes, sir, the address is 15679 Fern Road in Heavenly, British Columbia. It is the camp there, the small home, the third one on the left. It is near woods, that's what the little girl, Deirdre told her uncle," Lily said into her cell phone.

"Thank-you, Lily." Emmett said, "Now tell the police officers to go to the closet in the master bedroom and say this nursery rhyme: *"There was a little girl who had a little curl right in the middle of her forehead and when she was good,*

This Little Girl Had a Little Curl
By S. G. Lee

***she was very, very good; but when she
was bad, she was rotten,"*** Emmett stated.

Speaking into his home phone he said,
"You did good Deirdre. You and Jacob
stay in that closet room, until you hear a
voice say to you at the hidden door,
***"There was a little girl who had a little
curl right in the middle of a forehead
and when she was good, she was very,
very, good and when she was ..."***

"***Bad, she was rotten***! Mommy said that
all the time she said you used to tease her
with it. Mommy said I look just like her,"
Deirdre exclaimed.

"Really? Then you must be very pretty.
Now how old are you, Deirdre?" asked
Emmett.

"I'm four, but I'll be five soon. I'm really
very big," Deirdre replied.

"How old is Jacob?" Emmett asked
worrying sick about his niece and
nephew.

This Little Girl Had a Little Curl
By S. G. Lee

"Jacob is not that old. He was my Christmas present," Deirdre stated.

"Last Christmas, Jacob was your Christmas present? Or the Christmas before?" Emmett asked.

"It was last Christmas, silly Unca Emwett! Becky made the turkey, so mama could rest. She was sick," Deirdre stated.

"This past Christmas, your mother had your baby brother? Jacob is almost six months old? Who is Becky?" asked Emmett.

"Becky is my sister, silly. She's bosseee, that's what Joseph says all the time," Deirdre answered.

"How old is Rebecca? And who's Joseph?"

"Youse really silly, Unca Emwett. Rebecca and Joseph are twins. They are twelve. They are my brudder and sister. Mama had some brudders and sisters after them, before me, but they all died," Deirdre said exasperated.

"Where are Rebecca and Joseph?" Emmett demanded.

"There are more children?" Lily asked, but Emmett waved her off.

"Rebecca and Joseph are at school. It's Monday. I go in da afternoon; but mama said I didn't have to go today. Then the bad mens come and scare mama and she said go hide…"

"The Royal Canadian Mounted Police are on their way, Emmett. They should be there within the half hour." Lily stated, "Keep her talking so she isn't scared."

"What is your daddy's name?" Emmett enquired.

"Brother Parsons."

"What do other people call your Mommy?" Emmett asked.

This Little Girl Had a Little Curl
By S. G. Lee

"Sister Dianna, silly," Deirdre stated "I hear a noise that sounded like this, whoop, whoop, whoop!"

"That could be the police coming. Please, just wait there, until you hear the rhyme," Emmett stated.

"Daddy said the powleese is all bad mans; but mommy said that wasn't true. We were at the library and mama showed me a paper at the library and how you helped other people. I want you, not these powleese. I thought youse was coming not powleese. I thought you'd say *'she was rotten',* not somebody who was stranger powleese," Deirdre reproached.

"I promise you on my word as your uncle, that you can trust these people, honey; as long as they say the rhyme," Emmett stated.

"But I want you!!" Deirdre sobbed.

"I'm really faraway, baby doll. As soon as they get you and your brother safe, I'll take a plane and get to you and we'll get your sister and brother from school."

"Youse promise, Unca Emwettt? You'll come here, really fast?" Deirdre begged.

"I promise Deirdre, I'm coming to help you, just like mommy said; but I have to take a plane to get there; so, it will take a little while. You be a good girl, until I can get there," Emmett insisted.

"Good, because I'm weally scared," Deirdre responded.

"Hang in there, baby doll. It's going to be okay."

"I like it when you call me baby doll, that's what mommy calls me too."

In the background Emmett heard someone say, *"There was a little girl who had a little curl right in the middle of her forehead and when she was good, she was very, very good but when she was bad, she was rotten."*

This Little Girl Had a Little Curl
By S. G. Lee

The phone was then picked up and a voice asked, "Is this Sergeant Detective Rogers?"

"It is," Emmett answered.

"This is Detective Inspector Georges with the RCMP, your niece is safe. The baby Deirdre was talking about it's a doll; it cries like a real baby. I think there may be more to the story there; but I'm not sure what it is yet. Will you be making your way here now?" Inspector Georges asked.

"Yes, sir!" Emmett responded, "Have you found my other niece, Rebecca and my nephew, Joseph? Deirdre said they are twelve years old and at school down the road there."

"Excuse me a second. Deirdre, you go with the nice policeman right there and he'll take you to a place you can wait for your uncle."

This Little Girl Had a Little Curl
By S. G. Lee

"Is it okay to go with this policeman Unca Emwettt?" Deirdre shouted obviously taking the phone.

"Yes, sweetie. I'll be there soon. Now let me talk to the nice policeman."

"Kay. I'll go with him, but come fast you pwomised."

"I will sweetie."

A second later Emmett heard a slight rustle and then Inspector Georges was back on the phone and stated, "I don't know how else to tell you this Rogers; there has been a mass murder here. We'll try to keep Deirdre from seeing any of this; but she knows something has happened and may see more than she should."

The cop then hesitated here and took a huge breath before continuing, "Sorry, that there's nothing, but bad news about any of this. Being a cop like myself I think you can handle it. So, I'm going to

This Little Girl Had a Little Curl
By S. G. Lee

tell you it like it is… your sister is
hanging on barely to her life, but hurry. I
don't know if she will survive."

"Oh my God no…," Emmett muttered
and Lily hugged his arm knowing
something bad had happened.

"All the other bodies we have found are
just that bodies… they are all dead."

"The other bodies? How many?"

"The whole town is gone. It is likely that
your niece and nephew are one of the
victims in the schoolhouse. We will have
to identify the bodies, before we can
determine their identities."

"Oh, lord!" Emmett said, as Lily
overheard and covered her mouth in
horror.

"I'll be there as soon as possible; but I do
live in Ontario, so I'm a few hours away
by plane. I also have to secure the next
flight. Where should I meet you?"
Emmett asked.

This Little Girl Had a Little Curl
By S. G. Lee

"We'll see you at R.C.M.P. headquarters at Revelstoke, until then the child protection agency will take care of your niece," Inspector Georges replied.

"Thank-you please take care of my niece and tell my sister even if she can't hear you that I'm coming."

"I'm sorry Rogers; but I'll make sure your sister and your niece is well cared for until you arrive."

"See you soon," Emmett said and hung up the phone.

Emmett dialled Caleb's cell phone by memory no answer. Where was that kid? Why wasn't he answering. He looked at the time. Of course, he was at school. Caleb probably turned off his phone in class as per his teacher's instructions; but where did that leave Emmett?

He needed to reach Caleb. Maybe he should call the school? No, that would make Caleb mad and the kid was mad enough as it was his grief was making him angry and combative at times. He should probably get Caleb into some grief counselling it seemed to have done Rose and Carol some good.

~0~

Chapter 2 - Parting is such sweet sorrow

"**E**mmett you need to leave now!"

Lily insisted.

"What about Caleb? I can't get a hold of him. He's still grieving for his mother. I can't just leave him, can I? He should be coming with me," Emmett said guilty.

"I'll help with Caleb. I'll explain all of this to him. He is welcome to stay here with Rose and me. If he wishes, he can stay part time with Dafydd too," Lily reassured.

"I wish you could come with me," Emmett begged.

"So, do I; but I can't leave my job right now. I've taken off so much time the last year that my job could be in jeopardy," Lily explained.

"I just wish you could come."

"I would, if I could..."

"I need to make arrangements with the airlines to get there."

Lily picked up her cell phone and began dialing.

"Who are you calling?" Emmett asked surprised.

"Hello, Grandpa Terrence? Can you do me a favour? Emmett needs to go to British Columbia and he needs someone with him that knows the law. Emmett's sister has been found. Uh, huh, the one that went missing. She's been shot. No, we don't know exactly what happened; but she has three children. Two of them are missing... presumed dead. Her daughter needs Emmett. No, I told you Grandpa Terrence; we don't know what happened, or what has happened to her over the years; but that's what Emmett has to find out." Lily explained on the phone, "You are up to it and you will? Oh, thank you, Grandpa Terrence. Emmett will need all the help he can get and I can't leave. Okay. Bye now, see you in ten minutes."

"Ten minutes? The man can be ready in ten minutes? It takes me ten minutes to find my keys, some days," Emmett said stunned.

"He said he's getting some clothes already packed, and he was throwing some stuff suitable for an airplane trip into a bag," Lily answered.

"He knows about the restrictions; doesn't he? You can't bring certain things on a plane," Emmett replied distracted.

"Emmett, we were on a plane at Christmas, the man knows," Lily answered.

This Little Girl Had a Little Curl
By S. G. Lee

"I can't believe I finally find my sister
and then they say she's going to die,"
Emmett bemoaned, as he frantically tried
to book airplane tickets online.

"I'm so sorry Emmett. I know how hard
this is for you. I can't imagine the
emotions you must be going through; but
that little girl Deirdre needs you." Lily
said, "Now did you get a seat on the next
plane?"

"No, and I have to find two seats. Oh my
God! I didn't tell my sisters."

Emmett then covered his mouth and
looked ashen.

"How am I going to tell them? I have to
call my sisters Suzy and Paula. I suppose
I should tell Paula's husband, too. Oh,
damn; I forgot. Jason was deployed to
Afghanistan last week."

"Afghanistan? Oh, that's scary. How is Paula taking that? Where does Paula live, anyway? You told me; but I forgot," Lily asked.

"She was living in Borden, Ontario; but they just moved to London, Ontario. Her husband ,Jason Spriet is a career soldier. He was deployed to Afghanistan. They've got two sons. Austin is fourteen years old; their son Greg is eighteen, or is nineteen? Paula is pregnant now again, with a baby girl. A surprise baby; obviously and she's due in September." Emmett answered.

"Obviously? You really should comment on that Emmett. People are blessed with children, some unplanned. You know you hardly ever talk about Paula. I know I've talked to her a few times over the phone and met her once at Suzy's baby shower; but you hardly ever mention Paula, why is that?" Lily asked.

"Paula married Jason, when she was eighteen years old, simply because she was pregnant with Greg. I didn't want them to get married."

"Paula must have loved him, or they wouldn't have married, so, you don't like Jason," Lily guessed.

"Jason is a bit of an ass, to put it bluntly. He really isn't there for my sister. All he cares about is his army games and his career in the army. He doesn't care about how any of this affects Paula and his kids. Paula doesn't talk to me a lot, because of him. I also suspect Jason's a closet wife beater, and if I could prove it, I'd lay charges against the bastard," Emmett replied angrily.

"He sounds like a piece of work."

"Paula is damaged; she thinks it's normal behaviour in a man, because of my dad. My Dad was a hard man, a real disciplinarian, but I think he was hardest on my sisters. He threw Paula out of the house, when he found out she was pregnant. At the time that happened I had a small apartment and was about to stat working as a patrol officer and I offered her a home; but she refused and moved in with Jason. Then they married," Emmett explained.

"Oh, Emmett, I'm so sorry that your father was like that."

"He really was a good father, at times. I think he had undiagnosed mental health issues," Emmett added defending his father.

"Do your think your dad threw Dianna out; that maybe she was pregnant, too? Then Dianna picked someone out who was a bigger problem than your dad?" Lily asked.

"Maybe, I don't know. I just know Dad and Dianna were always clashing heads," Emmett explained rubbing his hand, through his dark brown hair.

"Maybe she'll be able to fill you in," Lily stated going over and hugging Emmett.

This Little Girl Had a Little Curl
By S. G. Lee

"Hopefully she'll have time to fill me in. She has along recovery… if she lives, but either way someone's going to have to look after those children. How am I going to look after five-year-old and two twelve-year olds?"

"We'll manage. Emmett and Grandpa Terrence will make sure you get custody; if the worst happens. That's the main thing, but we can take it one day at a time until then."

The doorbell rang and Emmett ran to answer it; letting in Terrence.

"Are you ready to go Emmett?" Terrence asked.

"I haven't been able to book our tickets online. Lily's internet service is spotty," Emmett complained holding a laptop in his hands and looking frazzled.

"Sorry, Emmett, I'm switching to a new provider this week; although that won't help you right now.

"Not to worry, Emmett, it's already done," Terrence explained

"How?" Asked Emmett surprised.

"Simply one-word Grandma Katha. That woman is a whiz on the computer," Terrence bragged.

"That she is Grandpa Terrence. I've never had anyone get things done so fast in any medium," Lily agreed.

"I've also filled a temporary guardianship for Lily to look after Caleb's interests, so Caleb will be fine, Emmett."

"Thank-you so much Terrence. I would never have thought of that and what would have happened if Lily needed that?"

"He'll be just fine. Now this just covers any contingency; until you get back," Terrence told Emmett, then turning to

This Little Girl Had a Little Curl
By S. G. Lee

Lily he said, "Don't you worry; I'll take care of our boy. See you soon, Lily."

"Goodbye, Emmett. I love you. Call me when you get everything settled," Lily said kissing Emmett passionately.

"Wow, with a kiss like that I'll be back. I love you too, Lily," Emmett replied then left with Terrence.

Lily watched them get into a cab to go to the airport and prayed that everything would work out okay. She prayed that Dianna would live, not only because Emmett loved her; but because three more children would really be a stress on their relationship. She wasn't sure she was ready to be mom to that many more children, not when she was keeping such a big secret from Emmett. Maybe it wasn't a secret, maybe she was wrong to keep her own counsel, but she'd had to know for sure because right now Emmett had enough on his plate.

~0~

Chapter 3 – Maybe Baby

Lily closed the front door and raced

to the bathroom taking out the item. Taking it out quickly, before she could change her mind, she waited for the symbol to show, plus, or minus. Had it only been a half-hour; since Emmett left? It seemed much longer, as she'd already left the house, gone to the Tim Horton's to buy coffee, and discretely bought the pregnancy test at the drug store, next door to it.

Later this afternoon, she had an appointment with her doctor. Lily had been feeling sick and light headed; but it hadn't occurred to her, (until Emmett was talking on the phone to his niece) that it might be symptoms of pregnancy. Did she want to know?

Yes, she was sure, that she wanted to know now. She stared at the test. She was pregnant, there was a positive sign. Was this good, or bad? Emmett might be bringing back a six-year-old, and two twelve-year olds and in six, or was it seven months , that there would be another child? Could they handle five kids, with Caleb and Rose and a baby? She'd have to hire a nanny just to handle work and the six kids. Even with the year off that she could take with the employment regulations (to be with her baby), it wouldn't be easy.

Marriage and a new baby, but maybe she was getting ahead of herself? Just because she thought two parents should be married would Emmett? The fact was she and Emmett hadn't talked about permanency, let alone a baby. Emmett had said he was moving in, but he hadn't said anything about marriage again. Did he still want to marry her? If she told him about the baby would he just marry her because she was pregnant? Did she really want Emmett to feel obligated to marry her? What bad timing for all of this? How could she even think that way? Lily thought. His sister, his beloved sister who had been missing had been found, but she was at death's door and all Lily was thinking of was herself? What kind of person did that make Lily?

She should have found a way to get time off and go with Emmett. He needed her, and she felt like she was letting him down. She'd keep the pregnancy to herself. She needed confirmation from the doctor anyway, but even then, she couldn't be more than three months; they had six more months; telling Emmett could wait a little longer. Caleb needed someone too and she'd promised Emmett she'd look after him. Lily had enough to do right now. Baby talk would wait.

Caleb's mother, Sherry-Anne had been brutally murdered and the killer still hadn't been found. Sherry-Anne had fought hard enough to live so, that little Daniel had survived. Caleb's little brother was doing well, they had even been able to bring him home from the hospital.

Dafydd was deliriously happy to have his son, Daniel home; but he kept asking why the culprit hadn't been found. If it had been a robbery very little had been taken, at least that's what the police investigating the crime had told Emmett even though they weren't suppose to share information. Maybe the actual killing had been an accident? Was Sherry-Anne just in the wrong place and the wrong time? No, that didn't explain the fingerprints.

The evidence said either a woman, or a man with small hands had pushed Sherry-Anne down the stairs. Lily was just glad they'd been able to prove that it wasn't Lily that pushed Sherry-Anne down the stairs.

Emmett had tried to solve the case, but he'd gotten reprimanded for working on a case he too much interest in. Six months had passed, and the worst part of it was the police were almost ready to have the case declared a cold case.

Lily wished they would find the culprit, so she could prosecute them to the fullest extent of the law. In the meantime, Lily had Caleb to think of. Now that he wasn't as focused on helping his little brother Daniel survive his grief, the death of his mother was starting to hit him. Emmett had tried to get him to go to a counsellor; but so far Caleb had resisted. Caleb was so angry so much so that Lily had made an appointment with a psychiatrist for him. Doctor Frobisher had an opening at 2 p. m .

Lily was sincerely worried that he was going to get himself into trouble. Lily heard the home phone ring, and she realized it was almost noon. It was longer than a half hour since Emmett left where had the time gone? Lily had somehow stumbled absentmindedly into the kitchen and still hadn't eaten. Lily would have to go get Caleb soon and drive him home then to his appointment ,where she hoped he would go, wouldn't argue but go willingly. A soon to be step-mom could dream, couldn't she?

"Can I speak to Emmett Rogers please?" The voice asked on the phone as Lily answered it.

"I'm sorry he's not available. He's out of town," Lily replied.

"I'm afraid I urgently need to speak to the legal guardian of Caleb Rogers!" insisted the voice on the phone.

"I'm his step-mother," Lily lied.

Why had she lied? Thought Lily. Terrence had given her temporary guardianship papers that would probably have been enough to talk to this principal. Somehow that had just tumbled out of her mouth. Oh well, it wasn't really a lie; she reasoned she soon would be his step-mother if all went well.

"This is Ms. Christina Lovett, the principal at Trudeau High School." Christina explained.

"And ….?" Lily asked.

"I'm sorry to say; we have had to suspend Caleb from school for fighting. Normally we would also call the police."

"Oh, no."

"Given the minor infraction and that Caleb great record at the school, added to his suffering from the loss of his mother; we are inclined to give him leniency."

"Thank –you we appreciate that. You said Caleb hit someone. Is he okay? Are they okay?" Lily asked shocked.

"He seems fine, physically; but we must speak in person, Mrs. Rogers about this matter."

"What do you want to talk about?"

"We can speak more when you arrive; but right now, as I said Caleb is looking at a suspension," Christina Lovett said sadly.

"I'll be there within the half hour," Lily announced.

Lily arrived at the school a half an hour later. She felt slightly nauseated and worried that she might be late for her doctor's appointment and Caleb might be late for his. If she hurried, she could handle this and just make it. She could drop Caleb at Dr. Frobisher office; so he could get the help he needed. He couldn't go on this way. He needed to talk to someone about his anger issues stemming from his mother's death. She hoped he would go of his own volition and that he wouldn't be too angry about his father leaving.

Emmett had tried to call him, before he went to the airport; but Caleb was already at school with his phone off. He didn't even know that Emmett had left. How would he feel to find out his cousin/cousins were possibly moving in with him? Lily had promised Emmett that she would explain. Did he even know Dianna existed? Lily went over the scenarios in her mind of how to explain this to Caleb without alarming him, but there wasn't an easy way to tell him his long-lost aunt was dying and that his cousins were missing.

How did she explain this to Caleb so he also didn't feel abandoned? Caleb needed his dad too!

Lily opened the door of the school office and announced herself to the administrative assistant.

"I'm Lily Rogers." Lily said keeping up the ruse, "I'm Caleb's step-mother."

"I'll let the principal know you're here. They are waiting for you in the office," the administrative assistant replied.

"Principal Lovett will see you, now," the assistant said after coming back from the other office. The administrative assistant then took her through to the principal's office.

Caleb stood up and said in surprise, "Lily, what are you doing here? I thought they called Dad."

"We will discuss that when we are finished here. For now, sit down and let me handle this," Lily said quietly and firmly.

"I'm sorry, Lily. I'm so sorry!" Caleb said hugging her and crying, "Please don't tell my Dad. He'll kill me."

"It's going to get better, Caleb," Lily said.

"I'm Principal Christina Lovett. We are very alarmed at what Caleb has done today."

"I'd like to know exactly what happened here today."

"Caleb shoved another boy and then punched him, placing him in a locker. Then he closed and locked it," Christina Lovett exclaimed.

This Little Girl Had a Little Curl
By S. G. Lee

"Caleb! You didn't!" Lily cried.

"It's not as bad as it seems. Larry was a jerk and had harassed some people. I called him on it and he decided to hassle me."

"I'm sure there's some more to the story, but Caleb refuses to share with my administration. We need to discuss this kind of behaviour and address it, so it never happens again."

"Can I talk to Lily alone for a moment?" Caleb begged.

"I'll give you five minutes, then," Carol announced leaving the office.

"If my Dad loves me, where is he?"

"He had some news today stunning news that required him to…," Lily began before being interrupted.

"Everything and everyone will take precedence over me. Mom was always there for me, and now she is not there. It hurts so damn bad," Caleb exclaimed crying.

"I know it's hard now, honey. I'm not your mother and I never will be; but I want to be your friend and an adult you can talk to and I can explain about your father's absence."

"I'm in a lot of trouble, Lily. I hit someone and shoved them into a locker." You heard Ms. Lovett; Caleb explained.

"Who did you hit? And why did you hit them?"

"I hit Larry Harrow. He said I didn't have a family anymore. My mom was dead and my Dad had moved on, and soon my step-dad would move on too," Caleb replied.

"You know that's not true, don't you? Was there more to it?" Lily demanded.

"He said my Dad was hanging out with that black widow slut, Lily Kelly and that she'll cause my Dad to be killed like all her other husbands," Caleb admitted.

This Little Girl Had a Little Curl
By S. G. Lee

"Is that all he said?" Lily asked shocked, but hiding it.

"No, he said he was going to go after Rose and bag that little hottie," Caleb replied blushing.

"What a nasty piece of work he is." Lily replied horrified, "You have to tell them what he said. He should get suspended as well. Besides that, he threatened Rose."

"I can't be a snitch and he won't lay a hand on Rose. That son of bitch is scared of me now."

"Caleb, he shouldn't go unpunished, and you shouldn't swear," Lily persisted.

"Sorry, about the swearing. But drop it Lily. I'm not going to tell them."

"I could tell them."

"But you won't! I'll take my punishment and even go to this shrink. I won't let him hurt Rose. Now tell me what's up with Dad."

This Little Girl Had a Little Curl
By S. G. Lee

"Did your Dad ever talk to you about his older sister, Dianna?" Lily asked.

"Yes, she's the one that went missing right? Wait a minute, did they find her body? Oh shit, sorry, I promised not to swear. Was she one of those in the wall of the Beyer building? Poor dad."

"No, they identified all of those women they found. Dianna was found in British Columbia. She was the victim of a crime," Lily explained.

"Aunt Dianna was murdered in British Columbia?" asked Caleb sadly.

"She's alive, barely. I don't know all the details just yet. It seems she was living in some kind of religious commune, or something and someone shot everyone there, everyone that is except her daughter Deirdre, who is five years old, her other two children are missing presumed dead," Lily explained.

"What! That's crazy! But you're saying Aunt Dianna is alive?" Caleb asked stunned.

"For now; but the doctors don't think she's going to make it."

"Oh no, like I said poor, Dad."

"There's more to it," Lily continued.

"What more? Oh, yah her daughter, my new cousin Deidre. Who is going to look after her? Oh, for Pete's sake, of course my dad! Dad's going to… he's gone to say goodbye to Aunt Dianna, hasn't he? He's going to bring the kid home, so we can play some more happy families. Why didn't he take me?" Caleb cried bitterly.

"He tried to call you, but you were at school."

"Sometimes it seems like everything, and everyone comes before me, when it comes to dad."

"That's not fair. Deirdre was all alone in the middle of a tragedy and she's only four. You know we are all there for you, Caleb, Your Dad trusted me to be there for you. So, can you trust me too? A parent can love more than one child and if Deirdre needs someone then your father will step up and still find time for you, too. We both will."

"Fine, I trust you Lily. Let's get this over then. Do you think they'll kick me out of school? How can I explain this to dad? He'll hate me," Caleb asked hanging his head like a hound dog.

"Not if I can help it," Lily promised.

"Thanks, Lily."

The principal knocked on the door then walked in.

"I want to apoligize for my behaviour today Mrs. Lovett. It was out of character and won't happen again," Caleb stated immediately.

"I trust that it won't Mr. Rogers." Ms. Lovett replied then turning to Lily she said "As long as Caleb gets help for his anger issues with our psychologist, we are prepared to only give him a week's suspension from school."

"I've made an appointment for him with an eminent psychiatrist. He'll see his own doctor," Lily replied.

"What? I didn't agree to that Lily," Caleb protested.

"Caleb, I love you. Your father loves you. We both love you enough to want you to get some help, to deal with these difficult times and situations you are going through. I've been to one. it's not a weakness; but a strength to ask for help to deal with grief," Lily said turning to Caleb.

"I'll go, but I don't have to like it."

"Then Mr. Rogers, I hope you use your week's suspension wisely. Just realize Mr. Rogers that I'm giving you a break. I don't want to see you in my office ever again, understand?"

This Little Girl Had a Little Curl
By S. G. Lee

"Ms. Lovett, you won't see me in this office again," Caleb stated politely agreeing.

Lily just wished he was able to tell Ms. Lovett what the other child had done. Larry Harrow might try this on another girl who didn't have someone like Caleb in her corner.

Both Lily and Caleb breathed a sigh of relief however, as they left, thankful that Caleb wasn't removed permanently from the school. After getting in and both of them buckling up, Lily drove them to their appointments. Lily dropped Caleb at Doctor Frobisher and told Caleb she'd be back in an hour hoping that the session with Doctor Frobisher would work out and help Caleb. Then she sent to her appointment and hoped it wouldn't go past the hour.

~0~

Chapter 4 – Revelations

Emmett gripped the seat as the plane

landed. Beautiful British Columbia, Emmett remembered the motto of this province, with its majestic mountains and beautiful trees and fields. However, he wasn't here to enjoy nature; he reminded himself. Like, he really needed one to be reminded. He'd always wondered was Dianna okay, or if she'd been murdered. Now his beloved sister was found alive; but for how long? What had she been doing all this time? Why didn't she contact him or his parents when they were alive? Did family only matter when she needed someone to take care of her daughter? No, he would think that way.

This Little Girl Had A Little Curl
By S. G. Lee

Dianna was his sister. Someone had kept her from them; that was the only answer.

Dianna had loved Emmett and he had worshiped her like a younger brother did; showing that love by tormenting her with frog and snakes; but Dianna had only smiled and encouraged his love of science and creatures by buying him a terrarium with money she made working at a fast-food store. This was the same sister who had babysat him when he was young. The same sister, he had spied on when she was dating, just to irritate her. Dianna had then turned around and spent her allowance on candy that she shared with him. Dianna saved to buy him something special for his birthday the year she disappeared.

Emmett had wanted a He-Man and Dianna had bought the Castle Grayskull, He-Man and Skeletor. Emmett had been overjoyed. He never thought he would have any of those toys. His father had said he would never buy those trashy,

This Little Girl Had A Little Curl
By S. G. Lee

gimmicky toys. Emmett still had those toys in a box somewhere; maybe he should break them out for Deirdre? Did five-year-old girls play with those kinds of toys?

Dianna seemed so full of love and generosity; but Emmett wondered when she came to grips with what had happened would she be the same?

"Dianna, why did you leave me? Why didn't you try to contact me?" Emmett thought mournfully, "Did you mean more to me; than I did to you?"

"Emmett, old man, buck up. I know it's damn hard; but you've got to be strong for this child. Her mom has probably spun her stories of big strong Uncle Emmett, and that's the man they are expecting to see," Terrence exclaimed.

"Sorry, Terrence; I know you are right. It's just that I haven't seen Dianna in over twenty plus years. She turned thirty-nine last week," Emmett replied looking far away.

"I'm sorry, Emmett. It must have been heartbreaking for your family; not knowing where your sister was. I know my Katha suffered for years, not knowing how her boy was, or what had happened to him," Terrence said with sympathy.

"How is Faraj doing?" Emmett asked as they get in the rented car.

"He's actually had some good news. The new trial drug that he's on seems to be helping. They're not saying remission; yet but it's looking very promising."

"That is good news. Grandma Katha must be very happy."

"She is. I had to tell her to not get her hopes up, but I have my hopes up, so how could Grandma Katha not?" Terrence explained.

"It's hard not to Terrence. A person has got to believe, that it is possible to beat cancer," Emmett agreed.

"That is true enough, Emmett." Terrence replied, "We're here now; that's the hospital."

Emmett sighed, straightened his shoulders, and strode into the hospital. He was supposed to go to the R.C.M.P. headquarters first; but he couldn't wait to see Dianna. He also knew they wouldn't release Deirdre to him, until Dianna signed over custody to him. Terrence would do the paperwork and then he could get his niece and take care of her. The halls seemed endless, but soon he was at Dianna's room and showing his identification to the policeman outside the room.

Dianna connected to tubes and machines, looked small and frail in the bed. Dianna's red gold, long curly hair, lay spun across the pillow. It looked to be about waist length and as beautiful as he

This Little Girl Had A Little Curl
By S. G. Lee

remembered. When Emmett was a boy
and Dianna let him braid it. It took some
doing to learn how to do it and the other
boys teased him that he could braid hair.
Would he braid hair again with Deirdre?

"Di? It's Emmett I'm here," Emmett
cried, gently taking Dianna's hand.

"Emmett? You're here? Really here,"
stuttered Dianna.

"Don't try to talk too much, sweetie,"
Emmett said patting her hand.

"Have to…have to tell you what really
occurred. I'm so sorry Emmett. Wouldn't
have left you for the world," Dianna
replied regretfully.

"It will be okay, Dianna. I'm just so glad
to have you back," Emmett said tearing
up and choking back the tears.

"Love you, little bro."

"I love you. too, Dianna."

"Sorry for running away from home. Daddy knew...why," Dianna explained choking for air.

"Dad knew what?" Emmett demanded to know.

"Daddy kicked me out.... pregnant wouldn't let me see Mom."

"Dad did what? Lily was right!"

"Lily?"

"My girlfriend."

"I'm glad brother I hope she makes you happy."

"But dad said he had no idea why you didn't come home. I should have guessed it was him. That asshole!!" Emmett exclaimed shocked.

"He knew...he threw out some clothes at me and said be gone. I went to Vancouver with Bobby Trent. He was the father...of

my baby," Dianna explained gasping for
air.

"Where is the baby?" asked Emmett.

"Lost it …when Bobby left me on
streets…so hungry …begging for food,"
Dianna replied gasping for the words.

"Oh, my God, Dianna. That's so horrible.
I'm so sorry that happened to you."

"Lost… so lost and I couldn't find food,
or shelter. Henry promised me a family in
the religious community he was starting.
He called it Heavenly and at first it was,"
Dianna explained grasping for air she
motioned for water.

Emmett handed her the water and put the
straw to her mouth.

"He said we had to set example and
marry. He married us. Then I found out
what his so-called religion was really all
about…it was a cult; where he took all the
people's property when they joined. I
tried to escape, but he brought me back. I

couldn't escape and leave my children to him. He took more than one wife. I escaped with the kids and he'd drag me back, keep me locked up and starve me; until I agreed to behave. The more I fought back, the more he'd threatened to kill the kids. He kept me prisoner in the community the other wives told him everything I did," Dianna explained pausing to get back her breath.

"You said wives?"

"I was one of three sister wives. We all lived in different homes in the community, but we ate dinner together every day, and spent all our time together; until it was bedtime then he would decide which wife he'd sleep with. Sometimes he'd sleep with all three of us. I'm so ashamed Emmett."

"Dianna, you have nothing to be ashamed of. Deirdre said you went to library; couldn't you have emailed someone, or called the police?" Emmett asked.

This Little Girl Had A Little Curl
By S. G. Lee

"I knew you didn't mean it ;you're ashamed of me."

"I'm not ashamed of you. I just want to know what happened."

"I couldn't call anyone or email anyone, they spied on me as I said. I wasn't allowed near any computers. You've grown," she said changing the subject and then taking a steadying breath she continued, "Into a great man, little brother. That's good, my children need you."

"They won't need me that much with you around," Emmett replied lying.

"Emmett, I know I'm dying. Please, I want to see my kids to say goodbye." Dianna demanded.

Emmett tried to act like the adult he was, but he felt like that nine-year-old boy whose sister went missing all over again.

This Little Girl Had A Little Curl
By S. G. Lee

"I don't want you to go Di," Emmett
sobbed.

"Don't want to go...but have no choice.
God picks the time... It's my time now,
little brother. Now dry your tears and
think of me as I once was, your loving
older sister. Think of me with joy and
happiness, not sadness, and tell my
children stories of me. Now I have to
make plans for my children for after I'm
gone," Dianna insisted slowly getting out
what she needed to say.

"I brought a lawyer. His name is Terrence
Stewart. He has papers which will give
me custody of your child ....er
...children," Emmett said, going to the
door and motioning to Terrence to come
in.

"Hello, I'm Terrence Stewart. I'm a
friend of Emmett's. I'm also a former
judge; but I still am a lawyer and I'd like
to help you cement your child's future."

This Little Girl Had A Little Curl
By S. G. Lee

"Child? You mean children… and are you allowed to practice here… if you're from Ontario like Emmett?"

"I have a permit which allows me to practice law here in British Columbia for the next 100 days," Terrence answered ducking the question about the children.

"Dianna believes that Joseph and Rebecca have been found," Emmett whispered to Terrence in a warning tone.

"Emm…ett thinks that I don't know they haven't been found yet. He doesn't believe it; but they've found them. I know they have. They must have skipped school…ran into the woods …heard shots...were scared …and hid until they saw lots of policemen. I had always told… them policemen were good… that my brother, Emmett was one. I knew they would come out and trusted them…," Dianna started coughing and grasping for breath again.

This Little Girl Had A Little Curl
By S. G. Lee

"You rest your voice Dianna. I hope you don't mind me calling you that?" Terrence said as Dianna nodded.

"They were found? That's wonderful. I'll add their names to this document and you initial here. Sign here and sign here. Emmett then gets custody of your three children, since Henry is dead," Terrence explained placing the pen in her hand and showing Dianna exactly where to sign.

"Thank -you." Dianna stated, "So much."

"Emmett is a good man. He will take good care of your children, Deirdre, Rebecca and Joseph," Terrence reassured.

"No one can take them away with these papers?" Dianna demanded to know.

"No, it says that you as their legal guardian and mother give custody to their uncle Emmett." Terrence stated, "Is there someone you are worried about?"

"Henry's mother, Henrietta lives in Vancouver. She's in her seventies; but she has money. A lot of money," Dianna explained then gasping for air.

"You think she may petition for custody?" Terrence asked.

"Yes."

"Not to worry. Emmett will have custody, rest easy."

"Emmett, go get my children. Make them feel safe. Explain to them about me," Dianna demanded taking a rattling breath "Bring them back to me. I have to say goodbye."

"I will Di. I'll go get them now. We have the papers they should give them to us; right Terrence?" Emmett said reassured his sister.

"That's right; we will go right now. Hang in there until we get back Dianna."

"Don't come back without my babies!" Dianna demanded.

This Little Girl Had A Little Curl
By S. G. Lee

"We will Di. I'll bring them to you. I promise," Emmett replied turning his back to leave and hiding the tears that are now streaming down his face.

As Emmett and Terrence walked down the outside steps of the hospital to go the RCMP police station Terrence motioned Emmett aside and said, "Dianna's mother-in-law, Henrietta could be a problem. We have custody rights from Dianna, but she has rights too. You are single, something the courts could hold against you, simply because you are man."

"That is not fair."

"No, it's not; but it some ways the courts are archaic," Terrence explained.

"Would it be better if I were a married man?" asked Emmett.

"Are you and Lily ready for that?"

"I asked her before; but things got messed up. Hopefully this time she'd say yes and not just because of the kids," Emmett declared.

"You need a bigger place. You'll have four children to raise," Terrence cautioned.

"I know it won't be easy; but with Lily by my side, anything is possible." Emmett declared, "We could always find a new house. I hope Dianna is right about her two oldest children."

"She sounded sure that they were alive."

"I know that; but she's dying. She wouldn't want to think that they were gone too. She could have imagined them safe; I won't believe their safe; until I hear it from law enforcement," Emmett replied sadly.

"I know this is hard on you too, Emmett but don't you think you should be talking to Lily about this? These decisions should be jointly made."

"I will right after we get Deirdre."

This Little Girl Had A Little Curl
By S. G. Lee

"You are going to need to hire a nanny temporarily," Terrence explained as his phone beeped with a message.

"Ha-ha, it looks like Katha-has already covered that. She apparently hired a woman from a reputable agency here. Her name is Laura Lynwood and she's meeting us at the Revelstoke RCMP station to assist with the care of the children. Katha says Ms. Lynwood has glowing child care reviews."

"Grandma Katha is amazing. I can see where Lily gets her spunk and kindness."

"Just see that you treat my great-granddaughter right, Emmett Rogers. Like Katha she is a jewel and you're lucky to have her," Terrence said.

"Don't I know that!

~0~

This Little Girl Had A Little Curl
By S. G. Lee

Emmett and Terrence got into the

rental car. Terrence pointed the car towards Revelstoke. Emmett was surprised how little time it took, until they were at the Revelstoke police station.

Emmett and Terrence entered the police station. Emmett wondered how he could explain to Dianna that she just imagined that they found her two children Rebecca and Joseph if they weren't alive.

"Detective Rogers, I presume?" stated a plainclothes officer. Tall and over six feet trim with dark black hair and indigenous features he oozes strength.

"That's correct and you are? "Emmett asked.

This Little Girl Had A Little Curl
By S. G. Lee

"Inspector Trevor Georges, I spoke to you
on the phone," explained Inspector
Georges.

"It's nice to meet you, Inspector George.
I'm Terrence Stewart, Emmett's friend
and lawyer," Terrence said stepping right
up and putting out his hand.

"It was nice of you to go out of your way
and wait for us. You even and met us at
the door," Emmett declared suspiciously.

"I have a guard on your sister, until we
find the perpetrator. Obviously, meeting
you is a courtesy, given that you are a
police colleague from another
jurisdiction. I also want to caution though
Detective Rogers it is my jurisdiction. I
will book no interference in my
investigation," Inspector Georges
announced.

"I'm here for my sister and her child. Any
other time I might have wanted to be
involved, but that little girl comes first.
She and all of us have to deal with their

mother dying and frankly, I only have time for that," Emmett retorted.

"Just see that it stays that way. I looked into your background and I've seen you've solved quite a lot of cases, but not this one. You do understand Rogers that this one is mine."

"My sister is not doing all that well. Terrence spoke to the doctor," Emmett replied gulping and trying to hold back his emotions, "The doctor doesn't think my sister has long. I'd like to collect Deirdre and take her to see her mother before she... dies."

"What about the other two children? It was my understanding; that you would take custody of them as well," Inspector Georges explained.

Emmett paled, then looked excited, as he realized that this meant the older twins were alive.

This Little Girl Had A Little Curl
By S. G. Lee

"Then Dianna didn't imagine it? Rebecca and Joseph are alive? But how did they explain escaping the massacre you described to me on the phone? You said that every household, every place, even the school in the compound of Heavenly was filled with dead bodies." Emmett inquired afraid to believe.

"Rebecca and Joseph walked out of the woods last night. They were cold and hungry. They even thought they'd get in trouble for skipping school. Devastated to find out that their father was dead, and the mother was shot; they stopped talking about school and just cried until we brought them here. I think they'll be glad to find that you are here. Rebecca has apparently been talking non-stop, about how we should contact her Uncle Emmett who lives in Happy Valley, Ontario. Joseph is mouthy and belligerent however, so you may have trouble with that boy. He seems to have serious anger issues. If his sister hadn't vouched for him being in the woods with her all day, I might have though the lad had the anger to commit the murders," Inspector Georges exclaimed.

"How dare you? That child has been through hell, and you have the audacity to assume that he might have killed an entire compound of people? I should sue your department," Terrence angrily stated.

"The mouthpiece, huh? Cool your jets. The boy is safe and not suspected anymore."

Emmett was very happy to know that the children were alive; but he bit back his anger and tried hard not to yell at Inspector Georges. How dare he degrade the boy? The child just lost his (denigrate) father and his mother was dying. Of course, the boy was acting out ,what child wouldn't? He needed to stay on the inspector's good side at least until the children were with Emmett.

This Little Girl Had A Little Curl
By S. G. Lee

Emmett was sure with enough love from
him and with Caleb's help Joseph would
be able to be himself. Caleb after all had
just lost his mother who better to
understand losing a mother? Then there
was Lily. Sweet Lily who had welcomed
Caleb with open arms. Would she then
welcome his two nieces and his nephew?
Of course, she would even though with
Caleb and Rose that would make five
children. It was almost like the Brady
Bunch; even if they were short one child.
He loved that show in reruns when he was
a child. His mother had insisted on
watching it and had gotten him hooked on
it. She said it was the number one show
when she was a child. So, he knew he
could handle this; couldn't he?

Would Lily finally agree to marry him?
They'd discussed him moving in; but not
marriage again. Emmett wanted to marry
Lily. He wanted for almost a year now;
since he'd met her when she was another
man's widow. He could admit that now.

This Little Girl Had A Little Curl
By S. G. Lee

Lily's husband had been murdered and he
had tried to deal with his growing feelings
for the new widow, by accusing her of the
murder. That had not been an auspicious
start to a relationship; but then Lily hadn't
been ready to move on anyway. Lily had
been loyal, even to a husband who
deserved none of that loyalty. She'd
fought her feelings for Emmett all the
way. Then Caleb's mother had gotten in
the way. Sherry-Anne had drugged him
and set it up to look like Emmett had slept
with Sherry-Anne. Lily was heartbroken
and had refused to speak with him. Given
her history of her two husbands cheating
on her, Emmett couldn't blame her.

Emmett had kept secrets and that had also
made things difficult for their
relationship, but just as they were finally
back on track this happened; but they
were happy again and that counted.

He loved Dianna and was glad beyond
belief to see her again if only for a short
time. However, it was a huge

responsibility to take on three more children. Was he ready for this? Would Lily take on four more children? Lily was the woman he'd always waited for. He hoped that this wouldn't make her walk away. It would make a lot of woman walk away.

"Emmett, are you paying attention?" Terrence asked.

"Sorry, did you say something?" Emmett enquired.

"The nanny has apparently beaten us here." Terrence replied, "She's in the next room with the kids and a social worker."

"Nanny? The woman that Grandma Katha hired for us? She's here all the way from Ontario all ready? How did she manage that?" Emmett wondered.

"Katha apparently hired her, here in British Columbia. I told you that I guess you didn't take that in." Terrence

This Little Girl Had A Little Curl
By S. G. Lee

answered, "She is with the children already."

"I hope she's good with grieving children."

"Katha said she was. She had good references."

"I guess we are about to find out," Emmett exclaimed entering the next room.

"Unca Emwettt? I knew you'd come just like you promised." The little girl said the spitting image of her mother.

Emmett stared at this little whirlwind wrapped around his legs. She was adorable. Her hair was red gold, in two braids on either side of her head; but a curl had escaped right in the middle of her forehead. The curl seemed to curl all on its own. This had to be Deirdre, he thought as he recognized the voice.

Deirdre was dressed in a homespun dress, a flowered blue primrose pattern. The

This Little Girl Had A Little Curl
By S. G. Lee

shoes on her feet were so tiny; he noticed, as his stared at her feet. Emmett had no idea they made black oxfords that small. Tears streaked the little girl's face.

"Hello Deirdre. I said I would come, and here I am," Emmett announced prying the little girl off his legs and hugging her in his arms.

"I wanted to see Mommy but they won't let me. They think I'm too little, but I'm not. I don't like it here; some kid broke my Jacob doll. The lady threw him out. I hate it them! I heard them talking they want to take me away from you to some strange place away from my mommy. You'll make them let me see my mommy. Won't you, Unca Emwettt?" Deirdre shouted stamping her foot.

This whirling dervish reminded Emmett of Dianna stamping her feet, when she was younger and he had to suppress a laugh.

This Little Girl Had A Little Curl
By S. G. Lee

"It's going to be okay honey. I'm sorry about your doll, do you want a new one?"

"No, I gots a new one when the real widdle brother, Jacob died, it wasn't the same. I know Mommy's hurt. She's goin die, isn't she? Like widdle brother Jacob? You hafta take me to see my mommy now!" Deirdre yelled turning purple in the face.

"Deirdre, honey, we talked about this remember? You have to wait a little; then I'm sure your Uncle will take you to see your mother." A woman said coming up to Deirdre.

"Don't care. Waura youse lied...I want my mommy...you said I'd see my mommy!!!!" screamed Deirdre throwing her hands out. One of the swinging hands hit the woman.

Deirdre then began stamping her feet; then abruptly she quit yelling, and just started to cry huge heartbreaking sobs.

This Little Girl Had A Little Curl
By S. G. Lee

The woman held her in her arms and let her cry.

"Deirdre, you had better stop that right now! Or, I'm going to make you sorry!" A young boy demanded entering the room.

The boy was dressed in a white dress shirt, and black trousers with boots picking out beneath them. His hair was red and his eyes were blue, like Deirdre. He took the belt off his pants; as if he would hit Deirdre with it.

"Hey, none of that Joseph. You are Joseph, aren't you? I'm your Uncle Emmett. You can't hit your sister with a belt! Put down that belt, now!" Emmett demanded taking the belt out of Joseph's hands.

"She's a brat. Father would have already smacked her with the belt," Joseph announced defiantly.

This Little Girl Had A Little Curl
By S. G. Lee

"I'm sure your father was a good man;
but he was wrong to do that. You cannot
use physical threat on people," Emmett
explained quietly.

"What do you know? I've never even
seen you before. You probably don't even
read the bible. Father says I shouldn't
trust people that don't have faith in their
lives."

"That's where you're wrong, faith guides
my life and it brought me back to your
mother, your sisters and you."

"Then you know the bible says spare the
rod and spoil the child. Father always
used to read that to us every time he had
to punish us. He also said it hurt him,
more than it hurt us. I was doing Dee a
favour. I am after all her father figure
now that father is gone." Joseph retorted.

"It doesn't say that anywhere in the bible
that's a misquote, it was actually said by a
poet, Samuel Butler who corrupted a
Proverb."

"What about Proverbs 13:24? *"He that spareth his rod hateth his son: but he that loveth him chasteneth him betimes."*

"I told you it a corruption; we don't hit people. especially in my house Joseph. We treat those we love with kindness."

"Get over here Rebecca; so, Uncle Emmett can meet you. Come on hop to it. Or I'll swat you one. At least Dee had the manners to come to him," Joseph shouted ignoring his uncle.

Rebecca slightly smaller than her twin, has red gold hair that curls slightly like her mother and sister Deirdre. She looked a lot like Emmett remembered Dianna looking, before she left home. She obeyed immediately and left the corner coming to Emmett.

"Thank you, Rebecca." Emmett said then turned to Joseph.

"You are all going to come live with me. That means you will have to live by my rules. And my first rule is no physical violence. You will not harm your siblings and you will not threaten them. If any punishment is to be given out, I will do it. Do we understand each other Joseph?" Emmett demanded his voice booking no refusal.

"You are not my father. I am the head of my family, not you. We don't even know you and Father said you were a heathen," Joseph declared defiantly.

"Your father didn't know me, simply because he chose not to know me. But I am here for you and your siblings. I'm here to take care of you all, and see that you are treated well. I am not heathen as your father called me. I go to church every Sunday; unless I'm called out on a case. You will get to know me, but for now you will talk to me with respect and your siblings with respect. Do we understand one another, Joseph?" Emmett stated.

"I guess so, but I don't have to like this."

This Little Girl Had A Little Curl
By S. G. Lee

"You'll adjust. Now you and your siblings have to be prepared. Your mother is very ill…."

"Don't lie to us. She's dying just like Father did. Isn't she?" Joseph exclaimed "And don't think you are going to have us say goodbye to our Mother, then drag us off to the wilds of Ontario. Because we are not going, are we Rebecca?"

"I want to go Joseph. If we don't go, we will go into foster care and live without Dee. They might separate us up too," Rebecca replied in a small quiet voice.

"They wouldn't dare," Joseph crowed sticking out his chest.

"They'd dare son." Terrence exclaimed, "If you aren't in the home of a relative that child services takes you into custody and they can send you all to one place or put you in separate homes."

"Who are you to say that old man?"

This Little Girl Had A Little Curl
By S. G. Lee

"I am your mother's lawyer; Terrence Stewart and I am here to see that you and your siblings end up safe with your uncle."

"I don't want to go to a home; especially not his. Why can't I just go back to Heavenly with my siblings? We can survive on our own."

"You know that won't happen son," Emmett replied.

"It's not fair. I'm a man." Joseph whined, "And don't call me son. I'm not your son."

"I know you are not my son; but maybe someday you may feel we are more connected and that we are as close as an uncle and nephew could be. I know you are getting older and feel like a man, but part of being a man is to know when to fold your cards. You have to step up to help your sisters and your brother and then help me take care of them, "Emmett declared.

This Little Girl Had A Little Curl
By S. G. Lee

"I hate Ontario, and I hate you."

"It's okay to hate me. Now let us go see your Mother. She really wants to see you all."

"I love my Mother…. of course, we want to see her." Joseph insisted, "I'm seeing my mother first, though by myself."

"I'm sure that will be fine. You can all see her one at a time if you'd like."

"We will go in a minute. I have to speak with Miss Lynnwood first."

"I'm sorry I wasn't very helpful." Laura exclaimed, "I'll promise I'll be a better nanny. This is my first position; but I do have child care training from college. Please give me another chance."

Emmett stared hard at Laura. She was petite about five feet two inches and painfully thin. Her arms were tiny as… what was the expression? Oh yes, Emmett thought as tiny as a bird's. As Emmett watched Laura nervously threw her dark curly hair over her shoulder. Emmett thought she was pretty if you liked that type, he didn't, besides she was the children's nanny and he had Lily. She had a tight little curl right in the middle of her forehead. If he didn't know better, he'd think she was a teenager herself. Emmett was wondering though if Grandma Katha had made her first mistake in this woman. She didn't look strong enough to care for three children. In fact, she looked like a strong wind would knock her over.

"I'm not sure…" Emmett began.

"Please Mr. Rogers, I really need this job and I am a good nanny. I'm just having a bad day." Laura begged.

"If you could get the children ready to go to the hospital, I'm ready to give you another chance." Emmett replied relenting and feeling bad about his quick thought to get rid of her.

"Thank you, Mr. Rogers. I won't let you down, I promise and I'll get Joseph to come around," Laura answered a huge smile transforming her face, making her appear, stunningly beautiful.

Terrence also stared at Laura and thought this girl could be trouble. She's way too good looking to be a nanny. Katha was in a hurry and had made a mistake; he then thought about all the sensitivity training they made him and the other judges take. He wondered if he had fashioned a snap judgment based on Laura looks, something he cautioned himself never to do.

"Mr. Stewart, oh it's so nice to meet you. I *Skyped* with your wife, Katha and she hurried me to the first flight out of Vancouver so I could be with the children," Laura said finally appearing to notice Terrence.

"Nice to meet you too, young lady. Are you sure you can handle three children?" asked Terrence still not convinced.

This Little Girl Had A Little Curl
By S. G. Lee

"I promise I can look after them. I'm just a nervous."

"I guess anybody would be," Terrence conceded.

"The guy is more than a lawyer to you. Who is the old dude and who's this Grandma Katha that Laura is talking about is she your mother?" Joseph demanded to know.

"This is Terrence Stewart, a good friend of mine. His wife is Grandma Katha, also a good friend of mine too." Emmett explained, "My mother, your grandmother, died a long time ago."

"So, Grandma Rogers is dead. Did Grandpa kill her? He's not alive, is he? Because I heard from mom that he was really mean and wicked. Dad said he was just making sure mom behaved, but I thought he was a creep," Joseph demanded.

This Little Girl Had A Little Curl
By S. G. Lee

"My Dad, your grandfather died at the same time as your grandmother, in a car accident. But your grandmother would have died anyway, she had breast cancer," Emmett answered.

"Mom said she had sisters too, our Aunts. Where are they?" Rebecca piped up.

"Your Aunt Suzanne (we call her Suzy) has two little babies that are a few months old. Their names are Abigail and Emma. She lives in Happy Valley, right across town from me; but we see each other often. Your Aunt Paula is married to a soldier, your Uncle Jason, who is in Afghanistan. They have two sons, Austin who is thirteen Greg who is just turned eighteen and is expecting another She lives in London, Ontario right now," Emmett answered

"Are you married Uncle Emwettt?" asked Deirdre.

"No sweetie, but I'm hoping to be. Lily, is my girlfriend."

This Little Girl Had A Little Curl
By S. G. Lee

"You gots no kids?" Deirdre asked her fingers in her mouth.

"Good grief, Dee, Father hates er…hated when you put your fingers in your mouth and didn't speak clearly," Joseph rebuked.

"So, how do I ask him?"

"Like this, Uncle Emmett. do you have any children?"

"That's rude; we shouldn't ask that Joseph," insisted Rebecca.

"Do you Unca Emwett?"

"Oh, for Pete's sake, speak clearly," Joseph demanded.

"I have a son, Caleb who lives with me part time," Emmett answered.

"Why?"

"What do you want to know Deirdre?" Emmett asked puzzled.

This Little Girl Had A Little Curl
By S. G. Lee

"Why doesn't he live all the time with you? Don't you love him?" Deirdre demanded to know her eyes big and troubled.

"Of course, I love him. He's my son and family just as you and your sister and brother are." Emmett declared, "His mother died and he wants to spend time with his little brother whose Daddy is his step-daddy."

"His brother has a different Daddy?" Deirdre asked then thinking hard and expression of worry came across her face.

"Yes, Daniel's Daddy is Doctor Dafydd Jones."

"Oh, so if you take us home; you won't give us away?"

"No honey. When you come home with me, all three of you; you are coming home to stay," Emmett reassured.

"Do you know what happened to the other children, Unca Emwett?"

This Little Girl Had A Little Curl
By S. G. Lee

"I'm sorry honey there is no easy way to say this…. the people that hurt your Mom and Dad…."

"Killed…. they killed Daddy." Deirdre clarified sadly, not sounding like she really understood.

"Like duh. You are so stupid Deidre. Do you have to keep saying it?" Rebecca asked.

"We don't call people stupid, and especially, not your little sister. Do you understand me, Rebecca?"

"Yes, I see the little prissy, Deirdre can do no wrong. She has you wrapped around her finger, all ready." Rebecca declared angrily.

"Rebecca, I care about you too, honey; you are all my family," Emmett announced gently.

"You've said what two words to me and lots to them."

This Little Girl Had A Little Curl
By S. G. Lee

"Rebecca, I want to get to know you too."

"Really?"

"Yes, really. I love your mom and I want to get to know and love all of you. I promise."

Rebecca seemed mollified and sat back down. Emmett was worried about how angry Joseph and Rebecca are. They re not handling this well. Maybe they had survivor's guilt? They needed a lot of tender care; was he up to it? He only hoped Lily would be there to help him because he couldn't handle this on his own.

"We have no family, only each other. My Dad is dead and my Mom is leaving us too. This is awful," Rebecca cried then sobbed loudly.

Emmett was surprised he thought she'd accepted what he'd said but he leaned in and hugged her in sympathy.

This Little Girl Had A Little Curl
By S. G. Lee

"Youse always got me. I lob you even when you are mean to me, Rebecca," Deirdre replied and then hugged her sister, too.

"I love you too, pipsqueak," Rebecca declared drying her tears.

"We've got Unca Emwett too; don't forget. He pwomised. Mommy told me all kind of stories of tings they did when he was little. She had pic-a-nicks in the backyard with him. And they did all kind of other stuff too. But youse was naughty Unca Emwett like Joseph because Mommy said you caught garter snakes. Then you put them on her to make her scream like Joseph does to me," Deidre recalled.

"Did you really do that?" Joseph asked looking at Emmett like he thought that was cool.

"I did do that, but it was very mean. I shouldn't have done that. My mother punished me."

This Little Girl Had A Little Curl
By S. G. Lee

"What did your mommy do?" Deirdre
asked.

"My mother made me apoligize to my
sister and then she took the television
away for a week," Emmett recalled.

"A whole week that's all? We only watch
television once a week when services
were on," Joseph replied.

"My father thought you were right
Joseph, he took his belt to my backside,"
Emmett remembered.

"But you said you didn't believe in
violence," Joseph retorted.

"I don't, but my father did. He was a very
troubled man and he believed all life's
problems could be solved with a belt. I
don't believe that. I believe that violence,
only begets violence. I've seen it in my
work."

"Fathers discipline you, that is what it
says in the good book. What of it?" and
then changing the subject Joseph asked,

This Little Girl Had A Little Curl
By S. G. Lee

"So you're a cop? Do you have a gun? Have you shot people? Did you kill anyone?"

"I have a gun, that's always with me, or under lock and key. And killing someone is not something I want to talk about…ever," Emmett explained, "None of you ever touch my lock box; do you understand?"

"As if I would want to touch your stupid gun," Joseph said offended.

"We won't touch it will we, Dee?" Rebecca pleaded.

"No guns are really bad…. Mommy's not coming. She's joining Daddy in heaben isn't she?" Deirdre asked as both Rebecca and Joseph listened intently.

"Yes, Deirdre; but she wants to say goodbye. Do you understand?" Emmett asked bending down to the little girl.

"Mommy is going to be with Daddy and God in heaben. I wish she could stay here

instead," Deirdre retorted her eyes
scrunching up like she's would cry again.

"So, do I, pumpkin; but we all have to put
on a brave face and go see your mother.
Do you all understand?" Emmett
requested of the three older children.

"We understand. Don't we girls?" Joseph
asked, "Does she have to come though?"
as he indicated Laura.

"Are you speaking of Laura? We need a
nanny for Dee and someone has to watch
you when I can't," Emmett explained.

"The nanny is for Dee, then that's okay.
You do realize Rebecca and I are too old
for a nanny or a babysitter, don't you?"
Joseph demanded.

"Of course, I do Joseph, but the law does
state because of your age someone has to
be there to look after you," Emmett
retorted.

This Little Girl Had A Little Curl
By S. G. Lee

"She better not boss me around. I'm not a child. I'm a man!" Joseph insisted, "And I'm seeing my mother by myself."

"Okay, you can have time with her alone. I understand why you want to see her by yourself," Emmett reassured him.

"Right like you care. You haven't seen mother in years." Joseph said under his breath.

"I didn't know where your mother was. I love her, very much; but we can talk about this more later. Now let's all go see your mom now," Emmett said taking custody of them from the social worker.

~0~

Chapter 5 – Who Killed Sherry-Anne?

Lily wondered if she should call

Emmett and tell him how she had to masquerade as his wife to look after Caleb. Poor Emmett was going through so much and now she was going to add to that. She was three and half months, possibly four months pregnant. In December they would have a baby. Maybe she should call him? She was torn.

She hoped that Emmett would be as overjoyed as she was about the baby; but it was a huge step having Caleb, and Deirdre come to live with him let alone taking on Lily, Rose and now... a new baby.

This Little Girl had a Little Curl
By S. G. Lee

Lily picked up the phone and hoped she
didn't reach Emmett at the wrong time.

"Hello." she said as she heard Emmett's
voice.

"You have reached Emmett Rogers. I'm
not available. Please leave a message at
the tone," was all she heard.

He must be with Dianna. Poor Emmett his
sister was dying; he was taking on the
responsibility of another child. She should
fly out to him; surely, she could rearrange
her schedule. What was she thinking? She
couldn't rearrange anything; she'd lose
her job if she took off any more time and
she liked her job. In order to get the years
maternity, she was due, she'd have to
work the next few months just to make
sure she had the number of weeks
required.

Thank goodness, Grandma Katha had
hired a nanny to help Emmett. What if the
nanny was good looking? Look at what

This Little Girl had a Little Curl
By S. G. Lee

happened to all those celebrities who
hired nannies and they walked off with
their famous employer. What was wrong
with her? Emmett wasn't like that. Lily
heard a noise at her front door and went
to answer it.

"Kendall, what are you doing here?" Lily
asked.

"It's official business. I'm looking into
Sherry-Anne's death on my own time.
This is Alan Barnes, he's assisting me.
Oh, sorry, do you know him?" Kendall
said hurriedly, noting that Lily smiled
welcomingly.

"Hi Lily; it's nice to see you again," Alan
said.

"Hello, Alan and Kendall. Please, both of
you come in and tell me how I can help
you," Lily offered ushering them both in.

"We're trying to piece together the night
of Sherry-Anne's death," Kendall
explained

"You know I didn't do it!" Lily protested.

"We know you've been eliminated, Lily. Personally, I never thought you did it; but we have to follow the letter of the law. That's not why we are here though. We're wondering if you, or anyone you know saw any suspicious people near Sherry Anne's home, say any time in the last few days before the killing?" Alan enquired.

"I hadn't been to Dafydd's, except for that one time. I really can't help you with this. I wish I could. I want you to find the culprit that took Sherry-Anne's life; so I can prosecute them to the fullest extent of the law," Lily stated fiercely.

"Thank-you, Lily. I'm sorry about arresting you. I hope you are not still angry with me," Kendall stated, trying to apologize awkwardly.

"That's okay, Kendall. I know you were trying to do your job," Lily stated mollifying the situation. After all Kendall was close to Emmett.

"I guess that's why Emmett cares about you. You are very generous, Thanks for being so understanding," Kendall stated.

Alan reached out and put an arm around Kendall; she pushed him away and gave him a look as if to say, not now we're working. Lily smiled, so they were together now. Good, Kendall needed someone; maybe Alan would be good for her.

"We'd like to interview Rose as well. I know Emmett is out of town, we'd like to know whether it would be okay to interview Caleb with you. Do you have the ability to give us permission?" Alan asked.

"Rose isn't here. You'll have to talk to Rose later, she's with her grandparents. As for Caleb I don't know; maybe I should call Emmett and ask him?" Lily exclaimed.

"Don't worry, Lily. I don't mind anything to find the bastard that killed my mom," Caleb said entering the living room.

Lily looked at Caleb troubled. Worried that this might be too stressful for Caleb; after all he's been through lately; she knows she can't trample on his choice to talk; especially given his age.

"I do have a temporary guardianship..." Lily began, but was interrupted by Caleb apologizing, "Sorry, I swore, Lily. I know you hate that."

"It's okay, honey. I understand how much this hurts you. I want them to find your mother's killer too," Lily stated.

"Are you sure? Mom was pretty mean to you," Caleb asked sounding surprised.

"Caleb, she was your mother and she loved you. Your Mother was trying to make it up to me, when someone took her life. She was happy and looking forward to having a life with Dafydd, your brother, and you. No one had the right to take that away from her, or any of you." Lily stated fiercely, "I want to find the person who did this and prosecute them to the fullest extent of the law."

"Thank-you, Lily." Caleb stated.

"No thank-you's are necessary. You can answer their questions, Caleb; but if at any time you feel uncomfortable; just stop okay?" Lily stated.

"You came home found your mother where?" asked Special Constable Alan Barnes.

"You know I found her at the bottom of the stairs." Caleb asked puzzled.

"And?" demanded Kendall, without any sympathy, clearly wanting more information.

This Little Girl had a Little Curl
By S. G. Lee

"She was unconscious…" Caleb paused here taking a breath as if not to cry, "Just a heap at the bottom of the stairs."

"What else did you see?" Asked Kendall.

"She had a pool of blood underneath her."

"Take your time, Caleb, and continue. I know this is hard, but try to visualize it like you're seeing a movie, noting any detail, so you can tell your friends later," Alan stated, seeing Caleb starting to crumble.

"I put my fingers to her neck and found a really low pulse. I picked up the phone and called for an ambulance. There was so much blood, and I was worried about Daniel," Caleb explained.

"Did you hear anyone in the house?" Kendall asked.

"No, I don't think so," Caleb stated clearly unsure.

"Did you hear any sounds? Think back Caleb!" Alan prodded.

"I don't know. I just don't know it was just so awful. You can't know how scared and horrified I was," Caleb stated.

"I think you two should quit badgering him and leave him alone. If he remembered anything, he'd tell you," Lily said stepping in.

"I'm okay, Lily. I want to answer their questions. Then turning to Alan, he continued, "I heard a creak like a window opening, then shutting," Caleb recalled.

"Which window?" Kendall demanded.

"I don't know. It's not like I went to check," Caleb explained.

"If you were to guess, what window do you think it was?" Alan asked.

"It could have been the kitchen window, I guess?" Caleb answered.

This Little Girl had a Little Curl
By S. G. Lee

"Thank-you," Alan said.

"Yes, thank-you Caleb. You've been very helpful," Kendall stated standing up.

"I have?" Caleb stated looking happy and surprised.

"Yes, you've confirmed for us that the footprints we found were probably the killer's," Alan answered, even though Kendall gave him an evil look for saying so.

"Thank-you, Lily, Caleb, we will be going now," Kendall stated.

Kendall and Allan then left, but Lily overheard them outside the window talking…, "There were small footprints in the garden under the kitchen window. "Why didn't want me to tell them that?" Alan protested.

"Alan, that why I'm Sergeant Detective and you're still a Special Constable." Kendall insisted, "You don't tell anyone who is not involved in the investigation what evidence we have."

"Don't you think your being a little harsh Kendall?" Alan asked.

"Alan if we are going to work together on this get this straight, I am in charge. I am the lead officer on this case. You work for me; so, what I say is the law, got it?" Kendall demanded angrily.

"I understand, that Detective Evans," Alan replied, angrily.

"Good thing, you didn't tell them that we are looking for a woman. Do you know that Caleb and Rose, Lily's daughter have been involved in solving crimes in the last year? I don't want them, or Lily Kelly anywhere near this case. Do you understand me Alan?" Kendall stated fiercely.

"You want all the glory. I got it," Alan said under his breath.

"What did you say?" Kendall asked angrily.

"I said yes, Kendall everything is hunky dory," Alan made up on the spot.

"Oh, okay then," Kendall said not sure what to believe, but choosing to believe Alan.

"So where do we go from here?" Alan asked.

"We have to go back and look at what evidence we have. It points to a woman. We proved it wasn't Lily Kelly."

"Was Emmett pissed at you?"

"Didn't matter my job as a cop is to follow the evidence, even if it's a friend."

Kendall considers me a friend, Lily thought surprised, good, I'd like to be friends.

"Why would another woman want Sherry-Anne dead?" Kendall asked.

"She saw something fishy at the hospital where she worked?" Alan speculated.

"I guess that's possible. We need to interview some of the people she worked with at the hospital again." Kendall replied, "Sherry-Anne must have ticked off a lot of people. She made me mad five seconds; after I met her."

"What about those people who were responsible for the murder of her sister?" Alan inquired.

"It wasn't her sister; it turns out that her sister, was really her mother."

Alan looked at Kendall like she had two heads.

"I know confusing isn't it?" Kendall commented.

"It's weird."

"It's like one of those old timey stories where the mother pretends, they are the

This Little Girl had a Little Curl
By S. G. Lee

sister and the grandmother raises them."
Kendall explained.

"What happened to her father?"

"He, the senator, is dead and his honey?
She's in jail for the murder of the senator
and the attempted murders."

"What about the Senator's kids; could it
have been one of them who killed Sherry-
Anne?" Alan asked.

"That's one of the inquiries will have to
make as well. We have to know whether
they were in this country and what kind of
alibis they have." Kendall stated.

"There's a lot of material to go through,
and all of this is on our free time?" Alan
stated sounding weary.

"Hey, you horned in on this Barnes. If
you don't want in on the investigation
then walk away now. But remember no
guts, no glory."

This Little Girl had a Little Curl
By S. G. Lee

"I thought I'd be working with Emmett Rogers." Alan stated.

"What am I chopped liver?" Kendall demanded.

"No, of course, you are not chopped liver," Alan stated backtracking.

"Let's go interview some hospital people then starting with some doctors and then some nurses."

"Do you have anyone in mind?" Alan asked.

"I think we should start with the doctor she worked with the most. Dr. Pope… Carla Pope." Kendall replied.

"I think you better tread lightly with this woman boss. Isn't Dr. Pope the one who just lost her mother and found out her sister was murdered by a couple of serial killers?"

This Little Girl had a Little Curl
By S. G. Lee

"You heard about that one, huh?" Kendall said proudly like she was the one to discover it all.

"I was part of the discovery too, Kendall. Remember!" Alan said annoyed.

"Oh yes, that's right, you came in at the end; when we had to take Roy away." Kendall stated, "You took him to jail."

"I can understand why you don't want to remember Kendall; after all you were involved with the guy," Alan commiserated.

"I dated him a long time ago; when I was young and impressionable. The guy was trying to get in good with me again, unlucky for him, I wasn't falling for it." Kendall denied, "Besides we are starting something aren't we?"

"We've had a couple of dates and I care, but do you?"

This Little Girl had a Little Curl
By S. G. Lee

"I do care; but it's new and you throwing Roy in my face isn't fair."

"I'm sorry I guess I'm jealous."

"Of him? There's nothing to be jealous of. There is nothing worse than a dirty cop. His actions were nothing short of evil."

"You are right in that Kendall. Dirty cops make us all look bad." Alan stated then changing the subject he said, "I heard something, that I thought you should know. There's a rumour going around at the station about you."

"There is a rumour about me? What the hell could anyone say about me?" Kendall demanded to know.

"They are saying that you are the Chief's daughter and that you didn't earn your position. Isn't that ridiculous?" Alan stated.

Alan saw the look on Kendall's face and he blurted, "It's true? Chief Stewart is your Dad?"

"Maybe, but I earned my rank. I've worked hard to live down the fact; that my Dad is the chief. It must have be Roy, that rat bastard. Have you ever heard of this before now?" Kendall demanded, "How dare anyone think that I would use this to get ahead?"

"A lot of people would use that position Kendall, but I think people who know you are going to know that's not true; you can weather this. Just hold up your chin and pretend you don't know why this would be an issue. You've got them scared now they won't cross you. They don't call you the Iron bitch for nothing." Alan stated.

"They call me the Iron bitch? Really?" Asked Kendall surprised and pleased, "Good. Then they won't try to take advantage of me. They don't know about us, do they? I want to keep that on the down low."

"No, I'm keeping quiet like you asked. Forget I said that they call you the Iron Bitch. The guys will rake me over the coals for letting you know," Alan replied looking embarrassed.

"Don't worry Alan; your secret is safe with me. I appreciate your friendship too." Kendall stated awkwardly, "You're a good friend and a good colleague and maybe when we're not working, good boyfriend material."

"Wow, compliments, I'm touched. Don't worry, Detective Evans; I haven't forgotten you are the boss," Alan said sensing her discomfort.

"Just don't ignore that. I'm sick of the men I work with(except for Emmett and possibly you) treating me like I'm a piece of meat, that they can sexual harass and fondle. I put those so-called men in their place. Women shouldn't have to contend with such blatant sexual attacks but I hear they have that throughout all police departments. I've earned my role as a top investigator and they should respect the badge and the authority," Kendall stated.

"I'm sorry that they are so immature."

"Immature? Are you kidding me? Their behaviour is bordering on criminal, but if I tell anyone I'm the narc, the woman cop who had to cry, because she couldn't handle the job making it even harder for other women."

"If it's that bad maybe you should tell your dad."

"That would look great wouldn't it? Whiny little girl has to tell daddy that the boys don't get along with her. It's bad enough that others know he's my dad. You men have no idea what women have to put up with and we shouldn't have to. But let's drop it and go talk to those people on our list. We need to figure out a way through this maze and find the perpetrator of this hideous crime. Now don't forget, when Emmett gets back, I'm updating him."

"Don't you think he's a little too close to the crime?" Alan asked.

"Emmett is my partner and overlook that. My first loyalty is to him. He is a brilliant problem solver. Much like Sherlock Holmes, he puts all the pieces together. We need his keen insight. It's that simple," Kendall stated.

"Fine, then Emmett's updated when he gets back. Let's go talk to some people. Boss!" Alan said trying to mollify her.

This Little Girl had a Little Curl
By S. G. Lee

Lily hurried away from the window; she
didn't want to be caught listening into the
investigation, but she hoped they found
Sherry-Anne's killer soon. As much as
she disliked Sherry-Anne, she hadn't
wished this on Sherry-Anne. Sherry-
Anne's poor little baby could have died.
Poor Caleb was suffering too, no one
should lose their mother so young. Lily
knew how much she missed her own
mother every day; Lily would try to help
Caleb deal with this great loss, if he'd let
her.

~0~

Chapter 6 – Missing Connections

Emmett sat down in the chair and turned the television on low; there was no way he could go to sleep yet. He needed to talk to Lily and Caleb. He knew that they were probably sound asleep; because of the time difference. He heard a noise in the bedroom of the hotel room and he startled; but since he had given Laura the night off to get some rest, he thought he'd better check out the noise. In the twin beds he saw Rebecca slumbering not making a noise except for her rhythmic breathing. Deirdre on the other hand, was half on, and half the bed, her new stuffed bear lay on the floor. He would have

This Little Girl had a Little Curl
By S. G. Lee

checked that she was still breathing, but
she was whimpering in her sleep.
Emmett's heart went out to this little girl.
Poor little Deirdre and the other children
had been through so much, especially
today. Dianna last thoughts had been for
her children and their welfare She had
managed to be alert enough from the fog
of the drugs, that kept her comfortable,
enough to reassure each child that she
loved them.

Dianna had promised to look down on
them from heaven. She had told them
Emmett was the best brother ever, that he
would be the best uncle ever, and making
sure they had all they needed. Emmett
had gulped back tears at this and had
reassured the children that what their
mother said was true. He loved them all
and would take care of them.

Emmett picked up the brown bear, the
very same one that he had picked up for
Deirdre today. Deirdre demanded to go to

the gift shop, the minute they got to the hospital. Emmett thought back to the moment thinking of how generous hearted his little niece was and how troubled the twins were.

"Uncle Emwettt we have to get mommy a present. When people are in hospital you get presents," Deirdre had insisted.

"You are ridiculous. What is wrong with you? Mommy's dying. What she going to do with a present?"

"Becky...," Joseph interjected even before Emmett could say anything.

"What Joseph? She is so pathetic and stupid. You know she is! Mommy is leaving us too; just like Daddy did. Don't look at me like that. Oh, I hate you all!" Rebecca said stalking off.

"I'll get her, Uncle Emmett. Don't worry, I can handle her," Joseph stated following after her.

This Little Girl had a Little Curl
By S. G. Lee

"Don't hit your sister, Joseph," Emmett cautioned.

"I heard you the first time. I think you're wrong about discipline ; but I won't hit her …this time. Mom wouldn't like it," Joseph stated.

"Thank- you I think," Emmett stated.

"Please Uncle Emwett, we need to go in the store. Mommy's going to be so lonely without us," Deirdre stated, putting her fingers in her mouth, "She needs a stuffy."

"What does she need honey?" Emmett asked confused.

"Mommy needs a stuffed toy to take to heaben," Deirdre answered.

"If that's what you want honey, then let's pick one out. Your sister and your brother are back, maybe your sister will help you pick out one," Emmett stated relieved to see them both back but feeling adrift at comforting a small child.

"You'll help Dee pick out something won't you Rebecca?" Joseph stated booking no refusal.

"Yes, okay." Rebecca stated wiping tears from her eyes, "Deirdre can pick what she wants for mommy and show me."

"Thank-you," Emmett mouthed to both Joseph and Rebecca.

Deirdre had looked intently at all the things in the store. She starred longingly at the brown bear and it was obvious she wanted it for herself; but she didn't pick it up; instead, she picked up a small white bear with a halo and wings.

"Is this bear, okay, Uncle Emwettt? It's not too spensive?" Deirdre asked her eyes looking worried.

"That one will be fine, honey," Emmett stated smiling.

This Little Girl had a Little Curl
By S. G. Lee

"Good, it's an angel like Mommy, so she will be able to take it to heaben," Deirdre stated.

Emmett grabbed up the brown bear and paid for both bears saying, "Here, honey, you have this."

"Oh, Uncle Emwettt, thank-you; I wanted him so much; but I didn't want to be gweedy," Deirdre stated, "I'm going to call him Em."

"Would you two like anything?" Emmett asked

"I'll have this!" Rebecca said snatching up some candy, then she added getting some for her siblings as well. "Here's some candy for Joseph and Dee, too,"

"Are you sure you don't want something Joseph?" Emmett asked.

"I'm good. Come on girls. Let's go see Mom," Joseph stated then he glared at Emmett.

This Little Girl had a Little Curl
By S. G. Lee

The children all went into say their
goodbye's one at a time. Dianna had one
last request… Emmett's presence, while
the goodbyes were said. They talked and
then Dianna seemed to go out like the
wick of candle. Her essence just seemed
to shimmer, then fade into the
netherworld. For a moment Emmett
thought the saw a light emanate from her
body, then float up past the ceiling.
Emmett felt stunned at how fast she went.
He couldn't imagine how bad the children
felt. This was their mother and she was
gone in the blink of an eye.

"Uncle Emwettt?" Deirdre had asked.

"Yes, Deirdre?" Emmett answered.

"This is like that thing that Daddy was
always talking about." Deirdre exclaimed.

"What was that Deirdre?" Emmett asked
trying to understand.

"You know that passage from the good
book," Deirdre said puzzled, that Emmett

This Little Girl had a Little Curl
By S. G. Lee

didn't know what she was talking about,
and then she whispered in Joseph's ear.

"Yes, Dee. I know it all," Joseph replied.

"Say it." Deirdre demanded.

"If it will make you happy Deirdre, I'll
say it."

*"To everything there is a season, and a
time to every purpose under the heaven:
A time to be born, and a time to die; a
time to plant, and a time to pluck up that
which is planted; A time to kill, and a
time to heal; a time to break down, and a
time to build up; A time to weep, and a
time to laugh; a time to mourn, and a time
to dance; A time to cast away stones, and
a time to gather stones together; a time to
embrace, and a time to refrain from
embracing; A time to get, and a time to
lose; a time to keep, and a time to cast
away; A time to rend, and a time to sew;
a time to keep silence, and a time to
speak; A time to love, and a time to hate;*

This Little Girl had a Little Curl
By S. G. Lee

a time of war, and a time of peace."
Joseph concluded reading from his bible
that he clasped.

"We gots love in Uncle Emwett. That's
what mommy said, right, Uncle
Emwett?" Deirdre said.

"Yes, honey and I'll be there for all for
you."

"Can we have funerals for my mom and
dad before we go to Ontario?" asked
Joseph.

"We can, but not for a few days," Emmett
replied.

"Are you okay Rebecca?" Emmett asked.

"Sure, why wouldn't I be? My mom and
dad are dead, my friends are all dead, and
I have to move way far, far away. I'm just
peachy," Rebecca said sarcastically.

"I'm sorry Rebecca," Emmett said trying
to comfort her.

This Little Girl had a Little Curl
By S. G. Lee

"If you were really sorry you wouldn't
have stayed away from my mom; so long.
She missed you," Rebecca censored.

"He didn't know where Mom was."
Joseph said defending Emmett, "Dad
didn't want her to see her family, so she
didn't."

"I didn't know that," Rebecca said.

"I know lots of things, you don't know!"

"I want my mommy," Deirdre stated,
finally realizing she really wasn't going to
see her mom again.

Emmett took her in his arms and she cried
herself to sleep. He carried her to the cab,
the other children following behind him.
Back at the hotel room and Emmett
tucked Deirdre into the bed putting the
bear in her arms.

Emmett grieved for Dianna and the life
she should have had, the time that both he
and the children should have had with

This Little Girl had a Little Curl
By S. G. Lee

her. Inspector Banks still hadn't let him
know who he thought had shot all of
them. Everyone at the complex had died
except for Dianna's children. Why?
Simply because Deirdre had hidden and
the two preteens had skipped school to
explore nature. Who was it that came in
and shot the entire cult community?

Dianna had told Inspector Banks that they
were a community; but to Emmett it had
sounded like a cult. Inspector Banks had
explained to Emmett that although Henry
has started up the community and had
allowed other to think they were modeled
after a religion; he was the sole law and
leader. Some of the things Deirdre had
commented had Emmett to understand the
awful life Dianna had been trapped in,
along with her children. Emmett would
make it up to Dianna's children and raise
them to be happy and secure. It was the
least he could do.

This Little Girl had a Little Curl
By S. G. Lee

Emmett couldn't stop wondering about
the murders; who had committed them?
All the present members were dead,
except for Dianna's children and frankly
Emmett was glad that God, or fate had
spared them. Detective Inspector Banks
said they were looking into whether a
former member had been the one to come
in and kill everyone in Heavenly. Henry
Parsons, from all Emmett had been able
to learn about him was a controlling
however, charismatic leader. He managed
to sway and control his subjects ruling
with an iron fist. Obviously, the man had
ticked off someone. After all he'd kept
Dianna prisoner; that gave someone a
great motive for murder.

Dianna had been a victim of whoever had
shot all the other victims. Emmett wished
he could go find the killer himself; but he
had four children to care for, all who had
lost their mothers. Poor Caleb, still hadn't
heard from his dad. What kind of dad did
that make him? Hell, who was he kidding

he hadn't even found the killer who had killed Sherry-Anne, even if Inspector Banks had allowed him in on the investigation, he'd lost his edge.

Enough! He couldn't think about this anymore. Dianna's death was killing him.

Emmett felt sick to his stomach and he hadn't been able to eat. He wanted to cry, but he couldn't do that in front of the kids. He needed to be strong. He needed to speak to Lily. She'd make him feel better, if only for a few moments. He needed to hear her voice it had been such a horrendous day.

"You've have reached Lily Kelly-Brooksfield and Rose Brooksfield, please leave a message at the beep." Emmett heard, as he put down the phone. He'd call her and Caleb in the morning; before the children were up about four a.m. would be the time in British Columbia, seven a.m. the time in Ontario.

This Little Girl had a Little Curl
By S. G. Lee

He missed Lily so much. Emmett was
sorry, she hadn't been able to come with
him; but at least he knew Caleb was in
good hands with her. His poor son had
been through so much. Caleb insisted he
was fine; but Emmett was sure he wasn't.
Losing your mother at any age was hard,
but as a child? Caleb seemed angry and
withdrawn. He needed his Dad there, not
in British Columbia. As soon as they
could get Dianna buried, they'd head
home. It would be hard having four
grieving children but he'd manage with
Lily's help. Look how far Rose had come
in grieving for her father.

Good grief, he was talking about burying
Dianna, like it was nothing. Yet it hurt so
bad; he felt like his heart had been ripped
out of his chest. All the what-ifs were
killing him. Why could he have found
Dianna sooner?

This Little Girl had a Little Curl
By S. G. Lee

He should have searched for her in British Columbia, then maybe he would have found her before...Emmett thought as he lay down on his bed, closed his eyes and drifted off to a troubled sleep.

~0~

Chapter 7 – A Killer's View

I missed my Dafydd. I wish, I could see

him in person, but it was far too soon. He was grieving *for that witch*! I hate that!!I'm taking stock right now and making my plans. But never you fear, Dafydd; I'll be back soon. I will stick to part of the original plan, and improvise just a little, even though it was so hard to be away from you, my beloved. I will give you him the time to get over her.

Why, he grieved her, I didn't know!! My Dafydd was better off ;without that lying cheating bitch! Dafydd was my rock. He kept me grounded; when the world around me seemed to kaleidoscope. Without Dafydd, I felt like I was drifting

This Little Girl had a Little Curl
S. G. Lee

flying away; like those million pieces into the stratosphere.

I needed him; probably more than he needed me, but I'd accept even a piece of Dafydd. As long as I didn't have to share him with another woman. I share him only with baby Daniel. That baby was adorable and so like his daddy.

My mother had died when I was young, leaving me all alone with daddy. Then daddy had gone too. I loved Dafydd, even though he left me, just like everyone else. Everyone leaves me; but my actions would change that now. That bitch would have kept him from me forever. She hated the very thought of me. I fixed her…one push down the stairs and it was goodbye Sherry-Anne. That should be a song. Would it make a good one? ♫ Goodbye Sherry-Anne. You'll never have a man. Just one push was all it took ♫ I didn't sound quite musical; but ha-ha it was too funny!!

This Little Girl had a Little Curl
S. G. Lee

The best part was she had no idea why, or
who I was, and yet should have known. If
she'd truly loved Dafydd, even the
smallest amount she'd have known about
me. She'd asked why I tried to kill her
and begged me to call for help for the
baby's life. I'd saved little Daniel, hadn't
I? What kind of a monster did she think I
was?

I hadn't known Sherry-Anne was
pregnant. I wouldn't kill innocents. Now
as for Sherry-Anne she deserved what she
got!! She was just playing at being
Dafydd's wife. She probably had a rich
doctor at her work that she kept on a
string. She'd only told Dafydd she loved
him, because Emmett Roger's had
discovered her true nature and would
have nothing to do with her. Obviously,
she'd used the oldest trick in the book to
trap my Dafydd.

Poor Dafydd; the woman was a temptress,
a vile witch in sheep's clothing.
Recognizably, the kind my governess had
warned me about (before mommy and

This Little Girl had a Little Curl
S. G. Lee

daddy had fired her for her practicing her religion with a seven-year-old me). Frankly, I don't know what mommy and daddy's problem was, sticking pins in voodoo dolls was so much more accepted in polite society, then dissecting the small rodents that I had been embalming at the time. I'd since learned to hide my proclivities. Daddy had asked me (at the time) why I embalmed things and I'd told him because I could and it felt good. He was horrified and hired the nanny. But my mind wanders and I must not go back to my childhood... my shrink says so; it makes my disposition worse; he claims.

Sherry-Anne had to go. I just know Sherry-Anne was the reason why Dafydd hadn't come to see me in so long. When I'd finally saw him Dafydd hadn't looked himself he seemed troubled and unhappy. Where had his wonderful smile gone? Sherry-Anne had taken it way replacing it with frowns and sighs. No matter I had fixed the problem. Dafydd could be happy now.

This Little Girl had a Little Curl
S. G. Lee

Now Daniel was simply too precious and looked like Dafydd. He could stay with us. I'd help raise him, when the time was right. After all, I'd called for help to come and save the little baby. Then the boy had come. Caleb was a handsome young man almost an adult, too bad for him; but he'd soon be off to university. Though Sherry-Anne claimed he was hers; I had grasped instantly, that he was cloned from his father, Emmett Rogers. None of Sherry-Anne's evil tainted him. So, I'd spared him.

I felt bad that Dafydd and yes, even, Caleb who also grieved for that bitch, but they'd get over her. Hadn't Dafydd got over Ellen Robertson? Ellen had told him to choose her, or me. Ha, ha Ellen, Dafydd had chosen me.

Sherry-Anne hadn't been his bed, that long anyway. She panted away for Emmett Rogers. I had evidence that she was found in his hotel room; by that simpering Lily Kelly. Why that woman didn't have the guts to rip out Sherry-

This Little Girl had a Little Curl
S. G. Lee

Anne's heart when she found her with her man, I didn't know. Dafydd had been interested in Lily for all of five minutes, but I still had my eye on that woman. Obviously, Lily was one of those frail simpering women that man fawned over, those kinds were dangerous to men. Lily had better stay away from Dafydd, if she knew what was good for her.

As for Emmett Rogers? The jury was still out on him. As long as he didn't threaten Dafydd, he would be safe. The poor man had to put up with that bitch, Sherry-Anne, so, I could give him some leeway. Sherry-Anne had even ruined Emmett's relationship with that mouse Lily. Sherry-Anne was probably the instigator; but he could have said no and not gotten in bed with that trash; although I wouldn't put it past the manipulating Sherry-Anne to have drugged him. That's probably what happened. Emmett Rogers seemed too nice to cheat on anyone. Dafydd, however, came first. Emmett Rogers, better hope he was as nice as I assumed, he was, or Emmett would pay if he

This Little Girl had a Little Curl
S. G. Lee

betrayed Dafydd. No one hurt my
Dafydd. No one and lived!! Sherry-Anne
had found that out the hard way. She'd
betrayed Dafydd and paid the ultimate
price. Tee, hee, hee.

Dafydd had the gift I'd left him. I hadn't
taken his son's life, only hers. I'd called
for help and got away before it came, but
Daniel lived. I didn't feel guilty, I didn't!!
The baby was safe that all that mattered.
Dafydd would appreciate my generosity.

That kid of Emmett Rogers, better not get
in my way, in any thing I had planned.
Frankly, I didn't like the way Caleb was
spending all his time with Dafydd. He
claimed that Daniel was his brother; but
any blood connection there through his
sleazy mother was diluted. Daniel was all
Jones; he had none of that Mobley blood.
Although from what I've seen of the boy
Caleb; he didn't share any of that blood
either. It was strange how he took after
his father, that Emmett Rogers; but it was
definitely lucky for him.

This Little Girl had a Little Curl
S. G. Lee

Emmett Rogers was very handsome and kind. However, that didn't excuse Sherry-Anne. The only reason Dafydd could have married Sherry-Anne was his misplaced chivalry. He thought he loved her; but his love was only for his baby, Daniel. He wanted his child and now he had him and didn't have to share with *her*! I gave that to him! He should be happy, instead he moped around whining about her!!

I'd done him a favour; he'd see that soon. Sherry-Anne would have climbed in the next man's bed and Dafydd would have had to sue for custody of his child. Now he didn't have to do that. I protected my Dafydd. No one hurts my Dafydd and gets away with it.

Daniel was such a cute baby. I snuck into his room several times since he was born. He slept in his crib and looked so much like Dafydd; my heart turned over. His hair was curly and fuzzy on his head and his tiny body, with those little fingers and toes, so gorgeous. I left gifts for him and

This Little Girl had a Little Curl
S. G. Lee

Dafydd hadn't even noticed my offerings.
Has he forgotten me all ready? Or, did he
think Caleb had bought them. No matter.

It was just too easy to get into Daniel's
room. You'd think that Dafydd would
have put an alarm on the windows.
Frankly, I was glad he hadn't because it
gave me easy access but still, I worried
were they safe? Why was Dafydd still
grieving for that woman? What had she
offered him but grief and aggravation?
She'd given him a baby. So, what? Any
woman could have a baby. Why did it
have to be her that he thought he loved?

I hated to see him cry. My sweet, Dafydd,
you should have no fears. I will protect
you, Dafydd, in your weakened state. My
plans to keep you safe and protected from
those who would keep you from me are
concrete. Never forget though, Dafydd
you are mine! When the time is right, we
will be together again. You, me and
Daniel will have all the love.~0~

Chapter 8 – Why hasn't he called?

Lily glanced at the home phone and

then her cell phone. With two phones Emmett could have reached Lily, somehow. Emmett had no excuse. Why hadn't he called? Grandpa Terrence had called her. Why couldn't Emmett make a simple five second call? Terrence had filed the papers so that Emmett could look after the orphaned, three young children. This was a huge responsibility; but the nanny, Grandma Katha-had sent seemed to be helping. They'd manage to raise all of the children…that is if he'd talk to Lily. Why wasn't he reaching out to her? Was it possible that Dianna had already died and he wasn't coping with his own grief and the three children's? Was he so overcome with grief that he couldn't talk to anyone? If so then what good was he to the children? Lily should have gone with him. To hell with her job!

Terrence had said Dianna was hanging on by a thread, when Terrence himself had left. Lily swivelled the chair in her office so she could look out the window; but all she saw was Emmett in her mind's eye. If only Terrence could have stayed with Emmett longer. Unfortunately, Terrence had to leave Emmett alone and high tail it back to Happy Valley, just because of the Beyer building. That damn building was cursed. Terrence wanted to tear it down, as he considered it a place of evil and not the home he had hoped for his family. Finding bodies buried in the walls made the place seem haunted, if it wasn't already.

He wasn't the only one in Happy Valley to feel this way; but Alberto Cozino the acting Mayor; the former comptroller of Happy Valley was going out of his way to make tearing down the building impossible. All those poor dead, murdered girls found in the walls and all that man cared about was political maneuvers.

Alberto Cozino had even tried to have the site declared a heritage site. It wasn't a heritage site and Alberto knew that. He just hated that in a few months after the election Grandma Katha would be mayor if the people had their way. Grandma Katha-had earned her votes. The investigation into the election had proven that the election votes had been stolen from her. Grandma Katha was the legal mayor and that meant that the acting mayor hadn't a leg to stand on. Albert Cozino fought that in the courts and refused to relinquish the mayor's job. He had somehow convinced the people of Happy Valley; that therc should be another election.

What a worm that man was; he was making Lily's life difficult, too. He was expropriating the properties on Lily's street, so far; they'd fought it, but probably sometime next year, Grandma Katha, Terrence, Amelia, Rose and Lily would all have to move. Then their homes would be torn down for widening of the road. That jerk actually thought, he could interfere in the office of the Crown Attorney in their cases. Lily had politely told Albert Cozino to butt out, but Lily was starting to wonder if she had a spy in her office. Alberto seemed to know too much of what was going on in the office and her cases.

Frankly, all these headaches were getting too be too much. If that Albert Cozino won the election, she would have to quit her job and go into private practice. The hours were getting longer and the cases were leaving her too long hours and not having enough time to properly prepare for cases. The only reason that the courts were working at all in Happy Valley was due to Crown attorneys, defence lawyers, police, judges and court administrative staff. The underfunding in this province was getting ridiculous, cutback, cutback,

and cutbacks. Every time the economy
floundered the money dwindled some
more. Somehow, scheduling for twelve,
or sixteen hours, during a six-hour court
day just didn't work. What brilliant
person thought it would? It was always
the same with governments the court
systems got the cuts. What they didn't
seem to realize was that there wasn't any
more to cut.

Lily swiveled her chair again to face her
office door. She really should be looking
at the Carson case; but she had so much
on her mind that she just couldn't
concentrate.

Colleen, Lily's assistant and very good
friend, suddenly appeared in Lily's office,
"Zebadiah Rockwood's lawyer has filed
for parole for him,"

"It's only been a year does Michael
Taylor think Amani Sulimani's life was
only worth a year? Stupid drunk driver."

"They already filed and the verdict is
coming down today."

"Why wasn't I informed?"

"The scuttle is the higher ups thought you were too close to the Sulimani family and you were off sick."

"Let me know when the information comes in."

"I'll have to keep track of the calls the answering machine from the phone company is on the frizz. Some people think we haven't returned their calls on purpose."

"What nonsense! I always return calls if I get them."

"I'll make that clear, now I'll leave you to study the arson case some more. I think Alberto Cozino is behind this. Someone said they saw some workers in the building allegedly fixing the phone lines; but now the lines aren't working."

"It's ridiculous, how is this man getting away with so much? We should call the police."

"The problem is Lily, there is no proof only speculation and rumour. Even if we found the lines damaged, we couldn't prove he hired someone to do it. If you need me just buzz. That seems to be working, for now," Colleen exclaimed leaving through the door and shutting it behind her.

Lily sat there for an hour reading over the Carson file. She was ready to prosecute him for fraud and theft over $500; this should be a slam dunk. There was nothing to worry her here. She stared at her phones they hadn't rang; maybe Emmett had rang her home phone? Was the office phone on the fritz the problem? No, he had three phones he could reach, she dialled into her messages. There were none; he hadn't called. Why didn't he call, or even answer his phone? Lily wondered. She'd called and called again; why didn't he answer? Was he okay? She was almost ready to chuck her job and get on a plane right now.

150
This Little Girl Had a Little Curl
S. G. Lee

Three more children… Lily and Emmett would have a full house with Rose, Caleb the new baby and the three other children. Huge responsibilities… maybe she should quit her job? Someone should be there for those poor children who just lost their mother. Lily remembered vaguely how she felt when her mother had disappeared, the anger and how she had turned it all inward. Three volatile children who had newly lost their mother and then add in Caleb and Rose who also suffered losses and it was going to take a lot of parenting to help them. The nanny would help for now; but when the baby came Lily was taking the year that unemployment offered and then after that she would decide whether she wanted to go back to her job.

The nanny would help for now; but when the baby came Lily was taking the year that unemployment offered and then after that she would decide whether she wanted to go back to her job.

This Little Girl Had a Little Curl
S. G. Lee

A baby! She was having a baby; she still couldn't believe it. She was so overjoyed to have a child especially with Emmett. He'd make a great father. She really wished though that she had been able to reach him and tell him.

If she waited too much longer Emmett would guess. Her little mound would soon be showing. Already her clothes were a little snug and that button on her dress pants? She'd had to move that over and put on an elastic just to wear them. She hadn't told anyone her secret yet; since she wanted Emmett to be the first to know. Grandma Katha was giving her sideways glances though. Did she suspect that Lily was pregnant? Amelia hadn't said anything; Lily guessed she didn't suspect either.

Rose was oblivious to it too. She seemed to be focused more on the cheerleader tryouts. Lily was surprised Rose always said cheerleading was sexist; but all of a sudden, she wanted to be a cheerleader. Could a sudden interest in a football player have caused the sudden interest in cheerleading? Rose seemed happy in any case so if this made her happy then Lily was all for it.

Lily's office door opened again.

"Lily why aren't you ready? Did you forget about our lunch date? Was it that Rockwell getting parole?" asked Grandma Katha, "What a travesty! Sometimes judges get it wrong; but money shouldn't buy a get out of jail free card."

"Hush. while I don't agree with parole, you shouldn't say he bought his freedom. You could be sued."

"Our courts can make mistakes; but we must trust in the system."

"Better you then me. I think you're looking a little peaked, my love; maybe you should see a doctor."

This Little Girl Had a Little Curl
S. G. Lee

"Why thank-you, Grandma Katha, everyone loves to be told they look peaked," Lily exclaimed.

"I love you darling, that's why I can say these things. You've been doing so much lately and you had heart surgery only a few months ago. I 'm worried that you are pushing yourself too hard. There isn't more damage from that bullet is there?" Grandma Katha stated looking scared.

"Not to worry, Grandma Katha, I'm fine." Lily said smiling then seeing and smelling the coffee Grandma Katha is carrying, Lily turned green and had to bite back the bile.

"You don't look fine,in fact the last time I saw someone looking like you... Don't tell me you're going to make me one of the happiest women alive and give me another great-great-grandbaby?" Grandma Katha exclaimed excitedly, her eyes shining, "I'm right aren't I?"

This Little Girl Had a Little Curl
S. G. Lee

"I haven't told anyone yet; not even Emmett you can't tell anyone," Lily stated.

"Just Terrence," Grandma Katha pleaded.

"No, you can't tell Grandpa Terrence. He's a wonderful charming man; but he can't keep a secret to save his life. Please, Grandma Katha, I want Emmett to know first," Lily pleaded.

"If that's what you want dear. I'm just so happy for you and Emmett. I can keep a secret, even if it's from Terrence. For you honey, I would walk a thousand seas; you know that," Grandma Katha exclaimed.

"I love you, Grandma Katha. What would I ever do without you?" Lily stated.

"You'll never have to find out." Grandma Katha stated, "Now let's go feed my new grand-baby and make it grow big and strong. You have to eat some vegetables, and some meat and potatoes, those are the best foods to grow healthy babies. And for desert Jell-O. You make the baby stronger in the womb that way."

"Thank-you Grandma Katha, even though you are fussing a little too much. Jell-O huh! One of those old folk remedies of yours I assume. I'll try that. I want this baby to be very healthy. I'm so glad I have you, because with all these kids in the house Emmett and I are going to need a little help." Lily fretted.

"You'll have it honey. We'll give those kids a warm Kelly welcome. After all they are Kellys as well as Rogers now. Now let's go eat lunch. I've got lots to celebrate five new grand-babies with these three, Caleb, and the new one coming. Wow, I'll have six great-great-grand-babies counting Rose. I'm so blessed."

"I'm starving, let's go," Lily stated.

~0~

Chapter 9 – Missing Lily

E mmett couldn't understand why he

kept missing Lily. He'd try to phone several times. He'd even called her office; but Colleen hadn't answered. No one was answering the phone; so, he'd left a message; or should he say messages?

Lily had to be either at her office, or at home he'd thought; but he couldn't reach her. The answer service must be on the fritz at her work; but was something also wrong with her cell phone, maybe the battery? Sure, she was in court a lot; but he wished just once he could have touched base with her. Why hadn't she called? Was she mad at him? Had he expected too much of Lily? Was she avoiding him to keep from making a decision on him and the children? Was she moving away from him?

Maybe he dialled the wrong cell number? He just wanted to be home in Happy Valley in Lily's arms. Today had been such a long day, yet again. They had cremated Dianna; after a funeral for the children's benefit. The children had born up very well; but Deirdre was clinging to him, like he was her only lifeline.

He was also worried about Rebecca; she seemed to be holding it all in, and from his experience; that's when people tended to go off like a lit fuse with all their emotions coming to force. Joseph was laid back and trying to blend into the background at times. Emmett was sure what to make of him. He was difficult child to get to know. Joseph was at that age, like a caged tiger ;where he was private and snarly at the same time. The thing parents fear most, a teen with attitude. Luckily, he already handled some of that with his sisters, and Caleb.

"Mr. Rogers?" Laura stated breaking up his thoughts.

"I thought we had this straightened out before, you are to call me Emmett. Please." Emmett stated.

"Thank-you, Emmett."

Laura all but purred, making Emmett very uncomfortable. That's all he needed, a nanny with a crush. He needed Laura to help with the kids; maybe he could steer her away to another option, once they returned to Happy Valley.

"Deirdre is asking for you," Laura continued.

"Oh."

"You go into her. I'll order us some dinner, since only the children have eaten. What would you like?" Laura asked eagerly.

"Anything will do, thank-you Laura," Emmett stated.

Emmett was obliviously unaware to the nuances of the subtle hints Laura was giving, that she was interested in him; but Rebecca saw it and was disgusted with Laura. She slipped into her sister's room and sat beside Deirdre's bed, soon Joseph joined her.

"Right, see you in awhile, Emmett," Laura stated picking up the phone in the hotel.

Emmett went into Deirdre's bedroom to check on her.

"I thought you were all in bed? That's what Laura said," Emmett stated surprised.

"We just were talking." Joseph stated defensively.

"Oh, okay. Deirdre you wanted me?" Emmett asked.

"I wants a story," Deirdre cried her fingers in her mouth.

"It's wanted a story and you should say, I would like a story and add a please," Joseph stated.

"Okay tanks Joseph," Deirdre said.

"Tell me a story about He-Man and She-Ra. Mommy used to tell us stories about them. She said you had a castle she bought you, sumpin called Castle Grayskull. Can I play with your Castle Grayskull when we get to Tario?"

"Good grief, it's in Ontario, stupid, and he probably got rid of it a long time ago. He's all grown up. Grown –ups don't have toys," Rebecca stated angrily.

"Actually, I still have it. I can get it out of storage," Emmett stated smiling.

"I can play with it then?" begged Deirdre.

"Gee whiz, Dee how many times do you have to be so stupid? He said he'd get it out of storage for you. Now shut-up, all right, all ready," Rebecca yelled.

Joseph violently shoved Rebecca and then raised his arm back. Emmett guessed his intentions, reached out and pulled back the left hand that was about to hit Rebecca.

"We talked about this remember Joseph? You cannot lose your temper and harm your sister, or sisters. You are bigger and stronger than her, and it is unfair to use your strength against her. Real men deal with their feelings better and channel it productively; so, it harms no one." Emmett stated, "You have to find a way to express your displeasure with anyone's behaviour without violence. What you may interpret as wrong could very well be the correct way, or just a child behaving in a way, that is normal for them. The point is, it is not your job to correct their behaviour, but mine."

This Little Girl had a Little Curl
S. G. Lee

"Rebecca you can't speak to your sister that way, either," Emmett chided Rebecca.

"I'm sorry, I didn't mean to make you all mad. I just wanted to play with the Castle." Deirdre stated starting to cry.

"Oh Dee, no, I'm sorry." Rebecca stated crying.

Emmett tried to comfort both Rebecca and Deirdre, but only Dee will let him hug her. Rebecca shoved Emmett away and continued gulping and crying loud heartbreaking sobs.

Joseph reached out to Rebecca and said, "I'm sorry for getting mad at you; but you have to stop calling Dee stupid. She's little that's all and doesn't know everything yet. I love you even when I'm mad at you. You big lunk. You are my twin sister and that makes you pretty special. We will get through this and you'll always have me for your brother,"

Joseph said hugging and comforting his sister.

Silently pleased, Emmett is glad that Joseph apologized to his sister . Joseph was defending Deirdre in his own way. Emmett wondered, had Joseph been defending his siblings for a long time? Poor kid, he needed a better role model. Hopefully, Emmett could leave up to Joseph's ideals. Emmett knew he had a lot to deal with if the children needed some extra help, he'd send them to a psychologist. Maybe he should have taken Caleb to one?

The kids were watching television; some sort of superhero show that he'd never seen before. Was it suitable for Deirdre? Was he already terrible at this parenting thing letting the television babysit them, while Laura was getting her things together to go to Happy Valley? No, they seem okay; it was okay for them to watch a little television and this looked tame.

This Little Girl had a Little Curl
S. G. Lee

Who could have murdered Sherry-Anne
anyway? All signs (according to Kendall
who was keeping him in the loop, thank
goodness) were pointing to a woman
having committed the murder. Who of
Sherry-Anne's acquaintance had wanted
her dead? That was the question that Alan
and Kendall were working on.

Emmett wished he could be in two places
at once, no make that all three places.
He'd like to be here with Dianna's
children; but he'd also like to be
analyzing and investigating Sherry-
Anne's murder and be with Caleb too. He
heaved a sigh as he realized he'd left out
time with Lily and Rose as well. Five
different places, he'd better get used to it.
He would be raising five children if Lily
would join him as his wife.

Emmett heaved a sigh wishing he could
reach Lily and talk to her. Dratted
invention! All this technology and yet he
couldn't reach Lily. Suddenly he had an
idea he would send Lily a telegram, since

he couldn't get her on the phone. He knew it was old fashion; but somehow, he thought if he sent her one that she would be thrilled and accept his proposal especially if it said…,

You are the best thing in my life.

Marry me

Love your Emmett

Of course, he should have included the fact that he and the children were taking out an early morning flight to Happy Valley, Ontario and winging their way back to her tomorrow, but in his excitement, he forgot. Oh well, it was too late now. Surely Terrence had told Lily by now; that there were two more children alive (since he hadn't been able to) if not it would be a great surprise, wouldn't it?

Emmett considered the matter for a moment, fingering the box with the

This Little Girl had a Little Curl
S. G. Lee

engagement ring, he planned to give Lily in his pocket. He'd forgotten it was in his pocket when he boarded the plane and the security officer had demanded to know why he had it.

Emmett considered the matter for a moment, fingering the box with the engagement ring, he planned to give Lily in his pocket. He'd forgotten it was in his pocket when he boarded the plane and the security officer had demanded to know why he had it. He'd explained that he was winging his way to his dying sister and forgotten it in his coat pocket and how he'd planned to propose when he was called. He'd thought he probably sounded suspicious rambling so much, but the security officer had wished him good luck; when he actually proposed. Emmett picked up the phone and placed the telegram order while still with the children.

"You should get her some flowers too. Girls like flowers," commented Joseph as he heard the telegram recited over the phone.

"Good idea, I'll send her favourite roses with a few lilies."

"Roses for her Rosey and Lily for her? I like that," Deirdre stated.

"I would want a diamond ring. Do you have one Uncle Emmett?" Rebecca demanded.

"Yes. See," Emmett said opening the ring box.

"Oooh, it's pretty and all sparkly," Deirdre exclaimed.

"Yes, it is lovely. How many carats is it?" asked Rebecca sounding knowledgeable.

"Eighteen carats," Emmett said proudly.

"Is that good?" asked Joseph of Rebecca.

"It's very good especially on a cop's salary. You must have saved for a long time, unless you owe a lot of money," Rebecca stated.

"I think they prefer to be called policeman," Joseph chided.

"Thank-you Joseph, Rebecca and Deirdre I owe you one. I'll order some flowers delivered too and I'll keep the ring here safe with me. Thank-you all, for reminding me. Now it's time for bed," Emmett commented. He then picked the phone up again calling the florist and placed an order for red roses with white baby's breath.

"Why baby's breath flowers Uncle Emmett? I thought you said her favourites were roses and lilies?" Rebecca asked.

"Baby's breath is for sincerity, and honesty, humility, and devotion. I'm saying, I honestly love her by sending red roses, baby's breath and a lily; at least that's what it said what I looked it up on the internet," Emmett replied.

"You must really love this Lily," Joseph uttered.

"He told me about her; she's sounds nice. Her little girl is fourteen and her name is Lily," Deirdre offered.

"You love her?" Rebecca asked.

"I do love her." Emmett stated, "Now it's late and we have an early start. Goodnight Joseph, Rebecca ,and Deirdre," Emmett announced.

"Goodnight, Uncle Emmett." All three children echoed.

"Goodnight, pumpkins," Emmett said closing the door and entering the living room area only to find the lights dimmed.

"Laura?" He asked confused.

"You came out too soon. I haven't got the candles lit yet," Laura answered smiling sweetly.

"That's okay. I'm just going to put on the light." Emmett stated sounding really unnerved.

"Sure, that's fine. I was just trying to make it look like grown-up dinner. I ordered steak and potatoes for you. I hope that was okay?"

"I guess that will be okay but…"

"I'm sorry. I went too far. Forgive me?"

"Sure Laura."

Laura had tried passing it off, but Emmett could tell she went to a lot of trouble to make the room look different. Did she have designs on him he wondered? No, he was just being a foolish, flattered old man in his almost mid- thirties, wasn't he?

He stared as Laura unfurled the food from under the metal covers keeping it warm. Sure, enough it was steak and potatoes; he thought sitting down and then peeking under the other he saw cherry cheesecake.

How had she known his favourite dessert?
Lucky guess, he thought.

As he ate his food, Laura looked at him
through her long lashes and Emmett felt
disloyal to Lily, just looking at her. She
was interested in him; this was not a good
thing. She was young and beautiful…
keyword young, but even if he had been
interested and he wasn't, she felt way too
young for him. Besides he had Lily.
Didn't he? He did he never lose Lily, he'd
do what he needed to keep her. With Lily
he was at peace. She gave him refuge
from all the bad things he faced in life,
including his job. With Lily he could tell
her anything, she'd listen and advise if
necessary, or just lend an ear to his
worries; she never judged. He missed her
so much. Even the cheesecake reminded
him of her. She'd made some for him
only days before he'd left.

"How is everything? I hope I ordered all
your favourites," Laura commented.

This Little Girl had a Little Curl
S. G. Lee

"Yes, it is good thank-you Laura,"
Emmett said finishing his food.

Laura smiled as if she wanted to say
something; but Emmett decided he
needed to be alone and not give Laura any
ideas then said goodnight and left the
room to go to his room. Laura stared at
his departing back and frowned.

Deirdre who had spied on them wondered
if she should trust Wara er Laura. It was
so hard to say that name. Laura didn't
seem nice, and she was being too nice to
Unca Emwettt. Deirdre had seen another
woman do that with daddy, hoping he'd
take a fourth wife. Deirdre had heard
daddy complaining that Rochelle and
Beatrice were not doing their parts; as his
sister wives and that he'd have to marry
two new much younger woman, soon so
he'd have more children.

Deirdre had told Joseph about Laura and
he'd said not to worry, but Deirdre was
worried.

Maybe she should tell Joseph about what she thought about Wara? He'd know what to do and if they needed to be careful around Wara. Mommy said Unca Emwettt would protect them, Deirdre told herself she was safe, and she tiptoed back in the bedroom climbing in the big bed, beside Rebecca who was snoring. Closing her eyes, Deirdre fell asleep.

~0~

Chapter 10 – Acting Out

Rose entered the house, worried

about her mother. Mom wasn't looking herself, lately. She was not the strong Mother, take no prisoners' mother, Rose knew. Was she sick again? Rose had never been as scared, as when she heard that Mom had been shot earlier this year. Then later, that had been compounded, when Mom had to have heart surgery to correct the damage from the bullet.

Grandma Katha had always been there to confide and look after Rose; but she wanted and needed her mother Lily. Rose knew as a teenagers, other teenagers said they didn't need their parents but they hadn't lost their father or their biological mother to jail. The only good thing to come out of all this was that Emmett was getting closer to her mother. She felt disloyal to her dad, but mom was young and she needed someone and not just any someone.

Emmett was kind and he seemed interested in being not only Mom's boyfriend; but he listened to Rose and all her problems... at least he had until Sherry-Anne was murdered. Caleb needed his dad right now; so, Emmett was spending a lot of time with him. Now though Emmett had to worry about these kids his nieces and nephew.

Emmett was a good man; he'd make mom happy. Emmett had even moved in. She'd push them to get married. Then everyone would be happy. Rose was thrilled about Emmett moving in. He was a great guy and now if they married, Caleb could be her brother. They'd planned it last year after Christmas; but Caleb's mom had tricked Emmett and mom into thinking Emmett had cheated on mom. Rose still hated the dead Sherry-Anne for all she'd done to her mother; but she wasn't about to tell Caleb, or Emmett that. Sometimes you needed to keep these things to yourself. Was Emmett, the reason mom was looking so worried and frazzled, or was she worried about these children he was bringing home? Frankly. Rose wasn't thrilled about those children coming either. For one thing their home was not big enough and Rose was not sharing a bedroom with Rebecca a twelve-year-old, especially since she had never even met her.

The little girl Deirdre probably would be fun to have around; but Rebecca and Joseph were twelve- years old and pre-teens were a pain. Pre-teens were a bundle of nerves, just waiting to spout off and cause havoc. They would probably take up all mom's time too. The more she thought about it, the more Rose wished they weren't coming to live with them. Was that bad of her; that she didn't want to share her mother? She was already sharing mom with Emmett, and Caleb, wasn't that enough?

Rose walked down the stairs. Rose set her backpack down at the door and ran back upstairs and into the bathroom. Darn, there was no toilet paper left. She would just have to use Mom's en-suite bathroom. Mom's bathroom would have toilet paper. Mom wouldn't mind. Rose entered the bathroom and did her business. Then going to the sink, she washed her hands, and saw a pill bottle out on the counter. Rose dried her hands and picked it up.

What the...? But these were prenatal vitamins and there were some gone. Mom was pregnant? So, that was it! Why hadn't she said anything to Rose? Did Emmett know? If Mom had her own child, where did that leave Rose? She wasn't her flesh and blood child. Would Mom care more about a child that she and Emmett had created? And now with all these other children here (including Caleb) how would she find time for

This Little Girl Had a Little Curl
S. G. Lee

Rose? Rose would be the last on the list;
that is if she was remembered at all. Just
because she didn't act up and act out,
didn't mean she shouldn't be noticed.

A baby, a newborn, would be in their
small house. It looked like she wouldn't
be having a social life anymore; someone
would have to look after these children
and with Mom's job, who was going to be
there all the time? Oh yes, that's right
good old Rose.

You know what? Good old Rose was not
going to be pushed around anymore. No,
it wasn't her children and her
responsibility. Mom was just going to
have to hire someone to help and maybe
take some time away from her job,
because Rose had a life now with Derek.
Sure, it was only a week that they'd been
dating; but Derek said he loved her.
Derek was her steady boyfriend now, and
she wanted to see him every moment of
the day because at least he paid attention
to her and the other girls were jealous of
her. In fact, if she didn't hurry, she would

be late for their date at the ice cream
shop. Rose hurried down the stairs,
grabbing her coat and sailing out the front
door, forgetting to lock the door.

~0~

This Little Girl Had a Little Curl
S. G. Lee

Rose thought about how Carol had

been distant and standoffish. Carol
claimed it was because she had a busy life
now, between living with the chief of
police and working with Aunt Amelia;
but Rose knew that Carol was moving
away from her. She'd seen her hanging
out with some other girls. It didn't matter
anymore; because now she had very little
time for Carol; because she had Derek.
She wasn't substituting Carol for Derek,
or because she wanted a boyfriend to
show off like her new friend Amy said.
She loved Derek okay so she really,
really, liked him but it could be love
someday…maybe and she had a
boyfriend, unlike most girls at school.

Getting back to Carol, she wouldn't be
any help anyway, with the baby and all
those children, nieces and that nephew of
Emmett's either. Carol was working a lot

with Aunt Amelia at Quirks (Amelia's hobby store.) In fact, Carol was working there tonight. Carol had always been available to talk to before; but now she was busy, busy, busy... with either Aunt Amelia, or her store. At least Rose left a note for mom which said she would be home after eleven p. m...

Rose probably would arrive home, before mom though; because mom kept working very late hours. How she expected to raise a baby with such long hours, Rose didn't know; but it was definitely not going to be Rose looking after all the children. Not at all, Rose repeated to herself. Rose felt really alone. She knew she shouldn't feel alone; it was good that Carol was getting to know Aunt Amelia; but it felt like she was moving away from Rose. She wanted to talk to Carol about all the ins and outs of dating, Rose wanted that easy friendship they always had.

Rose continued walking to the ice cream store thinking. She was worried about the pressure that Derek was putting on her to sleep with him. She'd have to love someone to sleep with them and really, she'd always pictured that happening with a ring on her finger. She'd told Derek she wasn't ready for that; but Derek felt that she would be ready soon and she didn't know how to tell him that she wouldn't. How do you tell a guy that you want to wait; until you are married without scaring them off? Maybe being a virgin until marriage was archaic; but that was how she felt.

Rose entered the ice cream shop, noting that it was really busy. It was six o'clock in the afternoon, why was everyone in town here? She wanted private moments with Derek, not moments where everyone could watch; except if Sarah Keller was here, Rose would like to see her surprise that Rose was with Derek. She wished she'd dare bring Derek back to her house, but mom had a rule, no boys in the house when she wasn't home. In fact, she hadn't even told mom about the fact that Derek and she were exclusive. Mom had promised to meet him weeks ago; but she hadn't found time in her busy schedule. It was Rose's delicious secret; that Derek loved Rose enough to call her his girlfriend. Carol didn't even know; but that was her fault. It would soon be all over the school.

She entered the ice cream shop and smiled. There was Derek standing near a table, trying to get her attention. His long lanky frame was leaning up against a wall. He was extremely tall for sixteen, being over six feet tall. Derek said his dad was six-feet-six. Rose wondered if Derek would be that tall too? She stared at his chin length, strawberry blonde hair and thought I wish he'd get rid of his Justin Bieber haircut; it would make him so much more attractive. After all he was an older man, having had his birthday two weeks ago. He was younger, the Biebs; but he shouldn't look like a Bicbcr want to be. He was so much more than a carbon copy, wasn't he? His personality certainly wasn't the same; sometimes he could be mean; but he always was nice afterward.

This Little Girl Had a Little Curl
S. G. Lee

"Hey good, you're here. Let's get a cone to go. Larry Harrow's having a party and we are invited. It started a half hour ago," Derek stated.

"I can't go to a party. I didn't let my Mom know," protested Rose.

"Geesh, Rose, don't be a wet blanket."

"I can't go until I talk my mom and get permission."

"Do I have to spell it out for you? Your friends are throwing you a party. Now you've spoiled the surprise; it's your birthday party," Derek complained.

"It's my birthday party? But Larry hates me!"

"Not really! Larry is just Larry; besides he knows you are my girlfriend now; so. he wanted to throw you a party."

"Really? You all remembered? I think everyone else forgot. I know my Mom did," complained Rose.

"Sorry about that; but not me babe. Look I even got you a present," Derek said holding out a wrapped box.

"For me? Oh thank-you, Derek. You're the best boyfriend, ever," Rose stated, smiling.

"Well open it, for Pete's sake," Derek demanded.

Rose opened it to a charm bracelet with a charm of a gun on it.

"Do you like it? I thought since you said your mom's boyfriend calls you Annie Oakley, you'd like it," Derek asked expectantly.

"I love it Derek." Rose said, "Let's go to that party I told my mom I wouldn't be home until after eleven. Mom will probably be asleep anyway."

Hours later, Rose tiptoed into Lily's house. Her shirt was buttoned incorrectly. She had tears streaked across her face and she was feeling hungover. It's four a.m, and Lily is fast asleep.

"I hate you, Derek Pember. You got me drunk and try to take advantage. I'm never speaking to you again. "Rose stated aloud, "Sweet sixteen, it was not! No one who I cared about remembered my birthday. Happy Birthday to me!"

Rose tore the charm bracelet off her wrist breaking the clasp, as she threw it on the floor missing the garbage can.

~0~

Chapter 11 –
Homeward Bound

Emmett awakened in his hotel, to his room phone ringing. He wondered who could be calling this early as he glanced at the clock and saw that it flashed five a.m... Drat, he was hoping to sleep another hour.

"Hello?" Emmett stated into the phone.

"Oh, did I wake you?" Kendall asked.

"What's wrong?" Emmett responded.

"Damn, I forgot the time change, didn't I?" Kendall stated with regret.

"It appears you did, Kendall. There is a
three-hour time difference, you know."
Emmett scolded.

"Sorry, boss." Kendall said then laughed.

"So, what's up?" Emmett asked again.

"I just wanted to fill you in on the case, so
far. We interviewed Louise Moore, but
she's still doing time for the murders of
Elizabeth Renfrew, Trent Byrant, Alfred
Getts, Fred Parcell, and the attempted
murder of Sherry-Anne Mobley. The
Senator's wife and children are accounted
for, and have not been in Canada since
the Senator died. Bette Renfrew and Belle
Renfrew are staying with their maternal
grandmother and although they saw their
sister in early January, they have only
talked by phone since."

"So that rules them out."

"Uh huh, now we talked to some of
Sherry-Anne's colleagues at the hospital
one Dayita Patel and her brother Dr. Raj
Patel. You remember them."

"I do. Didn't we rule them out in the murder of Alexander Vincent Scholar, the music teacher at Rose's high school?"

"We did decide they weren't guilty. When we spoke to them recently, they both said they respected Sherry-Anne and said she was a great asset to the hospital. They really miss her warm friendly manner, as well. It seems Sherry-Anne had a calming effect on the patients."

"Any other people you spoke with?" Emmett enquired.

"We spoke with Dafydd, but he's pretty broken up about it. He seems to be focusing any what's left of himself on Daniel. Daniel's a cute baby by the way. I got to hold him," Kendall waxed.

"Daniel is a sweet baby. You must have talked to someone else."

"We spoke with inmates, Dr. Henry Thomas and Janet Thomas, in two separate prisons. They both were surprised and actually had sadness for the

demise of Sherry-Anne. Doctor. Thomas
expressed his belief that Sherry-Anne was
one of the best nurses he ever worked
with. Janet Thomas said that Sherry-Anne
was one of the few nurses that didn't
make a move on, either Doctor Henry
Thomas, or Alexander Scholar. Janet
Thomas seemed all broken up about the
death, if you can call a sociopath broken-
up," laughed Kendall

"I still can't believe she gotten into the
position of being a principal at the local
high school. She really hid her
sociopathic tendencies well," Emmett
admitted.

"She really seemed to like Sherry-Anne;
maybe because like attracts like?"

"You really didn't care for Sherry-Anne."

"No, I didn't. I didn't like they way she
treated you, or anyone else."

"There not letting that psychopath Janet
Thomas out anytime soon, are they?"

"Janet Thomas won't be getting out.
Those charges we got her on will keep her
jail for at least twenty-five years,"
Kendall insisted.

"Happy Valley's a better place for it,"
Emmett admitted.

"Did Lily tell you we interviewed Caleb?
Sorry about that boss; but we needed his
statement. It was just bad timing, what
with him getting suspended and all,"
Kendall continued, not realizing
Emmett's silence is, not because he's mad
at her; but because Lily didn't tell him
any of this.

Emmett took a deep breath and tried to
calm himself .Couldn't Lily have at least
texted him this bad news.

"Damn it! I go away and all hell breaks
loose and no one sees fit to tell me?"
Emmett stated angrily.

"Lily didn't tell you?" Kendall stated
shocked.

This Little Girl had a Little Curl
S. G. Lee

"I haven't been able to get a hold of her at all. It's really strange, almost like she's avoiding me." Emmett admitted ,"But I'm sure that will all change today, after she gets my flowers and telegram."

"You sent her flowers?" Kendall asked, "That was so sweet."

"I asked her to marry me again."

"You asked her by a telegram? That's really unusual," Kendall stated, sounding like she thought it was a bad idea.

"You don't think she'll like that?" Emmett asked, sounding hurt.

"Knowing Lily, she'll love it. She's quirky like you, Emmett. That's why you two are such a good match. I'm sure she has a good reason, for not telling you about Caleb's suspension. It wasn't his fault anyway, that boy egged him on I'm sure. He seems like a real piece of work. I'm sure we'll be hearing about him soon," Kendall stated trying to reassure Emmett.

"I hope you're correct, about this incident. I'm sure Lily will enlighten me when I finally speak to her."

"Lily's a good one; don't let her get away."

"I'm glad you approve of my proposal. I was afraid you were going to tell me it was huge mistake," Emmett said with relief.

"When are you coming home with your new brood?" Kendall enquired.

"Actually, this morning we have a ten-a.m. flight."

"Oh good, but you're going to have to find someone to look after them, so you can help me find Sherry- Anne's killer. "I'm not getting anywhere with my present help of Special Constable Alan Barnes," Kendall insisted.

"I have a nursemaid for them now, but I'm not sure she's going to work out."

"Oh buddy, you need someone. You can expect Lily to take on three young kids, plus Caleb and her own daughter, Rose. She really won't marry you, if you don't have someone to help. She's got a life and a job she's worked hard for. You can't throw everything at her to handle especially with our line of work," Kendall commented.

"I know that! I don't expect her to take on that many children without help; but Laura just isn't working out," Emmett insisted.

"Why that has she got a crush on teacher?" kidded Kendall.

Emmett sighed.

"Oh, my goodness she does? She likes you? She'll get over it, if you don't encourage her. If she doesn't, you'll have to fire her; but not before you find someone else to help me, Emmett," Kendall continued.

"I guess you're right I'll give her some time. She's young and impressionable. I'm probably her first crush," Emmett retorted.

"I have to admit I was crushing a little on you until, I got to know the real you," Kendall said then laughed.

"Funny, Kendall," Emmett responded sarcastically.

"I better let you go, so you can get the young things ready. It takes a while to get kids ready. They are not as fast as adults and they'll need breakfast then toys and snacks for the plane," Kendall stated.

"We don't want to forget Deirdre's new teddy bear," Emmett said in all seriousness.

"No, you don't want to forget it. See you are on top of it. A girl should never be parted from her teddy bear. See you soon Emmett."

"See you soon, Kendall."

~0~

Chapter 12 – They All Lied

Rose washed her clothes in the

washing machine and tried hard to forget completely about last night, but it was heavy on her mind. She felt dirty and used. Just thinking about it made her sick inside, and scared again. Why was Derek such a creep? It was awful all that clawing. She had said, *"No!"* **loudly!** Why hadn't he listened? Why had he hurt her so badly? It was attempted rape; but who could she tell? Who would believe her? If she hadn't gotten away and stumbled onto Caleb, (who sobered her up then brought her home) she could have passed out and been abused by anyone at that party. Some party! There was a crush there; but the girls were paired off with guys and she was sure some of them had wondered into the bedrooms and made out.

Rose had thought Derek was a good guy; but he wasn't and it wasn't like she could even complain it was attempted rape, but was it? She had been drinking underage and he was her boyfriend. I mean, wasn't it partly her fault? They'd just say she was asking for it.

She was just going to forget about and never speak to Derek again. It wasn't like she could talk to Carol. Carol was always busy now. She hardly ever saw her and Mom? Mom was focused on her career and now this new baby coming, and all those children? She didn't have time for Rose.

If her mom Lily found out ;would she blame Rose? After all she might think she was just being like her biological mother Cordelia. Cordelia had been into drugs and had moved in with her pimp. When

Cordelia had finally straightened herself
out, she had gotten an apartment with
Rose sharing custody with Rose's now
deceased father Horace. Then Cordelia's
former pimp had demanded that she come
back to him. He had kidnapped her
drugged her and lastly threatened Rose.
Cordelia had acted like any mother would
and had killed him. Rose didn't
understand why her mother Cordelia
hadn't gotten off; but she was serving
time now twenty-five years to life for
murder. Rose missed her.

That wasn't disloyal to Lily was it? Lily
had been there for her since she was nine
years old; but Rose loved her mother,
Cordelia. Rose wanted to see her mother;
maybe she'd go to the prison and tell
them she was eighteen now. Surely, they
would let her see her mother. It was a lie;
she was only sixteen years old; but they
didn't know that. Her mother Cordelia
would understand, better than Lily. Lily
wouldn't have been tricked by a
boyfriend into drinking alcohol, then

passing out. She wouldn't have awaked to her boyfriend attempting to rape her.

Lily had always cautioned her about underage drinking. Rose was so sure Lily had been the perfect teen; but when they dared Rose with one drink, she felt stupid and childish and she downed some of it. It was only one drink and she didn't drink all of it; why had she almost passed out? Of course, it had been drugged. Rose felt so stupid.

Her biological mom, Cordelia and had made mistakes; she would understand much better than her mom, Lily. They could speak about this clearly and she'd make sense of it all.

She could try to forget it; accept every time she closed her eyes, she remembered him tearing her shirt groping her trying to take what he wanted. She survived a serial killer who had wanted to do this; only to have someone she trusted… her so called boyfriend try to take what she wasn't ready to give. Thank God for

Caleb. Oh no, Caleb must think she was
an idiot how could she face him again?
She had to get away. She'd decided she
was going to visit her mother at the
penitentiary. She'd take the train and go
today. No one would know and she be
able to talk to her about all of this.

~0~

This Little Girl had a Little Curl
S. G. Lee

Rose boarded a bus after finding out

the train wasn't until evening. Rose
arrived at the prison with trepidation.
What if they wouldn't let her see her
mother? What if they figured out that she
was lying, that she wasn't eighteen years
old? That the identification she produced
was faked?

She was scared; but determined she had
to see this through, if she acted confident
then they'd believe her and she see her
Mother.

"Rose Brooksfield, to see Cordelia
Brooksfield," Rose stated to the guard
showing the fake identification.

"I'm sorry, miss, we don't have an inmate
here by that name," the guard stated
scanning her computer list.

"But you have to have her here. She's been here for almost six years," Rose protested, worrying that something had happened to her mother in prison and no one had told her.

"Just a moment. You look like a nice kid; but you shouldn't be showing that fake identification around it's going to get you in trouble." The guard stated sympathetically palming the identification, "I'll see if we can find out if she was transferred somewhere else; but you are not getting his identification back. I hope you have real identification."

"Thank-you," Rose said, though embarrassed that the guard knew she had faked her identification.

The guard spoke to another guard a female and then came back.

"You must have been a lot younger than that honey, and no one told you. The guard there said she was here in Happy Valley six years ago. She said Cordelia

Brooksfield is in the Mental Health
Centre in Pinecrest," the female guard
explained.

"That's impossible! She can't be Lily
would have told me. She wouldn't have
lied to me by omission," Rose stated
visibly shaken.

"Are you related to Cordelia? If you
contact them, they may be able to set up
an appointment for you to visit with
Cordelia. They do encourage visitation to
help the inmates," the guard continued
not noticing how upset Rose really is.

"Thank-you." Rose stated turning and
exiting the penitentiary.

Rose thought, everyone always kept what
they wanted to themselves. How many
other people knew about Cordelia? Knew
she was Rose's mother and that she was
in a mental health *' criminal'* facility; like
that evil Brad Owens. Were they in the
same facility? She certainly hoped not.
Were the whole world liars, like Lily?

Look at Grandma Katha she had children by a rapist. Her child was stolen and didn't tell anyone. Then she passed off the other child, as someone else's all these years. Maybe Grandma Katha would listen? No, she was old and somewhat set in her antique ways. She probably knew this secret too.

No, they were liars, all of them, even Aunt Amelia. Aunt Amelia didn't tell anyone about her family being murdered. Mom knew but Rose didn't. They probably all knew where Mommy Cordelia was and did, they tell Rose? No, they didn't tell her. Why didn't Daddy tell Rose that her mother was in a mental facility while he was alive? What about Lily she must have known? Was her mother that sick? There were scary criminals at that so-called mental facility. It was a place for the criminally insane after all why was Mom Cordelia there?

Mom Cordelia wasn't criminally insane like that freak Brad Owens. He had stalked Amelia and killed her family and several others. Now that was crazy!

Her mom, Cordelia had only protected her daughter ;that didn't make her crazy. There was also Barbara Franks residing there who had kidnapped Rose, Caleb and Carol. She murdered Carol's parents and grandfather. Dangerous people were there with her mother, was her mother truly safe? She couldn't believe she had called Lily mother. Rose felt she'd let her mother , Cordelia down, so badly. Lily had promised Rose her mother was safe. She'd said she was in prison for twenty-five years, but she'd lied. Rose couldn't trust her anymore.

"I hate the world! They are all filthy liars. Everyone just keeps things from me." She said muttering aloud and getting strange looks from people on the street as she left the jail and walked to the bus station.

At the bus stop she waited at she continued to mutter, "My mother Cordelia has been there for six years. All those

times Lily or daddy said they were
visiting my mother, were they really?"

Had Lily really kept my mother safe, or
did she really want to get rid of her and
out her in that place just to get my dad?
Did she ever really want me? Now that
she has her own baby and my dad is gone;
she probably doesn't want me and doesn't
know how to get rid of me; the way she
did my mother. My real mother!!! Not
that woman who pretended she loved me
and just lied and lied to my face.

Lily has another think coming if she
thinks she can continue to hide my
mother from me. I'm going to visit my
real mother. I'll help her get better and
when she gets better, I'll live with her, not
the two-faced woman, Lily Kelly who
calls herself my mother. Just you wait and
see.

With that Rose smiled a gruesome smile
that frightened the other passenger
waiting who thought about reporting the
strange acting teen to the police; but when

the bus came and Rose seemed quiet and normal again. Rose entered the bus and sat quietly at the back, the passenger then relaxed and forgot all about the strange teenager.

Rose took the city bus to the train station. She'd take a train to Pinecrest and see her mom, Cordelia soon, or her name wasn't Rose Brooksfield she vowed as she consulted the train schedule and took out her emergency credit card.

~0~

Chapter 13 – A Tangled Web of Lies

T he phone rang and Lily jumped, but answered it mid-jump. In a recorded message, a telemarketer said something about a sale at some store Lily used to shop at. It's not the time for this! I'm about to go out of my mind with worry. Rose is missing and no one, I've talked to has heard from Rose in the last eight hours. I still can't believe that the summer writer's class didn't called me, when Rose hadn't shown up. Maybe I'm expecting too much from them. They probably thought if someone blew off their class they were heading to the beach, or on some summer holiday. At least that's what the woman I spoke to seem to say.

Where was Rose? It wasn't like her not to let me know where she was. Had someone kidnapped her, again? That seemed like an unlikely supposition but where was Rose? These were the thoughts racing through Lily's mind. If only she hadn't spent all day in court. Her phone was blinking, thank God; maybe it was a message from Rose.

"Lily? Where are you Lily? Didn't you get my telegram? I'm home with the children. Call me. I'd like to bring them to live with you and Rose; but I don't want to impose as I've heard nothing from you. I know I'm talking too much for a mess….," The message broke off here.

"Oh thank, goodness, Emmett will help me find Rose." Lily thought, "She has to be safe."

Lily dialed the familiar cell phone number.

"Emmett?" Lily said as the phone answered.

"This is Emmett Rogers, please leave a message at the beep." the phone message said.

Lily hung up angrily and distraught.

"Why don't you answer your phone Emmett? Are you playing games? You wanted me to call you. Why aren't you answering? You claim you love me why aren't you ever available?

Lily frantically called Carol.

"Have you heard anything from Rose? Has she called you yet?" Lily demanded.

"I'm sorry, Aunt Lily, Rose hasn't called me. I've been working here at Quirks all day; but Aunt Amelia allowed me to keep my phone on, so, I would have gotten any text or call. I've tried texting Rose and calling her; but I think her phone must be off, or something because she doesn't respond to me," Carol answered.

"Give me your phone, Carol," Lily heard, Amelia state in the background.

"Lily do you want us to come over and help you look? I'll close the store," Amelia insisted.

"Yes, come over; but leave a message on your phone for Rose to call me in case she calls in," Lily answered.

"Lily?" Grandma Katha yelled from the front hallway.

"Grandma Katha?" Lily responded.

"Terrence and I came as soon as we got your message," Grandma Katha stated.

"I can't find her Grandma Katha. What can I do? How can I find her? Where is she?" Lily stated frantically.

"We will find her darling. She's got to be somewhere. When did you see her last?" Grandma Katha asked

"She left me a note; before she went out last night. Oh no, yesterday was her birthday. How could I have forgotten? What kind of parent forgets her own daughter's birthday? No wonder she's nowhere to be found; she probably ran away with that boyfriend of hers."

"Rose has a boyfriend? What's that boy's name?" asked Grandma Katha.

"His name is Derek Pember. I should have called him. She really likes this boy, maybe she's with him?" Lily said hopefully, then she said," Oh no, maybe she's with him?"

"Call him," Grandma Katha urged.

"I'm sure you'll find the dear girl is just upset about her birthday. Tell you what I'll arrange a party right now and you can tell her we had planned it all along for tonight as a surprise," Terrence stated.

"Thank you, my dear." Grandma Katha said patting his arm, "But that can wait until we find Rose.

"She is my granddaughter too. Don't you worry Lily; we will make this right. We will make her happy again. You just call that boy while I go in the other room, and make the arrangements, sparing no expense," Terrence stated confidently and he then left the room to make the arrangements.

"You're not listening," Grandma Katha said to his departing back.

"You told him, didn't you?" Lily asked

"I'm sorry dear, he guessed that you were pregnant; but I swore him to secrecy. He won't tell anyone," Grandma Katha explained.

"What is done is done, but he had better not say anything to Emmett. I haven't been able to talk to him yet," Lily admitted.

"Terrence won't; he knows how my wrath is when I am crossed. What is the phone number of the boy?" Grandma Katha stated matter of fact.

"I don't know. I can't believe I didn't get his number from her. All this time she's been calling him from her cell phone and I haven't any idea what his phone number is."

"Do you know where he lives? Maybe his family still has a landline as the kids call it…," Grandma Katha reasoned.

"It's four hundred and three, I think it's Simmons Street, or is it Simon Street. I'm such a bad mother, I don't even know where my daughter's boyfriend lives," Lily sobbed.

"We'll find him we will get to her and make her come home don't worry Lily," Grandma Katha stated comforting Lily.

"I'm sounding like a drama queen. I have to pull myself together and find Rose. I am a Kelly, after all," Lily exclaimed.

"That's the spirit."

"It's Simmons Street…I think. Let's look for that in the yellow pages online; they still exist I think."

"Here it is Charles Pember, four hundred and three Simmons Street," Grandma Katha stated excitedly pointing to the number in the yellow pages and then dialing the number on her cell phone.

"Hello this Katha Stewart, I was wondering if my granddaughter Rose Brooksfield is at your home?" Grandma Katha asked.

"Who?" asked the male voice.

"To whom am I speaking?" Grandma Katha asked imperiously.

"Charles Pember. This is my phone. Why would your granddaughter be here?" Charles Pember asked.

"She's dating your son." Grandma Katha answered.

"Really? That's news to me. The boy is secretive though. He doesn't tell his mother, or me anything; though he did come slinky in last night in the wee hours of the morning." Charles Pember admitted, "Just a minute, I'll ask the boy, if he's seen the girl."

Grandma Katha heard yelling and then a conversation.

"Derek have you seen the Brooksfield girl today? Her grandmother is looking for her." Charles demanded.

"I haven't seen her since last night. We broke up. I doubt I'll be seeing her again," Derek replied sounding bored

"Uncommon good sense you showed boy. Take what you want and dump the trash."

This Little Girl had a Little Curl
S. G. Lee

Katha couldn't believe what she was hearing this man and his son were scum.

"Sorry Ms. Stewart. I'm sure you heard that the boy isn't seeing her anymore. I hope you find out where she went, but really we are out of it," Charles stated hanging up the phone.

Grandma Katha couldn't believe the nerve of the man or the boy; how dare they speak of Rose that way. Was there more to the story then the boy was saying and what about this party? Had that evil boy sone something to Rose? Parties could be dangerous for young girls. Heaven knows she read enough about how young girls getting drunk, high, or drugged, at these kinds of parties. Now she was really alarmed.

"What a nasty man. I tell you the girl is well shed of that boyfriend, if he's like the father and he certainly sounded like him," Grandma Katha remarked as she hung up her cell phone.

"They split up? I forgot her birthday and on the same day I did that, her boyfriend dumps her? My poor little Rose. We have to find her," Lily exclaimed.

"Pull yourself together, Lily. This isn't like you." Grandma Katha stated, "Think where, could the child be?"

"Maybe she went to see her new shrink Dr. Frobisher? After all it was a stressful day," Lily replied.

"I take it she wasn't at the boy's house?" Terrence said coming back in the room "Dears have you used the home phone?"

"No, we used my cell phone," Lily answered.

"Don't worry I didn't do anything. I can arrange a party later. Now, did you try to see what the last number called on the house phone was? This phone has that capability of redialling the number instantly old technology but very useful."

Terrence then used the function and reached the prison.

"Oh no, she called the prison. Do you think she found out about her mother,Cordelia?" Terrence asked.

"That would explain why she isn't here; but Pinecrest is a long way away." Grandma Katha stated, "She would have had to go by train, or bus. The train leaves too early in the morning, so it would have to be the bus, unless she left this afternoon at 2 p. m..."

"Can we call the bus station and find out if she bought a ticket?" Lily asked.

"With the security now, you have to give identification to buy tickets. Now we should be able to find out that is if I use my connections as a judge and the father of the police chief," Terrence said, "Give me five minutes and I'll find out."

"Doesn't that child have an emergency credit card? Call the credit card company dear," Katha declared,

Terrence then walked into the other room while dialing his cell phone. A few minutes later, he came back in the room and said, "The bus arrived in Pinecrest, five minutes ago and Rose was on board. She took a taxi to the mental facility there. I've hired a private plane to fly us to Pinecrest. It departs as soon as we get there. I also got air clearance for the flight. Had to pull in favours for that, but it's done."

" I found out she used the credit card to buy a ticket and pay for a cab to take her to Pinecrest," Lily cried.

"Lily?" Amelia said as she entered the house with Carol.

"In here, Amelia." Lily replied,

"Have you found her?" They both asked excitedly.

"Yes and no. She knows Amelia. She knows about her mother," Lily stated sadly.

"Oh no, that's awful. How in the world did she find out where her mother was?" Amelia asked.

"She's always known her mother was in prison. What on earth are you talking about?" Carol said mystified.

"She's not in a prison. Rose's dad did not want her to know that her mother is in a mental facility and she doesn't recognize her daughter," Amelia replied without thinking.

"Oh no, Rose won't be able to handle that. Why didn't you people tell her? She's not a child. Rose thinks her mother is a heroine. She's told me so many times, how her mother saved her." Carol stated.

"I'll tell you the whole story; but you have to keep this to yourself," Amelia declared.

"I will, just tell me so I can help Rose."

"I'll explain this better Amelia," Katha uttered then turning to Carol she said, "Rose has a romanticized view of her mother. Rose's mom was an addict. She got off the stuff, briefly; but it didn't take. Any temptation by the pimp to get her hooking again, just to buy her drugs again, was followed by Cordelia. When she killed the pimp? Sure, the pimp threatened Rose; but that was because Cordelia had sold the drugs that the drug dealer was holding for a bagman. He was angry with Cordelia and he threatened Rose. Then he kept the coke away from Cordelia and she wanted it bad because she'd sold all the drugs. She offered him the money of course he wanted the true value of the drugs."

"Of course, you didn't learn this story, until after Cordelia went to the mental facility; did you Lily?" Grandma Katha asked.

"How did you know all that? That is kept under encrypted files on my computer and in my office. Despite her code breaking into my files; Rose didn't even know those files exist;" Lily asked Grandma Katha with great astonishment.

"I hired a private investigator, dear. I wanted to know something that I could hold over that woman's head; in case she ever tried to take Rose away from you, after Horace died." Grandma Katha responded, "I didn't think they would allow it her to take Rose; but if she got better you never know about the courts. Therefore, I got some ammunition just in case."

"I love you for that. Right now, however, we better go see to my daughter. She's going to be devastated if they allow her to see Cordelia." Lily stated.

"What about Caleb aren't you responsible for him?"

"Caleb 's visiting his baby brother, Daniel, Grandma Katha. He said he'd be there for the next two days."

"We will stay here and hold down the fort just in case Rose calls," Amelia stated.

"Or as all the trouble breaks out," Carol muttered under her breath.

"Thank-you, this means a lot to me," Lily said hugging them both and leaving.

"You are welcome. Now just go. I'll talk to Chief Stewart and Regan about Carol staying with me," Amelia stated.

Amelia ushered them all out the door.

"She might not listen. Rose is going to be sad, mad, and hurt. I hope that Aunt Lily can get through to her," stated Carol.

"Me too, Carol, because I can see how Rose might hold this against Lily, if she doesn't know all the facts," Amelia stated.

~0~

S. G. Lee

Chapter 14 – The Investigation Has Stalled

Kendall wasn't happy; Edward

Stewart, her father also the Chief of Police, had called her into his office. She glanced around the office noticing her fellow officers, CSI Brandy Calders, Constable Violet Garden, Constable Tricia Gallant Patrolwoman Jenni Hayes and Alan. Why didn't Alan say he was coming today? Dad didn't look happy to see her either. What had she done wrong?

"Lieutenant Evans, where are you at with the Sherry-Anne Jones investigation?" Chief Edward Stewart asked in front of the assembled officers there.

"I'm sure Alan could have told you Chief. This investigation has stagnated. We know it was a woman; but we have no

S. G. Lee

idea who. We have no one to compare the fingerprints to," Kendall replied.

"You are saying the investigation has completely stalled," Chief Stewart reiterated.

"That's correct, Chief," Kendall admitted.

"Brandy you were the CSI on scene; is this all the evidence you examined?" Chief Stewart demanded to know.

"Yes, sir. The footprints in the garden are petite and suggest a woman from the pressure and weight and size. See?" Brandy explained showing him a picture taken, and some papers that she had typed up.

"Where does that leave us Lieutenant Evans? Have we any suspects that fit this profile?" Chief Stewart demanded to know.

"No, sir! We have not been able to narrow down the suspect list to this person," Kendall admitted, as Alan hid his head.

This Little Girl had a Little Curl

S. G. Lee

"We are spending far too many resources on this Evans and Barnes, even if the two of you are allocating your own time for parts of this case. This is considered a cold case now," Chief Edwards stated.

"But...." Kendall began but is interrupted.

"No, buts I don't like it any better than any of you; but our policing budget has been cut back to the bone by the new acting Mayor Alberto Cozino. He was the former comptroller of Happy Valley and he believes in cutting back on public funding. I wouldn't be surprised to find that he cuts even more from our meagre budget and if that continues, I'll have to let some cops go. As it is, I have control of the budget; but a lot of my control over the policing has been taken away by the Ministry of the Solicitor General as they investigate. They tell me they're sending an Ontario Provincial police officer to oversee the investigation and my department. If you two want to continue to investigate it is without my knowledge and totally on your time; but I can't put any more resources and money towards this investigation, even if I want to," Edward stated.

"You came back after you resigned. Wasn't that good enough for them?" Alan demanded to know.

"No, they are under the impression, that because we had three serial killer cops under my watch. That we are all dirty." Edward said angrily, "Damn those three Roy Callahan, Silas Rentford and Brad Owens!"

"But we all told them that we had no idea. They were just that good at hiding their true natures. You can't control people's minds," Brandy protested.

"We did, but the chief is right. They think we are all dirty and they are looking for ways to get rid of us," Constable Violet Garden agreed.

S. G. Lee

Just then the door opened and an Ontario provincial police officer in full dress uniform strolled in.

"Secret meetings Chief and you didn't invite me? I think I'm insulted," Chief Superintendent Peter Brooks stated wryly.

"Chief Superintendent Brooks, so they sent you. This is hardly secret; I am in my office. We are discussing dropping a cold case," Chief Stewart stated gruffly.

"Really what case would this be?" Chief Superintendent Brooks demanded to know, "Maybe fresh eyes could be of assistance?"

Chief Stewart put his head down disguising a grimace, then his head came up slowly, as he nodded to Brandy to give her information to Chief Superintendent Brooks.

"Ah the Sherry-Anne Mobley-Jones case. I met the woman," stated Chief Superintendent Brooks, looking over the notes.

This Little Girl had a Little Curl

S. G. Lee

"Did you know she was married to our coroner, Dafydd Jones?" Patrolwoman Jenni Hayes offered eagerly.

"Really? I've met him too, He seemed like a nice fellow; but people can deceive you. Did you check out his alibi? Is he in the clear?" Chief Superintendent Brooks replied off the cuff.

"He's really sweet and very good looking," Patrolwoman Hayes proclaimed.

"Patrolwoman Hayes really that is quite enough. You are being totally unprofessional; maybe you should go back to the front desk and help the new hire, patrolwoman April Wan," Chief Stewart barked.

Once she was gone Chief Stewart said, "I apologize, Ms. Hayes means well; but that is why she hasn't advanced beyond the desk position," Chief Stewart explained quietly, but Kendall managed to hear it across the room anyway.

S. G. Lee

"Inspector Evans interviewed a number of people, but no key suspects. Why didn't they interview Dafydd Jones more? It's obvious someone who is in his life is responsible for this murder," Inspector Brooks demanded to know sounding like he thought them totally incompetent.

"He has been interviewed!" Alan protested.

"And you are?" Inspector Brooks demanded.

"Special Constable Alan Barnes." Alan stated proudly.

"You're the convict's son. Isn't your Father, Perkin Barnes the bank robber?" Chief Superintendent Brooks snarked.

"My father has nothing to do with my career, or my life. I am an honest police officer," Alan stated angrily.

"Good to know." Chief Superintendent Brooks stated dropping that subject, "I suggest you re-interview Doctor Jones. He must know something, that he just

S. G. Lee

isn't aware of, or his holding back on you. Either way, you've got to know you should re-interview him. On your own time of course though, as it's a cold case."

"That is exactly what I had planned to order Inspector Evans and Special Constable Barnes. However, thank you for your input, Chief Superintendent Brooks," Chief Stewart said with such cold politeness, that the other cops understood he didn't like Inspector Brooks.

Chief Superintendent Brooks however, ignored the jab, for as he left, he said, "We'll talk later Chief Stewart, please carry on."

In the hallway Inspector Brooks encountered Emmett Rogers heading for the Chief's office.

"Good, you are back," Inspector Brooks stated "Is the case solved?"

"I went there to assist my sister, not to solve a case." Emmett replied coldly.

This Little Girl had a Little Curl

S. G. Lee

"So how is your sister?" Inspector Brooks tried again, sorry for offending Emmett whom he respected.

"My sister died, leaving behind her three children. I've brought them to my home; where I'll be raising them, anymore questions?" Emmett stated uncharacteristically losing his cool.

"I'm terribly sorry, Emmett. I had hoped that they could save her. My sister died last year from cancer. I know that's not the same; but I know how rough that can be. My wife and I are raising her two children, as their father, my brother-in law, died as well," Inspector Brooks said sympathetically.

"I'm sorry, too. You were offering me sincere sympathy and I jumped you. I'm just so damn angry," Emmett explained.

"Emmett you need to take some time off to process all this. I think you need at least a week, maybe two, just to get your head around all of this. Please put in for leave," Inspector Brooks begged, "You

This Little Girl had a Little Curl

S. G. Lee

are a great cop, but if your head isn't in the game you are no good to anyone. It's not easy to lose so much in such a short time. "I promise I'll do everything I can to try to get any information on your sister's case and keep you informed."

"I know you are right, besides the kids need me." Emmett stated, "I'll put in for that leave."

"Before you put in for leave, I'd like to interview you about Sherry-Anne Mobley –Jones' murder, please?" Inspector Brooks asked.

I'm sorry for being so morose and hard to deal with. I don't know what more I can tell you about Sherry-Anne; but I'll be happy to help in any way. I'd like to see that culprit caught," Emmett admitted.

"Thank-you, can you come to my new office in this building, said the spider to the fly." laughed Chief Superintendent Brooks. "Emmett when it's just us two, call me Peter. I'd like to think we're friends."

This Little Girl had a Little Curl

S. G. Lee

"Thanks Peter, whatever it takes to nail him, or her we will do it," Emmett announced as they entered Peter's temporary office.

About a half-an hour later and after telling Peter all he knew, Emmett wandered again, why Lily hadn't called him. He checked his phone. It was dead, not only dead; but the screen was shattered and it was very wet inside. When was the last time he even looked at his cell phone? He'd answered the hotel room phone and used that the whole time he was gone, as he knew all his phone numbers off hand.

Did Deirdre play with his cell phone, get it wet and broken and was afraid to tell him? He'd have to speak with her about not touching his phone, gently of course. He'd buy another cell phone. Maybe he'd breakdown and get one of those smart phones. Caleb was always talking about. Caleb made fun of his ancient flip phone, even though Emmett had bought Caleb's .I-Phone. Should he get two phones one

S. G. Lee

for himself and an upgrade for Caleb?
Then again, maybe he should get a
cheaper phone for himself and warn
Caleb about light fingered Deirdre who
had obviously broke his phone.

Either way he needed a new phone; it was
off to the phone store. Then maybe he'd
drop in on Lily for a few minutes and find
out what was going on with her. Why was
she avoiding him?

Was it the children? Were five children
too much to handle with her career? He'd
do whatever it took to reassure her that
they could handle them all, that he would
be there… that Laura would help out.
Anything to make Lily understand he
couldn't live without her.

~0~

Chapter 15 – Cordelia

Rose entered the building with trepidation. What if they wouldn't let her see her mother? The guards look at her intimidatingly, with what Rose interpreted as suspicious, angry looks, as she went to the window. This made her very scared. Rose really needed to see for herself that her Mother was okay…that they had treated her mother kindly, and not with an iron hand.

"Identification please!" demanded the guard.

"Who are you here to see?" the other guard asked.

"I would like to see Cordelia Brooksfield, please," Rose added.

"You are not on the approved list," the guard insisted.

"Please, she's my mother. I'd like to see her," Rose begged.

"Wait, just a moment," the guard stated then picked up the phone.

"Dr. Ames? We have a teenager here who wants to see her mother, Cordelia Brooksfield. Yes, she has showed me identification that said she's eighteen; but I'd place her at about possibly fifteen, or possibly sixteen years old. Uh huh! Okay, yes, Doctor," The guard said concluding his call.

"Can I see her?" Rose asked eagerly,

"First you have to meet with the doctor," the guard stated

"Okay, I guess I can do that," Rose agreed.

"You go through the door to the second door on the right. This guard will escort you," the guard exclaimed.

Rose hid her fear as she entered the psychiatrist's inner office. The name on the door had said **Dr. Periodot Ames**. Why was she brought here to this doctor? Was this her mother's doctor? Or did she have a group of doctors? How did this work? Would her mother be happy to see her?

"Hello I'm Doctor Ames. I am the primary care doctor on your mother's case." Doctor Ames explained, "And you are Rose; are you not?"

"My mother has spoken of me?" Rose stated excited.

"If you're referring to my patient; no, she hasn't. It was your mother, Lily Kelly-Brooksfield," Doctor Ames replied.

Rose took a huge breath stamping down her anger at hearing Lily referred to as her mother. Rose realized that getting mad at Lily wouldn't get her in to see her real mother.

"I'd really like to see my Mom."

This Little Girl had a Little Curl
S. G. Lee

"I don't know how much your adopted mother has told you about her condition…," Doctor Ames began.

"Obviously, my adopted mother has tried to protect me; but now that I'm sixteen she has told me about my mother's incarceration here. Though, I don't actually know all the details; if you could fill me in that would be wonderful," Rose lied.

"Cordelia was very ill, when she first came here. The guilt she felt and the damage from the drugs she had taken impaired her mental facilities. Unfortunately, she got worse, instead of better," Doctor Ames explained.

"What do you mean? I don't think I understand," Rose exclaimed confused.

"You mother is not how you remember her. She is not quite aware of those around her. You have to be prepared. She probably won't recognize you. She doesn't really recognize anyone. If you

can accept that; then we can go see her,"
Doctor Ames continued.

"I just want to see my mom, please,"
Rose exclaimed, only half listening.

No one was going to keep her from her
mom, ever again, Rose vowed. Rose
followed the doctor down a long corridor;
where they entered an elevator that
operating with the doctor's key card.
Rose looked around and saw patients
dressed in scrub like clothes. No jail
clothes; that was good wasn't it? Then
she realized the colour of the scrubs
denoted that they were inmates. They
wore a khaki green colour. They were
easily identifiable as patients, no mistake
about that. She glanced around, thank
goodness Owens wasn't here.

Rose saw a woman sitting in the corner.
Her brown hair, with blonde streaks, had
some gray roots, and was a long, a little
unkempt, but clean and covering her face.
In her arms she held a doll which she
seemed to focus all her attentions.

This Little Girl had a Little Curl
S. G. Lee

"Cordelia you have a visitor," Doctor Ames exclaimed.

Rose stared hoping that her mother would look up at her; however, Cordelia continued looking at the doll and began singing to the doll. Rose recognizes the song as *Down in the Valley*".

"Cordelia look, your Rose is here. See," Doctor Ames said lifting Cordelia's chin.

Cordelia did not appear to see Rose even though she turned her head (almost like she would register her); but abruptly stared down at the figure in her arms and continued to rock the doll.

"Cordelia, Rose is her now. See her!" Doctor Ames repeated.

"Rose is a good baby. Aren't you my little Rosy?" she said rocking the doll again.

"Cordelia this is Rose. We talked about this remember? Rose has grown up. She's not a baby anymore." Doctor Ames stated.

"Oh, you are right…of course your right. Please no more drugs. I remember Rose is nine years old. They make me so loopy," Cordelia stated matter of fact looking confused and then she dropped the doll on the floor.

"She's not nine years old; she's sixteen. Remember she just had a birthday we had a cupcake in her honour."

Cordelia just shook her head in disbelief.

Horrified Rose didn't know at to do; her mother wasn't really there. She's turned into some person who was broken a long time ago and now thought a doll was Rose. Rose tried to rationalize this. She felt so bad for her mother, obviously being locked up here had made her go crazy. Lily had much to answer for. Who did she think she was stealing Rose and her father away from Cordelia in this cruel way? Rose picked up the doll and handed it to her mom humming, *"Down in the Valley"*, which was now stuck in her head.

"Rosy?" Cordelia asked looking very scared and confused, "How can you look like my Rosy? You are too old to be Rose."

"Mommy, it is me. It's your Rose," Rose stated throwing her arms around her mother.

Cordelia becomes agitated and tried to get away from the hug, clawing at Rose.

"Cordelia this is Rose. She's gotten older, like you have," Doctor Ames stated gently.

"Down in the valley, the valley so low." Rose began singing softly remembering the sweet words her mother had sung to her.

"Rose it is you; but I don't understand; how can she be so big?" Cordelia wondered.

Cordelia dropped the doll again and then hugged Rose. She looked boldly at Rose; touching her hair and Rose's arms like she couldn't believe her eyes.

"Time has passed Cordelia," Doctor Ames continued.

"But she can't be this old. She just can't," Cordelia whined.

"Time can't stay still. You've been very ill, Cordelia; but you are making the right step here," Doctor Ames encouraged.

"You were very little and we had an apartment. I tried to get free of the drugs; but I craved them so badly," Cordelia stated, then as if she didn't want Rose to hear what she had done Cordelia placed her hands over Rose's ears and said, "I don't want to talk about this anymore. She shouldn't hear this. I have to protect her."

"Shall I tell you what happened, Cordelia? I know you don't want to remember; but you went willingly to Darius," Doctor Ames insisted.

"Hush, she'll hear."

Rose thought the doctor was being unnecessarily cruel; but then she realized

This Little Girl had a Little Curl
S. G. Lee

Doctor Ames was trying to provoke a response… a memory to help her mother.

"Darius said I should do a few tricks and he'd buy me some drugs. I remember that," Cordelia replied, surprised.

"But that isn't what happened is it? Darius betrayed your trust," Doctor Ames stated.

"Not at first. No, he gave me the crack I needed; but I should have known it was a trick. He knew I'd be back a few days later for more. I needed the drug so bad it hurt. I was sweating and ill and he refused to provide me with any freebies."

"What did he do Cordelia?"

"He said I owed him, not only for the drugs he gave me, but for the drugs I took. I told him I had a daughter. I wasn't a hooker. He laughed at that. He said all I had to do was go to a party, sleep with one client and he'd supply me with the drugs I craved. I went to his party…. I am such a fool I went to the party!! I left

Rose with her Dad and I went. Darius had an auction going on for my services and a few other women, our services were sold to the highest bidder. I really don't want to talk about this anymore. I don't think Rose should hear this she'll know what an awful person I am. She'll hate me," Cordelia said.

"Then maybe she should leave?"

"But I don't want her to leave."

"I love you baby. You know that don't you?" Cordelia implored Rose.

"I know Mommy and I love you too. Whatever you have to say, I won't judge you." Rose reassured.

"What if Rose was to sit over there, where she won't be able to hear as much?" asked Doctor Ames.

"That would be okay. You won't leave though, will you Rose?" Cordelia demanded looking frantic and scared that Rose would do just that.

This Little Girl had a Little Curl
S. G. Lee

"I'm not going anywhere right now," Rose stated, "I will sit over there."

Rose walked over to the chair; but she realized that if she listened intently, she could still hear her mother's story. Rose wanted to hear it, so, she listened in.

"That man was cruel. Darius treated me like dirt. Like a doll, he'd bought. Darius hurt me so bad…. I had to go the hospital and get my jaw rewired and my broken ribs taped. He broke my wrist. He kept me for days away from my Rose." Cordelia cried, "When I went to pick up Rose, Horace was angry with me. He was also worried about me, but I wouldn't listen to him. He said even though he didn't love me anymore, he still cared. He begged me to go to rehab. He said he would pay for it, for Rose's sake. I didn't want to listen to him; but I had to pay attention when Horace changed his tone and started making threats. Horace said he was suing for custody. He said Rose wasn't safe with me…not anymore. Horace said if I ever dropped Rose off

like a sack of potatoes and then came
back looking all broken and beat up, he
said I'd never see Rose again, not even as
a visitor. I promised him I would never
put Rose in danger again. He took Rose
away for a month. He let me see her
again, when he was sure I was not using.

A month later, just when I was sure I was
off the drugs and feeling better; Darius
showed up. I didn't let him in he just
pushed his way into my apartment. Darius
said I had to go to his party; he was a
woman short."

"I said, "No I 'm not going."

"Don't you worry about the bruises;
make-up will cover them. You'll still be
beautiful," he said touching my face.

I said, "No" loudly.

"No one, says no to Darius Green. Listen
up bitch; you owe me. You will do what I
demand, understand? You will not
embarrass me and let me down," Darius
shouted at me.

This Little Girl had a Little Curl
S. G. Lee

"I can't Darius. I can't do that ever again; besides, I have Rose to think of."

"You are coming, because you owe me. Big Time, bitch!!" he said grabbing my arm.

"I said no, I had Rose with me. He pulled out a syringe and injected me with some stuff. He took Rose and me, somewhere. He held us in a small room for days, drugging me, whenever the medicine wore off. When he brought the johns, he took Rose out. I was more than scared. Darius had us both as prisoners. I couldn't even get to a phone; as he chained me to the bed when he wasn't there. I didn't know what was happening to Rose, when she wasn't with me; but the drugs kept in a state of mellowness, which made me forget about her most of the time."

"Rose said when she was returned; that she had watched television and coloured in a colouring book with Uncle Darius. She seemed unharmed; but how long would that last? You have to understand

This Little Girl had a Little Curl
S. G. Lee

Darius wasn't a good man. All he cared
about was the all-mighty dollar. As long
as he could think of making money, Rose
wasn't safe. You can guess the truth,
doctor. He threatened her; he told me he
knew some guys that liked little girls. He
said it was going to happen, accept it."

"I told him I'd kill him first and he said as
long as cooperated, she be safe. I didn't
trust or believe him; in my lucid moments
I knew I had to find something to fight
back with and save us. One day I heard
him on the phone he took from his pocket
and I knew he was planning to harm my
Rose. When he gave me my dinner and
my drugs, I didn't take the drugs. Instead,
I fought back. I took Rose's hand and we
ran to the door; but he stopped me and
beat me. He said Rose was his, accept it!
He was taking us both. We'd make him a
lot of money! I grabbed the knife from
my dinner tray as he pulled me by it. I
begged him one last time to let us go. He
shook his head and laughed at me and I
stabbed him through the heart. I stabbed
him again and again. I am so evil. There

was so much blood. Rivers of blood poured from his body. Rose kept asking me, "Mommy what did you do to Uncle Darius?"

"Then what happened, Cordelia?"

"I stepped through his blood, grabbing my daughter; but the neighbour called the police and I was arrested," Cordelia related in a quiet singsong voice like she couldn't believe this was all real.

"It is okay Cordelia. You did what you had to do to save yourself and your child." Doctor Ames reassured her.

"No, you don't understand. How can you understand? You are not a mother. How can Rose forgive me? I exposed her to that. I killed him in front of Rose. I am a murderess. How could I have taken someone's life?" Cordelia asked.

"Sometimes we are faced with unwinnable odds. We have to make a decision that can damage our mind to protect those we love and ourselves. It's okay to choose life over death, even if it means you have to take another life. The thing we have to do is to learn to forgive yourself and realize that you can move on from this," Doctor Ames stated.

"No, it's all too much I killed Darius. The blood…get it off; get it off my hands. Can't you see my hands are dripping in blood?" asked Cordelia.

As Rose watched in growing horror, Cordelia stood up and ran around the room wringing her hands. Cordelia seemed to be trying to get the blood off and then started picking at her hands; trying to rip off the invisible blood from her hands. Cordelia looked around a crazed maniac look. She continued moaning about blood being everywhere she looked. Holding her hand over her mouth to hold back cries of horror; Rose worried that she made Cordelia worse, that Cordelia would harm herself in this frenzy she now displayed. Dr. Ames took out a needle and calmly administered it. Rose watched as her mother's crazy actions slowed and Cordelia then sat down in a chair, closing her eyes.

"Will she be all right?" Rose asked as the orderly placed Cordelia in a wheelchair and turned to take her back to her room.

Soon her mother disappeared with the orderly down the hallway. Rose stood up as if to follow; but changed her mind.

"I'm sorry you had to see that Rose; but it was necessary Cordelia has come a long way, but when she remembers what happened it always seems to end the same way. I thought if she could speak of it in front of you even at a short distance, it might help. She hasn't been able to live with the guilt of killing Darius Green. Somewhere in there, she knows that she also lost you. She tries to harm herself and then she retreats into the world, where she was once happy in. The world where you are a baby and she cares for you," Doctor Ames explained.

"Are you saying, she won't remember any of this?" Rose asked.

"I don't know. We won't know until the medicine wears off; but usually she retreats into her fantasy world with her doll, Rose." Doctor Ames responded, "Why don't we talk about this some more in my office away from the other patients?"

"Oh, okay, I guess," Rose said, looking around and seeing the other patients looking a little distressed.

"They will look after her, I promise," Doctor Ames stated as Rose stared down the hall. As they are about to enter Doctor Ames office, Rose sat down in a nearby chair.

"Did you have to sedate her?" asked Rose asked.

"You saw how she was behaving. She could seriously harm herself in that state, or someone else. I'm sorry you had to see that." Doctor Ames stated, "Now we have to have a frank discussion. I think you are without your adoptive mother's permission, aren't you?"

"How did you know?" Rose asked shocked.

"I'm very aware of subtle signs. I sense that you are mad at your adoptive mother for keeping this from you? Am I right?" Doctor Ames replied.

"I'm very angry with her. She had no right to keep my mother away from me," Rose admitted.

"Your father didn't want Lily to tell you. Did you know that?" Doctor Ames stated softly.

"She just wanted my dad and me in her life. She saw her chance she dropped my mother off here and look what happened. She was around crazy people and she went crazy," Rose stated.

"That's not the truth and you know that deep down. Do you remember the actual killing Rose?" Doctor Ames asked.

"How do I know my mom actually killed anyone? Maybe she just had that drilled into her head by Lily Kelly, so she believes it," Rose stated, bitterly, "You can make someone believe anything, remember anything."

"You know you don't believe that Rose. You remember what happened, don't you?" Doctor Ames said intuitively.

"No, I don't remember," Rose stated, defiantly, but she can picture her mother with blood dripping from her hands.

"Are you saying you blocked it all out? That would be understandable. You must have been terrified knowing you were being held captive by someone you trusted, even if you were tiny. Then your mother killed your captor to get you away. That must have been difficult," soothed Doctor Ames.

"Don't you use that psychobabble on me!" Rose stated, "Lily lied to me! She said my mother was safe, in prison. It was all lies just to get me to forget all about my mother and accept her. I hate Lily. I'm never going to forgive her, as long as I live."

"As a parent, your father and Lily had to make difficult decisions to protect a small traumatized child from the knowledge that your mother didn't even recognize you. That Cordelia was very ill and couldn't see you as yourself. Think about it. If you had a child would you subject a small child to something that would harm their psyche; especially after they had been through so much?" Doctor Ames asked softly.

"I don't know; but I know I wouldn't lie to them."

"Do you remember meeting me; when you were a child?" Doctor Ames questioned.

"I met you when I was younger?" Rose asked, surprised then a memory came back to her and she cried, "Daddy and Lily and I went on a trip. We played in the park and then I met some doctor they took me to. That was you? It couldn't be, could it?"

"It was me." Doctor Ames admitted softly, "We talked a lot that day. Do you remember?"

"I don't remember meeting you clearly and I certainly don't remember talking with you," Rose stated angrily.

"Rose, you were traumatized. You weren't sleeping and they were worried. They'd taken you to see a doctor who recommended that you be allowed to see your mother." Doctor Ames explained, "So they brought you here to me. I took you into see your mother; but she didn't recognize you; she took your doll and called it Rose. Do you remember that?"

"I... oh my! I did come here ...I remember that doll she had today, "Rose stated shocked, but remembering.

Rose's eyes became glazed and she continued, "Mommy was sitting in a chair by the window. The sun was streaming in and she was sitting there looking into space. And she wouldn't see me... no matter what I did... she wouldn't see me.

This Little Girl had a Little Curl
S. G. Lee

I was invisible to her. I touched her and
she shrunk back, like I burnt her. I
dropped my doll and she reached for it
picking it up I thought she'd picked it up
for me… but it wasn't. She cradled the
doll like it was a baby, calling it by my
name. She forgot me… as if I never really
existed," Rose stated, crying huge tears.

Rose pulled herself together and looked at
the doctor, "Why does she keep forgetting
me? I thought she loved me but everyone
who loves me lets me down, or goes
away."

Rose she's not forgetting you, not really.
Cordelia never forgets you. Her mind
keeps you in her thoughts; that's why she
calls the doll Rose. Cordelia is deeply
troubled between what happened to her
and you that day. Do you want to talk
about your memories of that day?" Doctor
Ames asked.

"I don't remember that day at all; the only
thing I remember about that day is when

they arrested my mother and said she killed Uncle Darius."

"You remember nothing at all about that day?" prodded Doctor Ames.

"I said I don't remember it. Now drop it," Rose said defensively.

"Are you still seeing someone Rose?" Doctor Ames inquired almost sounding worried.

"I have a shrink, if that's what you're asking; but you know, you people ask too many nosy questions. I have to keep something of my own," Rose stated belligerently sounding unlike herself.

"Rose you've been through a lot. I followed some of the newspaper articles on your father's death and what has happened to you over the last year, being kidnapped three times. Once is traumatizing enough; but three? That has to be very hard on anyone."

"I told you to keep your psychobabble to yourself. I don't need, or want counseling. I am fine," Rose stated sounding anything but fine.

The door burst opened and Lily ran in shouting, "Oh, thank goodness. You are okay," Lily stated throwing her arms around Rose.

Rose pushed her away and crossed her arms then glared at her, not speaking one word.

"Oh, honey, I'm sorry I didn't tell you," Lily cried, then turning to Doctor Ames she said "I couldn't tell her, did you tell her?"

Doctor Ames shook her head behind Rose's back; as if to say don't tell her. Then she said, "I was just about to tell her I advised your husband and you not to tell her again about her mother."

"You should have told me anyway. You're not my mother; she is my mother, forever," Rose stated her voice breaking.

"I'm sorry, Rose. You know I wouldn't keep something from you; unless it was absolutely necessary." Lily stated, "Your dad and I agreed not to tell you unless your mother got well, or until your eighteenth birthday."

"Oh no, you don't Lily. Don't you dare try to bring my dad into this and blame this on him," Rose said incensed.

"Rose please…," Lily began.

"I don't want to hear it." Rose said, "In two years when I'm eighteen. I'm not going to live with you anymore. I'll come home with you; but don't expect me to like it. You took me away from my mother for six and half years and put her in this place. Don't expect me to forgive you anytime soon," Rose yelled, even though she knew she was being unfair.

"Rose, please don't be like this. I love you," Lily pleaded.

"Love? If this is love I want no part of your idea of love."

Rose said going then stamped through the door and bumped abruptly into Grandpa Terrence.

"She dragged you here, too? That figures," Rose stated.

"Can we talk honey?" Terrence asked.

"Fine, as long as we are not going to talk about her!" Rose stated staring daggers back at Lily.

"They'll be none of that missy. You may not agree with your Mom's choices; but Lily has looked after you. She's fed you, clothed you, and looked after you; loving you like a mother should. Now treat her with at least respect," Grandma Katha stated showing up behind Terrence.

"But…," Rose began before being interrupted.

"You are part of my family and the one thing we demand is that family members treat each other civilly." Grandma Katha stated, "Now let's talk about this."

"Fine, but I don't have to like it, or her."
Rose stated, then reconsidering she stated,
"You know what? I don't want to talk
about it, after all."

"When you cool off, we will talk about
this," Grandma Katha stated forcefully.

"We have to go now. We will come back
but we are need at home," Terrence
replied.

"Go? I'm not going anywhere. I have to
be here, when my mother wakes up. I'm
not going anywhere," Rose protested.

"Rose we can't stay. Cordelia has come
out of this before and she always retreats
back into her own world," Grandma
Katha insisted.

"You knew and you didn't say anything
either? Sure, she tells you, what to say
and do and you just do it," Rose
protested.

"Actually, she didn't, I hired a private
investigator," Grandma Katha admitted.

"Harrumph, she can't even share with you? Lily is so trustworthy."

"Rose you have to quit talking about your mother this way," Grandma Katha retorted angrily.

"If you are talking about Lily, she's not my mother. My mother is Cordelia Brooksfield, whom she, Lily Kelly cruelly abandoned here," Rose stated.

"That is ridiculous. She's been your mother for six and half years looking after you, feeding you, comforting you, loving you," Grandma Katha retorted.

"I don't want to talk about this anymore and I'm not going anywhere, until I see my mother again; so, don't hold your breath."

"I can understand that honey, maybe we can get a hotel room for the night so you can come back here tomorrow morning?" Lily asked.

"I can call the Hotel Francois. I use to stay there when I travelled in my job as

CEO of Terrabond. Let me call Cheryl
Turner the manager of the hotel."
Terrence demanded.

Terrence dialled the number on his new I-
phone and accidentally put the call on
speaker phone so Rose heard him clearly
ask, "Cheryl, this is Terrence O'Malley
here."

"Why Terrence, how lovely to hear from
you again, how are you?" the tinkling
crystal bell voice came clearly over the
phone.

Grandma Katha frowned and then tried to
hide her jealousy.

"I'm very well, Cheryl. I need some hotel
rooms. I was hoping you could help a
fellow out?" Terrence asked in a sweet
laid-back voice.

"For you, Terrence, anything. I'll rustle
up whatever you require. Now tell me one
room or two?" Cheryl demanded,
"Remember that night you only needed

the one. What a night that was maybe; we could do it again while you are in town?"

"Actually Cheryl, I'm married now." Terrence began.

"Oh, I'm very disappointed; but your wife must be a lucky woman," Cheryl stated.

"Actually, I'm the lucky one. Grandma Katha is a gem. A one-of-a-kind woman, the kind you wait your life for and hope she picks you."

Grandma Katha blushed then smiled.

"As I said she is with me, so you will. Now I really need three, is that possible?" Terrence asked.

"The Queen's suite is available, or is that too pricy now that you are retired?"

"That would be perfect. Thanks Cheryl we should be there within the hour. Bye for now," Terrence stated hanging up.

"The Queen's suite does have three bedrooms, correct? I'm not sharing with her!"

Rose then stood up and continued to still stare daggers at Lily.

"Rose this is a huge suite and yes, there are three bedrooms, a kitchen and several on-suite bathrooms."

"Thank you, Grandpa Terrence; that sounds perfect," Lily exclaimed.

"Come my dears; let's go. It's been a long day. We can order some room's service and then hit the hay," Terrence stated sounding tired.

"That sounds good to me." Grandma Katha stated, ushering Rose out the door and through the metal detector and into the waiting cab to go to the hotel.

~0~

Chapter 16 – Poisoned Waters

Emmett knocked on Lily's front door. What the heck? It's was after nine p. m., but no one answered. Did Lily take a trip somewhere and not tell him? Had something happened? No, if something bad had happened; Lily would have notified him. He had to hurry up; he needed to get home to the kids. He would just get in touch with Lily later; she'd understand she was probably just working late like she always did.

Deirdre loved to be tucked in by him. He was still working on liking the other two, Joseph and Rebecca. The twins could be short and difficult; he knew that was because they'd just lost their mom and were pre-teens; but they should have

come with a handbook. Joseph seemed to
have a cruel streak, which Emmett hoped
was learned and not genetic. Rebecca was
quiet at times; but sneaky in her
retaliation to her brother's barbs.
Sometimes, Joseph's behaviour spilled
over to Deirdre and hurt her; which
angered Emmett. He'd been working hard
to control that anger, just like he'd
learned all those years ago in his P. T. S.
D. therapy. It was working; he'd never be
like his father.

He'd given up drinking any alcohol, not
that he'd ever drank that much. From here
on end, he was a teetotaller.

He'd even gotten a punching bag…okay
so it was a blow-up clown(filled with
sand),which he used as a punching bag. If
his anger got to much, he'd use it; for
now, it was in the closet. He was grieving
all those years he lost with Dianna; but he
wouldn't show that to the children. They
needed him to be strong, and love him
and he'd do that. He'd show all the love

he could to these children. They'd been through too much.

Little Dee had stolen his heart, in such a short time. There was so much about her that reminded him of Dianna and she was so small needing his protection. He knew he was probably being unfair to the twins, but he couldn't help spoiling Deirdre.

He wondered again why hadn't heard from Lily. He'd been home two days with the children; maybe he should worry? No, it was just that his phone had been broken. She'd probably tried numerous times and then wondered why he hadn't called her back. He'd rectify that tomorrow and get those new phones for Caleb and himself. Then he'd call Lily and reach her and if not by phone then he'd show up at her office. After all Lily couldn't just be mad at him for not calling her, could she? Is that why she wouldn't answer the door? What was could she be so mad about anyway? Could it be the number of children now in their lives, or was it the marriage proposal? He had to quit thinking this way it was probably just a silly misunderstanding. But what if she was inside hurt and he was standing her on the doorstep and then walked away?

"Lily, please answer the door." Emmett stated, banging on it again.

Still no answer? What was going on? But what if she was inside hurt? He was standing on her on the doorstep and if he walked away; she might need help and then be harmed. How many times had heard about that happening? Emmett thought, as he worriedly pulled out his key and entered the house.

The house was eerily quiet and dark. Emmett didn't bother turning on the light, until he entered the living room to find Carol sleeping in a chair and Amelia beside her. The television was on low and it looked like *The Date* was on. They'd fallen asleep during their favourite show, how odd he thought. Why wasn't Carol with Chief Stewart and Regan? She

couldn't be visiting Rose, unless Rose
was in the washroom. Was Rose? Why
didn't they hear him come in? He hadn't
been quiet. It was just after nine p.m. and
they were asleep, all ready? Why didn't
they hear the front door, if the television
was on low? Emmett started feeling like
he had a horrible headache and found he
could hardly put two thoughts together;
but in his fog one clear thought came to
him, **"Gas, they've been gassed with
carbon dioxide."**

He'd been planning on buying Lily a new
carbon monoxide detector when he had
gotten back; since the other one would
soon expire. He should have bought it.
Lily? Where were Lily and Rose? He'd
better call 911, take them outside to
safety, and open all the windows.

"This is Emmett Rogers. Send an
ambulance and fire truck to 962
Beaconfield Drive. Possible…. carbon….
monoxide… poisoning suspected...,"
Emmett said as he collapsed.

Seconds later a figure arrived and entered the house.

"You weren't supposed to be hurt. She was supposed to be here," The figure said, touching Emmett's face gently; but Emmett didn't open his eyes.

The figure startled when they heard the fire trucks and ambulances. The figure grimaced, but continued throwing open all the windows. Then taking one longer lingering gaze back at Emmett; the figure quietly left before they were discovered.

The firemen entered and removed the victims to the front lawn where the EMT's attend them. Yellow tape was placed across the front door prohibiting entry until the fire department deemed it safe. Soon all three victims were loaded into the ambulances and taken to hospital.

~0~

Chapter 17 – Confusion Reigns

L ily awakened from a deep REM

sleep to a ringing cell phone. She glanced at the time; realizing she's been asleep, only a half an hour. It had been a long night. Rose refused to speak to Lily and just showed her the cold shoulder. Lily didn't know how she was going to make any of this right. Rose felt betrayed. Grandma Katha always said sleep on it and Lily had been working so hard and had so little energy with this pregnancy that she dropped off to sleep, despite herself. Lily heard her cell phone ring again and pulled herself together answering the unknown number.

"Is this Lily Kelly?" the voice asked tentatively.

"This is Lily Kelly."

"I'm calling from Happy Valley General Hospital. There's no easy way to put this, I have some bad news. We have two patients with your name listed as an emergency contact number," the voice explained.

"You have what?" Lily demanded to know coming fully aware, "Who do you have there?"

"We have an Amelia Kelly, and an Emmett Rogers, all of who were brought into the Emergency room a short time ago. You are listed as their emergency contact. Do you know where we can reach the guardian of Carol Banks?" The voice explained.

"The Chief of Police, Edward Stewart and his wife Regan are Carol's guardians. Now tell me what is wrong with them?

Were they in an accident?" Lily asked her heart pounding.

"No, Madame, they were found in a residence. We suspect carbon monoxide poisoning. Oops, you didn't hear me say that about Carol Banks, but since your Grandmother is on the board maybe you'll cut me some slack?" the woman explained.

"A gas leak in the summer? That makes no sense," Lily stated shocked.

"It's an unusually cool night; maybe they put on a gas fireplace?" The person pondered.

"I guess that could have happened. I meant to get a new carbon monoxide detector. Mine was set to expire next month. Why didn't I get one?"

"You are the next of kin for the other two? Do you have number I can reach Edward Stewart?"

"Yes, I'm the next of kin, as I said for Emmett and Amelia and this is the number for the Stewarts." Lily said rattling Edward's number off, "I'm four hours away, it will take some time to get there."

"Do we have your permission for treatment then?"

"Yes, of course you do, now I'll be there as soon as possible. In the meantime, do whatever you need to do for their care. I authorize it," Lily exclaimed.

"Thank-you Ms. Kelly. Please come to the nine-floor intensive care unit. We will expect you soon," the voice stated hanging up.

Lily dressed quickly bumping into the wall and bruising an elbow, as she hurriedly put her socks on over her swollen feet.

This Little Girl had a Little Curl
S. G. Lee

"Lily what is the matter? What is with all the noise? Are you okay?" Grandma Katha demanded entering the outer room living room.

"Something has happened to Amelia, Carol and Emmett."

"What?"

"Grandma Katha, I don't know how to say this; so, I'm just going to tell you. They've been gassed by carbon monoxide."

"Oh, no!"

"Why didn't I get a new detector sooner? This is entirely my fault," Lily stated wiping away tears.

"It's too late to blame yourself and it won't help anyone. We have to get there immediately!" Grandma Katha insisted, then she yelled into the bedroom, "Terrence, get out here,"

"What's happened? Did Rose take off again?" asked a bleary-eyed Terrence in a buttoned housecoat obviously from the hotel which he's knotting at the waist.

"No, it's not Rose. She's still asleep; but we have a huge problem. I can't be in two places at once and Amelia and Carol need me too," Grandma Katha blurted uncharacteristically upset.

"Dear, it is okay. Please sweetie, take a deep breath and explain to me what the problem is. We will find a way to solve this," Terrence stated calmly.

"Amelia was poisoned by gas and so were Carol and Emmett. There was some kind of gas leak at Lily's house. Carbon monoxide poisoning can kill! What if they are close to death and we are not there! We can't leave Rose; (she needs to see Cordelia) but we need to go to them. What can Lily and I do?" Grandma Katha moaned.

"I'm worried about them all too. I see your dilemma. I'd like to be there too; but I'll stay here. You can keep me updated about my granddaughter and niece, and I'll look after Rose. She's my great-great-granddaughter too. I'll take her to see her mother tomorrow and take good care of her. Don't you worry; even if Cordelia is unable to see her, I'll handle it. I'll phone my friend at the airport now and you can get a flight there in under an hour," Terrence insisted.

"Oh thank –you Terrence. You are the best husband, ever. We know Rose will be in good hands with you," Grandma Katha said, throwing her arms around Terrence.

"Just don't forget that and let some cute young doctor lure you away," Terrence joked.

Terrence then pulled away from Grandma Katha's embrace stepping into the bedroom to dial his friend.

"What's going on? Why are you people so noisy? I'm trying to sleep here," Rose stated coming out of her room.

"Rose there was an accident with the gas fireplace. Carol, Aunt Amelia and Emmett inhaled the gas," Lily said gently.

"Is Emmett okay?" Rose asked sounding scared.

"They took them to the hospital and they are treating them; but one of us has to be there for them. Grandma Katha can go by herself and update us if you want me to stay," Lily offered.

"Are you freakin' kidding me? I don't want you here; I rather have Grandpa Terrence. At least he cares about me. Hey, that's a great idea; you go abandon me for your real family and I'll stay here with Grandpa Terrence. You only care about Amelia and that baby anyway. Oops, that's right you didn't tell me that you were pregnant and you didn't need me anymore," Rose stated bitterly.

"She has to tell Emmett first," Grandma Katha defended Lily.

"You freakin' knew. She didn't tell me! Lily's always keeping secrets," Rose complained.

"Rose didn't you hear your mother? Carol and your Aunt Amelia were hurt too."

"Carol is hurt and so is Aunt Amelia, too? I thought only Emmett...?"

"I know you did; but we will make sure they are all okay and you can stay with Grandpa Terrence if you want and visit with your Mother, Cordelia," Grandma Katha stated.

"I should go see Carol and Aunt Amelia and Emmett; but Mom needs me too. I have to see that my mother is okay. Will Carol and Aunt Amelia understand that? I know Emmett would. He's really too nice; especially for the likes of her," Rose sniped, motioning to Lily.

"Rose you are being cruel. This isn't like you." Grandma Katha scolded.

"Sorree!" Rose said not really meaning it.

"Do you want to stay with Grandpa Terrence then?" asked Lily.

"Yah, I guess I do want to stay. You'll let me know as soon as they are all right, Grandma Katha?" Rose asked.

"Of course, I will." Grandma Katha stated, "That goes without saying."

"I hope Emmett's okay too, Lily," Rose added.

Lily tried to hide her hurt at being called Lily, instead of mom.

"Okay, your flight is ready; just get to the airport and Godspeed you two," Terrence cried.

"Thank –you Terrence. We'll call as soon as we know anything," Lily exclaimed.

Lily and Grandma Katha then went out the door only with their purses.

"Okay, now we can have some fun; the adults are gone. Do you want a pizza?" Terrence enquired.

"Yes, sure. Even though I'm worried, I could eat, I certainly couldn't sleep." Rose answered.

"Don't tell your Grandma Katha. She's got me eating all those darn health foods," Terrence half –kidded.

"Who me? I won't tell." Rose stated as Terrence dialled for a pizza.

"Good, because I'm thinking some deluxe pizza something with lots of meat. Sound good to you."

"Yum, yes."

~0~

Chapter 18 – Sabotage

K endall listened to the police radio

in disbelief; units had been dispatched to Lily's house. Kendall jumped her squad car and soon arrived at Lily's house. Kendall looked around the scene. Where could Lily be? Had Lily been harmed? Emmett would be devastated if he found Lilt harmed and frankly, Lily and her daughter had grown on Kendall. She was even beginning to consider Lily a friend.

Kendall had heard over the scanner that there were two victims. Please be okay, Lily and Rose, she thought. Emmett would be beside himself. Maybe, she should have gone to Emmett's first; but she wanted to find out all the relevant information and then inform Emmett.

Kendall thought it would be Special Constable George Razi assigned to the front door and she hoped to charm him into allowing her onto the scene so, she can find out the information; but it was a Special Constable she not seen before. He glanced at her identification and then stopped her from entering.

"Have the occupants of the home been taken to the hospital, already?" Kendall asked.

"Inspector Evans, I must inform you that Amelia Kelly and Carol Banks have been taken in as well as the Inspector," the Special Constable replied.

"Which Inspector was hurt? Was someone injured on scene?" Kendall demanded to know.

"It was Inspector Emmett Rogers. If he hadn't found the victims; they would have died."

"Where is Emmett then?" Kendall asked.

"I've been trying to tell you Inspector
Evans, Inspector Rogers found the
victims, then collapsed after calling in,"
the Special Constable answered.

"Is he going to be okay?" Kendall asked
stunned.

"We don't know yet; but the Fire
Marshall is on scene and he said there are
signs of someone tampering with the gas
line. This is an active crime scene. I can't
let you in without permission of Chief
Edward Stewart, or Inspector Peter
Brooks the Ontario Provincial Police
liaison. I probably shouldn't have told
you that much, but I've heard good things
about you and your partner Inspector
Rogers."

"Actually, Inspector Peter Brooks is not
an Inspector anymore. He just failed to let
any of us know, that he is a Chief
Superintendent now," Kendall stated a
little bitterly.

"We're all unhappy about a temporary
takeover of our station by the Ontario

Provincial Police, and how he is treating our police station; but we need to cooperate that's what Chief Stewart said so, this is me cooperating. Chief Superintendent Brooks is inside Inspector and he had ordered me not to let anyone enter without their permission. I'm sorry, but if I let you in, I'll be fired."

Kendall is puzzled and trying to solve this conundrum. First, Sherry-Anne is murdered; then someone tampered with Lily's gas line? They had to be connected. She had to look at the evidence and piece this together. She could solve a murder all by herself, if only she could get in. She would see Emmett, when she was done here. Surely, he was okay; after all he'd been able to call for help. Emmett would want her to stay and investigate discretely.

"What is your name Special Constable? I don't think I've met you before; have you been with Happy Valley police department long?" Kendall asked.

"I'm Robert Harris. I've been with the department for about three months I transferred in from London, Ontario," Robert answered.

"You transferred in after we discovered the serial killings of the young women in the wall?" Kendall asked.

"Yes, Inspector. Hey wait a minute, was that you and Inspector Rogers that solved that one? You are good."

"With the help of some of the department and some hard work on our parts; we were able to solve it," Kendall stated proudly.

"I'm sure Chief Superintendent Brooks didn't mean you. I mean you're a super star; you helped reveal a dirty cop as well," Robert Harris gushed.

"Inspector Evans? Who sent you here?" demanded Chief Superintendent Brooks sneaking up behind Harris.

"No one sir. I heard on the horn and hoped I might be of some assistance." Kendall stated.

"Hot dogging Kendall? You're a better cop than this," stated Chief Superintendent Brooks.

"I am not hot dogging as you put it, sir. My partner has been injured and I want to find the scum that did this," Kendall replied angrily.

"You know I might believe that; if you had cared to go to the hospital first," Chief Superintendent Brooks replied wryly.

"I didn't know Emmett had been injured, until I got here. I'm sure they fixed him up right away. He was able to call right away. Actually, to be honest, sir; I was worried about Lily Brooksfield Emmett's fiancée. Where is she?" Kendall responded looking around.

"Emmett is in the intensive care, Kendall; along with a Kelly woman and a young girl," Chief Superintendent Brooks hinted.

"Emmett's in intensive care and Lily and Rose are there too? That's impossible!" Kendall sputtered.

"Lily Brooksfield and her daughter aren't there."

"You were testing me?"

Chief Superintendent Brooks didn't answer, but Kendall saw how smug he was as she wiped tears from her face.

"The neighbour stated that Ms. Brooksfield left with Mrs. and Mr. Stewart in an agitated state this evening. It seems that Rose Brooksfield had run away from home. I think Amelia Kelly and Carol Banks were taking calls from people about the disappearance and collapsed. They are fighting for their lives in the intensive care unit. Emmett is holding his own for now in intensive care," stated Chief Superintendent Brooks gently.

"I have to go and see how Emmett is,"
Kendall stated stunned and upset.

"Yes, please go check on him and keep
me informed on Emmett's health, I
respect the man and I need to find out
who did this to him," Chief
Superintendent Brooks explained,
bending a little.

"I need to see my partner is okay; but I
have to be in on this investigation. You
have to let me find out who did this to my
partner. Please, I'm begging you, Chief
Superintendent Brooks," Kendall begged.

"Go see how your partner is then come
back tomorrow and I'll allow you to
assist. Try to get some sleep too," Chief
Superintendent Brooks agreed.

"Thank-you Chief Superintendent
Brooks, this means a lot to me. You don't
know how much," Kendall answered.

"I think I do. Now go before I change my
mind."

Kendall drove purposely to the hospital;
her mind dwelling on the case at hand.
Was it related to Sherry-Anne's murder?
They couldn't find the Sherry-Anne's
killer and now there had been an attempt
on Lily's life?

The only connection to both women was
Emmett, so, was someone in love with
Emmett and eliminating the competition?
What was going on? If the two cases
connected, they had to find this killer
before they struck again.

~0~

Chapter 19 – Hatred is the Madness in my Heart

Lord Byron had said it best, *"Hatred is the madness of my heart"*. I loved Emmett and she stood in my way. She found him first; but once he knew me, really knew me, then he'd love me and only me. I knew that in my heart of hearts.

Women flocked to him. He wasn't so much handsome and rugged, as kind. Look how he had so many women who cared about him. Even that woman cop, partner of his… loved him. Kendall was smart though. she knew she didn't have a chance now that I was on the scene. She must have sensed my interest somehow. I liked that woman, Kendall Evans. She only thought of him as a friend, which I could allow. She was good protection for him, when he was on the job. Someone needed to protect him from himself and his gallant deeds. I'd seen how he talked to people on the street and treated them with respect. A person, was a person in his book. He even treated criminals properly too.

Damn, now he was in the hospital and it was all Lily's fault. Why hadn't it been her? How I hated her. Lily Brooksfield just got in the way and brought trouble. I heard that she was a Jinx. It certainly seemed so. So many husbands; all dead! Emmett wouldn't be one. I wouldn't allow her to endanger my Emmett!!

I had to be smarter though. People were becoming suspicious and I could allow no suspicion to follow me. I'd done my due diligence. I'd wiped my fingerprints and used someone as cover. A simple slice in the pipe delivering the gas to the home and boom, carbon monoxide gas happened. It was simple; not too much over-thinking there. Emmett had to be all right. He really was a prince of a guy; too nice for the likes of a black widow like Lily Brooksfield. I'd seen the sparkler; he had for her. If I got my way, she'd never see it; but for now, I'd lay low. I hoped Dafydd was safe from her too.

Hide in plain sight, isn't that what they'd say in those old movies? I loved those old movies Tommy and Tuppence, such fun to watch and then of course Bogart playing Sam Spade. Sure, they were way before my time; but I loved the movies none the less. Maybe I'd sneak in nonchalant like in one of those movies and visit Emmett. I could finagle it. It wouldn't be too hard, after all I had the right credentials. My contact had made a number of identities, I could use at the ready.

Plan and execute carefully; that was my motto. I didn't want to get caught after all, but I would win my heart's desire in the end. If Lily Kelly got in my way then she would be sorry. I'd make it my mission to make her life hell and if she pushed too hard, then Lily would end up just like Sherry-Anne.

~0~

Chapter 20 – Troubled Waters Run Deep

"**I** need to call Laura before we get to the hospital to make sure Emmett's kids are looked after," Lily insisted.

"Go ahead, give her a call Lily."

"That's funny, she's not answering."

"Maybe she's at the hospital? The kids would be really worried," Grandma Katha answered.

"Yes, of course, that's probably it. Oh no, I didn't call Suzy and she needs to call Emmett's other sister, Paula. I don't have Paula's number," Lily stated.

Lily took her cell phone out of her phone and dialed.

"Suzy, hi it's Lily. Did you hear about Emmett?" Lily asked over the phone

Grandma Katha heard Suzy whisper, "I can't leave. It was Laura's day off and I was watching the kids for Emmett. I don't think he'd want Dee to know and I can't reach Laura either."

"Oh dear, Suzy. How are you managing with two small babies, five-year-old and two twelve-year olds?" Lily asked surprised.

"It certainly isn't easy. Dee has been amazing though. Do you know that little girl can change diapers better than most adults? She loves the babies." Suzy explained, "I'm a little worried about Joseph and Rebecca though. They overheard about Emmett and they are extremely upset, luckily though they haven't said anything to Deirdre."

"I've had some drama of my own with
Rose (we will talk later about that); but it
means I haven't even met the kids yet.
Would you mind keeping them; until I
can find a sitter for them?" Lily asked.

"Sure, it's not like I can take Abigail and
Emma to the hospital." Suzy stated,
"You'll let me know about my brother
though, won't you? I called Paula; she's
dealing with her own drama, as usual. Her
husband was home for a few days. I think
he's an abuser, but we can't get her any
help. She always denies it and the army
seems to protect him."

"I'm so sorry. I didn't know about Paula.
Suzy when I was talking a babysitter, I
was planning on two; so, they could
watch all the children. You need a break
and to visit Emmett too."

"Tell her I have two nannies coming from
a reputable agency in under an hour,"
Grandma Katha interjected.

"Tell your Grandmother Katha I heard
that and she's a lifesaver." Suzy

exclaimed with relief then added, "I have to tell you though to watch out for our sister Paula. That woman is mad at the world. It's not just because I called her on the abuse. She's worried sick about Jason going back to Afghanistan and she's taking it out on me and the general population. She actually had the nerve to blame you, for Emmett being at the hospital. Let me tell you, I put her straight; but I don't think it took."

"Paula is angry at me?" Lily interjected, her taxi pulling away from the airport on the way to the hospital.

"I know; it makes no sense. I don't think my sister has ever made sense in her twenty-five years." Suzy commented, "I told Paula, your cousin and her daughter got hurt and all she could say was that you Kellys should keep your curse to yourselves and not involve Emmett. She is so mean; sometimes I wondered if they switched her at the hospital. But she looks too much like our mother for that to be true. Oh, got to go; Dee said one of the babies is crying in the crib. Bye Lil. See you soon."

"What is wrong with Emmett's sister, Paula? I thought you talked to her on the phone; before when the babies were born. Does she even know you? Why does she say such awful things?" Grandma Katha stated as they step onto the elevator.

"She just doesn't know me at all Grandma Katha, but Emmett has been hurt several times since he met me," Lily stated.

"He is a police officer. Police officers get hurt sometimes on the job. What does she expect? She has no cause to blame everything on you," Grandma Katha stated angrily.

They then exited the taxi and look for the intensive care.

"I love you too, Grandma Katha."

"That goes both ways, honey," Grandma Katha answered.

"What was that?" asked Lily, as the elevator shook.

"It's an old hospital old elevator, nothing to worry about," Grandma Katha said as the elevator shuttered again and then came to a complete stop.

"Oh, no, Grandma Katha; I think you spoke to soon. "Lily responded

"What? But they reassured the hospital board that these elevators were safe and this wouldn't happen again. What if a sick patient was in them?" Grandma Katha ranted.

"Why hasn't someone come to get us out?" Lily asked visibly paling.

"I pushed the alarm. You heard it didn't you?" Grandma Katha asked.

"No, I did not. Push it again; shouldn't it be ringing, or something?" Lily asked sounding slightly panicked.

"I thought you got over your claustrophobic tendencies? Breathe use

your techniques. They'll come soon,"
Grandma Katha stated the emergency
button again.

"I hate small spaces. I don't know why;
but they make me feel very sick. Why
isn't that button working? I hear nothing,"
Lily replied.

"We will get out soon honey," Grandma
Katha reassured

"We have to get out." Lily said sinking to
the floor of the elevator, "Emmett,
Amelia and Carol need us."

"They have to know the elevator isn't
working; they'll come back," Grandma
Katha stated.

"Maybe someone can hear us," Lily
stated. then she began yelling, "Help we
are stuck in the elevator."

A few minutes later Grandma Katha said,
"I don't think anyone heard you; but they
must know the elevator isn't working
someone will check."

"That's not going to help, if they don't know were stuck in here. Doesn't that phone work?" asked Lily pointing to the phone on the wall.

"Wait a minute…. what am I thinking? We will just call the front desk of the hospital on my cell phone and let them know we are trapped here." Lily said taking out her phone and dialing.

Lily explained that they are stuck in the elevator.

"They said they are working on it. It could take an hour," Lily explained to Grandma Katha.

"Then we will just wait," Grandma Katha exclaimed.

Bored and trying to distract herself, Lily tried to hear anything and heard a conversation drifting into the elevator shaft, possibly from outside the elevator, or from in the elevator next door. She recognized the two voices as Dr. Claire

Callister and Dr. Carla Yates, two doctors she'd already met.

"Claire I was just coming to meet you. You wanted a consultation on a case?"

"I did. I have three carbon monoxide poisoning patients in the intensive care unit. There have just been too many cases of this lately. Were you aware that all of this could have been prevented by early detection with the use of a household carbon monoxide detector? Carbon monoxide poisoning is the most common type of fatal poisoning in many countries and yet people are not even aware of it? Thank goodness Ontario has made them mandatory? Yet here we are again," Claire said, sadly.

"I am very aware of the statistics, I'm afraid." Dr. Carla Yates stated, "I looked in on Amelia Kelly, Carol Banks and Emmett Rogers as you asked. You do know, that I know them personally, though? Faisal has been beside himself and we have no idea whether to talk to

Grandfather Faraj about the incident and the fact they are in the hospital. Grandfather Faraj is very close to Amelia, Lily and Grandma Katha Kelly, since they finally met."

"You know Lily and Grandma Katha?" Claire commented, sounding surprised.

"Of course, I do," Carla said with exasperation, then blurted, "Oh, you didn't know? Of course, you didn't. A lot of people aren't aware of the relationships. My grandfather- in- law, Faraj is Katha's son, making my husband her great-grandson. Amelia is related to us too of course. She's my husband's cousin, somehow," Carla explained.

"Wow, I had no idea. I met Katha Stewart when she came into the ER early this year remember?" Claire stated.

"Sorry, of course you met her right after…when my mother… killed people. I still can't believe what she did…….. trying to kill that police officer trying to kill…Weatherthorpe. I can understand

that; but a police officer even a bad one?"
Carla said with great sadness.

"I'm so sorry Carla. It could have been a
result of the brain tumour; you know,"
Claire sympathized.

"I know that; but it's hard to rationalize.
At least she saved Rose and Carol. Now
we have to save Carol, again. Her life
can't have been saved in vain. Carol is
just starting to become a young woman."

"It seems pretty grave though. I'm very
concerned that the oxygen isn't saturating
the blood. I think a hyperbaric chamber is
necessary; but three of them are necessary
and we only have two." Claire stated, "As
you saw on the chart, further treatment for
seizures, hypotension, cardiac
abnormalities, and pulmonary edema,
may be necessary in Carol's case. Carol is
the gravest. We are pushing the
intravenous fluids; but vasopressors may
be required to treat myocardial
depression. However, I am concerned that
treatment with sodium bicarbonate

acidosis may increase tissue oxygen availability."

"That is very concerning obviously Carol must have one of the chambers. Which one do you think can wait?" asked Carla.

"They all three need the treatment now; but if I had to pick Emmett would have to wait."

"This is the worst part of our job. We are trying our best; but the three of them are not in great shape. They have to take a turn for the better in the next few hours, or none of the treatments will do any good."

"Should we fly Emmett to London, Ontario?"

"We may have to; but let's just wait and see."

Lily heard the elevator next door ding and the two voices exit the elevator.

"Did you hear that Grandma Katha? All three of them are in trouble. They can't die. Emmett can't die. I haven't even told him about the baby yet," Lily said her voice trembling close to tears.

"Let's not borrow trouble, Lily. They are fighters. They are getting the best treatment and guess what? Your Grandfather Terrence's company, the one that he stepped down as CEO; still owns the majority of shares in Terrabond.... they have a subsidiary that makes medical products and I believe they may make hyperbaric chambers. I'm going to call your Grandfather now. He'll get us one of those hyperbaric chambers, even if he doesn't make them. That's what kind of man he is," Grandma Katha explained.

Grandma Katha took out her cell phone and called Terrence. She spoke for few minutes. explaining their predicament then explained how they needed the hyperbaric chamber. said goodbye and then hung up.

"Okay, we are all set. Your Grandpa Terrence is going to have one delivered from his subsidiary as soon as possible and he's sending a technician to get us out of this elevator," Grandma Katha explained.

"Thank goodness. Grandpa Terrence is a wonder. It's taking so long to get us out. It seems like it would take hours; before we get out of here," Lily responded, just as the doors opened between floors.

A repairman stuck his head down and, in the elevator, and said "Everyone okay in there?"

"Yes," Grandma Katha and Lily answered.

"We will have you out in about ten minutes; just got to make adjustments so the elevator comes up evenly," the repairman stated.

"Great, thank-you," Grandma Katha answered.

"Is it just me, or is it hot in here?" asked Lily

"No, it is a little warm dear; but don't worry we will be out in a jiffy. Let me help you off the floor."

"Thanks Grandma Katha. I appreciate the help, but I'm not that pregnant, yet," Lily said with a smile.

As Lily got to her feet the elevator lurched; but struggling and balancing her feet just right she managed to get her balance.

"Okay, ladies. There you go," the repairman said as the elevator door opened evenly on the floor.

Lily stepped out into the intensive care hallway and followed a long hall. Lily felt very warm, somewhat nauseous and faint. She decided to go near the doors for fresh air when to her surprise Paula, Emmett's sister came through them.

"You! You have the nerve to show your face here? Who do you think you are? If it wasn't for you, he wouldn't be here. People are right about you. You are a black widow," Paula spurted, without a breath her voice rising,

"There will be none of that Paula Rogers-Spriet. If you were so worried about Emmett where have you been all those other times, he needed you? Lily has been there every time in fact she is his fiancée," Grandma Katha stated fibbing a bit.

Lily just looked surprised at the attack and paled even more.

"Hello Paula." Kendall said, "I have to tell you Emmett would be very disappointed in you. You see Grandma Katha is telling the truth. Emmett proposed to Lily. They are engaged."

"You're engaged? When did this happen?" Paula asked turning back to Lily.

This Little Girl had a Little Curl
S. G. Lee

Grandma Katha is alarmed to find Lily in a heap on the floor.

Chapter 21 – Where am I?

Lily awoke to find a nurse checking a blood pressure cuff attached to her arm.

"What? Where am I?" Lily asked disoriented.

"It seems you had a worrisome spike in blood pressure. You just rest there quietly." The nurse stated nodding her head, "Yes, it is coming down. The doctor will be in soon."

"The baby…. is the baby all right?" Lily begged.

"Yes, for now. Now just relax and keep that blood pressure where we have gotten it to," the nurse answered.

This Little Girl had a Little Curl
S. G. Lee

"Emmett? How are Emmett, Amelia and Carol?" Lily demanded frantically.

"Wow, your Grandmother knows you well. She said to tell you first thing that Amelia is struggling; but hopefully getting better and Carol is awake." The nurse answered, "Now if I move this curtain here you can see for yourself that Emmett is holding his own."

"Emmett is right beside me? Oh, thank-you," Lily stated joyfully.

"Your Grandmother insisted on it. It seems like she is a mover and shaker here on the hospital board, so she demanded this and we conceded," the nurse replied.

"Grandma Katha is a wonder," Lily stated smiling

"Here she is. I knew she wouldn't be long away; despite us kicking her out; not more than fifteen minutes ago. We told her that there are only fifteen-minute visits in an hour; but she seems to think this means every fifteen minutes. Is she senile?

"No and don't say that in her presence if you like your job. Grandma Katha likes things her own way and if she doesn't like a rule, she bends it."

"Now, now Lily. Don't be telling things about your Grandmother out of school." scolded Grandma Katha, "I'm so glad you are all right my pet; but you have to take better care of yourself."

"I'm sorry," Lily stated big tears rolling from her eyes.

"If you are going to upset my patient hospital board, or no hospital board you won't be allowed in," the nurse stated interrupting.

"I'm not upsetting my girl. She just plain wore out with worry about everything. Her fiancé Emmett being so ill and her daughter running away have made her stressed, a little rest will do her good," Grandma Katha explained.

This Little Girl had a Little Curl
S. G. Lee

"Her daughter ran away as well? Oh dear," The nurse clucked.

"We found her daughter, just a misunderstanding; but you know how stressful raising children are. Now Emmett, dear Emmett being so ill…her cousin and her daughter Carol, of course she's upset; but she's going to think happy thoughts now. Aren't you my pet? Emmett will soon be right as rain, you'll see," Grandma Katha stated forcefully

Lily started to believe it ; after all Grandma Katha said it and Grandma Katha was a force of nature.

"Lily?" Lily heard.

"Why are you in a hospital bed? Why am I?" Emmett asked disoriented and trying to get out of bed.

"Emmett it's so good to see you, dear," Grandma Katha said hurrying to his side.

"What's going on?" Emmett asked again.

"Mr. Rogers, do you know where you are?" asked the nurse.

"Mr. Rogers? Oh yes I'm Mr. Rogers; but I don't have a button up sweater," chuckled Emmett at his own joke.

The nurse looked alarmed but tried to hide it.

"Still the same bad joke, I see," Lily answered.

"Lily what are you doing here? Why are you in that bed?" Emmett asked again; as if he hadn't already asked the same question.

"Why is he asking that again? Is he okay?" Lily wondered.

"Sometimes patients who have been exposed to carbon monoxide, can be a wee bit disoriented. It's nothing to worry about, unless it continues," the nurse explained.

"Lily, I am not confused. Why are we in hospital? I know that I was exposed to an odourless gas, but you? You didn't find me, did you?" Emmett asked sounding sensible.

"She was overcome when she heard about you, Emmett." Grandma Katha stated covering for Lily.

"Thank goodness! Then you are okay?" Emmett asked searching Lily's face.

"Grandma Katha is leaving something out Emmett. I wanted to tell you sooner, but things kept getting in the way," Lily replied but she's interrupted by Emmett.

"Please, Lily, whatever it was, we can make it right. I know it's a lot to ask you to take on three more children..."

"Actually, it's four more," Lily said quickly.

"But I only have three more.... wait a minute, are you saying what I think you are saying?" Emmett asked hopefully.

"We are having a baby in about three and half months," Lily said nodding.

"A baby? We are having a baby?"
Emmett asked with great joy in his voice.

"Yes," Lily replied.

"Then it's a good thing, I already asked
you to marry me, or you'd take my
proposal all wrong," Emmett stated.

"But that was so long ago," Lily said with
tears in her eyes.

"Not so long ago, just a couple of days
ago," Emmett said with humour in his
voice.

"What are you talking about?" asked Lily

"I sent you a telegram asking you to
marry me. Didn't you get it?" demanded
Emmett.

"I didn't receive a telegram," Lily replied
puzzled.

"That's really odd. I sent it to you."
Emmett stated totally perplexed, "Wait
minute, if you are pregnant and you're in

a hospital bed, then are you sure
everything is okay?"

"You two can talk all about this later.
Right now, it's time for your doctor to
look after you, Emmett." The nurse stated
looking up and seeing Dr. Carla Yates.

"When is the doctor coming to look after
Lily and our baby?" Emmett asked,
worried "Why aren't you looking after
her Doctor Yates?"

"Actually, my colleague Dr. Claire
Callister will attend Lily, until her
Obstetrician can get her." Carla stated,
"I'm going to put her mind at ease and
look after you, my patient."

"But...," Emmett protested.

"No, buts; if I have to get checked out so
do you," Lily said brooking no refusal.

"Fine, but I am fine," Emmett
complained.

"I'll decide that," stated Carla.

A few minutes later both doctors came out from behind the curtains.

"So, how are they?" asked a worried Grandma Katha

"With some time, Emmett will be fine," Carla replied talking to Grandma Katha in the corridor

"Thank you, dear and how is my grandson? He's been so busy the last week, I haven't heard from him," Grandma Katha complained.

"He's been very busy with his new case. He's hoping to win it you know and that would be a big boost to his career with Thomas, Brackenridge, and Forest," Carla explained.

"I certainly remember those days. Tell him I was asking after him and give him my love, dear," Grandma Katha stated hugging Carla.

"Oh, here's Claire. I think she wants to talk with you over there the way she's motioning to the chairs," Carla stated.

"Lily is rundown and this pregnancy is putting stress on her heart. Even though it was repaired earlier this year, this is a lot of stress. Her body is fighting back and her blood pressure then rises. If we can't get this under control better than we are already; we may have to hospitalize her for the rest of her pregnancy, or she may have to decide between the baby and herself," Claire explained.

"But she can have a healthy baby?" asked Grandma Katha.

"If we can't get this under control, we may have to make a choice to have the baby early. The baby may not survive," Claire stated.

"Do what you need to do and help both of them survive, please, Dr. Callister," begged Grandma Katha

"I'll do my best; but I'm not making promises," Claire stated.

"Does she know all of this?" asked Grandma Katha

"I've told her," stated Claire.

In the cubicle bed Lily cried softly. Emmett heard her and got up out of his bed and crawled in beside her.

"It will be all right Lily. Our baby is tough little pumpkin, like its parents. It's going to hang in there until it's time to be born. Wait and see," Emmett reassured her.

"Do you really believe that?" Lily asked hopefully.

"I do and so do you," Emmett stated patting her stomach. "Hang in there junior. This is your daddy talking. Now we want to see you in about three and half months understand?"

"Do you think they really hear us?" asked Lily.

"Of course, they do." Emmett replied, "Now I got your messages, did you find Rose?"

"She was visiting her mother," Lily answered

"Oh, boy!" Emmett responded.

"Oh, boy, indeed; she's really mad at me," Lily answered.

"It will all work out. She'll see that you were trying to protect her and she'll come around," Emmett stated.

"I hope so."

"So where is she now?"

"Rose is with Terrence and he'll take her to visit her mother," Lily answered.

"Mr. Rogers get back in your own bed," stated the nurse, as Lily and Emmett laugh in embarrassment.

"Love you," they both said as Emmett left Lily's bed and crawled in his.

"Both of you get some sleep now. I'm watching you," stated the nurse sternly.

This Little Girl had a Little Curl
S. G. Lee

Lily and Emmett closed their eyes obediently and are soon fast asleep. Grandma Katha kept a watchful eye on both of them. She continued to check on Amelia and Carol as well. She hoped and prayed that all will be alright soon. They were alive and on the mend that made it all right with the world.

~0~

Chapter 22 – Nothing is as it seems

One week later

Kendall frustrated and annoyed, couldn't understand why the case hadn't advanced. It should have been a slam dunk; they had a print, match it up and presto, they had the murderer, but the murderer's print wasn't in the system and once more the print; wasn't as clear as they'd like. Thank goodness it wasn't Lily. Emmett would never have accepted that; besides she grown to admire Lily a little, maybe even like her.

Kendall walked into the forensic lab where Brandy Calders was hard at work.

"Are you working on those fingerprints we found on Sherry-Anne's back?"

"Not at the moment. I do have other cases, you know," protested Brandy.

"I can't understand why we couldn't get a clear print. Why could forensics have given us some evidence, we could work with?" Kendall protested.

"We've called in Gerald Gates to work on it in a special office."

"Good grief, I mean it's not rocket science! I hear you can take D.N. A. and predict physical appearance helping me find the culprit."

"I don't have access to that kind of a program Kendall. That's all new and probably has a patent. We're not miracle workers; though we try to be. What Gerald has been looking at is the usual. We look at blood, semen, skin cells, tissue, bone, teeth, hair. He's been working at it over a week."

"But we don't have any of those. We have some hair I guess but the only other thing we have is the fingerprints."

"You're awful impatient, Kendall. We both wanted evidence we could work with; but Gerald Gates is one of the tops in his field if he couldn't find a print no one can."

"Really, it doesn't seem that hard. You look through a microscope examine prints and compare them to others. How hard is that?" Kendall asked.

Alan Barnes walked in.

"Sorry I've got to go now, "Brandy insisted

"That is an over simplification. Forensic Investigators don't have it easy. They have to constantly update their credentials to keep up with the latest finds," Alan stated annoyed.

"What is it to you, Alan, if I insult Forensic people?" Kendall spat.

"Number one, we work with these people and their evidence can mean the difference in nailing a suspect and one Gerald is my cousin, and two, I also like Brandy," Alan admitted.

"It seems that your cousin hasn't been that helpful. We have a perfectly good print from the Jones case and we haven't been able to nail that suspect; because they can't identify the perp. Now there are no other prints for an attempted murder at a police officer's girlfriend's home," Kendall griped.

"Hey, we are all mad about that Kendall. We'll nail the perpetrator even without prints. Someone had to have seen them outside the home." Alan stated fiercely, "Let's go get coffee; before you head back to the station.

"I could use one," Kendall agreed.

Kendall followed Alan to the nearby Tim
Hortons. They sat in a table where they
could see the door.

"Tell me how Emmett is doing?

"He's a lot better. He's going home with
Lily today. They are both going to be
staying at his house, since hers is a crime
scene." Kendall answered "Carol and
Amelia are on the mend too; although
they may keep them another week in
hospital."

"Who is going to look after Emmett and
Lily then? Won't Katha be spending most
of her time at the hospital? Isn't Lily on
bed rest for awhile?" Alan asked.

"You heard? Yes, Lily is on bed rest and
in fact both she and Emmett are to
recover in bed. Ha, ha. Actually, the
nursemaid Laura has offered to look after
them. I don't know how she's going to
manage to look after all those kids and
two adults." Kendall stated, "Frankly, I'm
not sure I like that woman, she gives me
bad vibes and I just don't like the looks

she's being giving Emmett. I told him he should hire a new nanny; but he said he doesn't have the energy right now to do so."

"Wow, that is a handful and more. I'm sure you're worried about the nanny, probably too much .The nanny will get over her crush. Emmett never notices women crushing on them and sooner, or later they find the man is human and get over themselves."

"I've seen that too. Thank-you Alan, I feel better."

"Is Caleb and Rose going to help out their parents?" Alan commented.

"I don't know about Rose; she's actually been gone for the last week. Something, hush- hush which Emmett and Lily wouldn't talk about. Probably has to do with the mother of Rose's," Kendall stated pensively.

"But I thought Lily was her mother?" Alan responded.

Kendall looked upset as she realized she said that out loud and Alan is asking questions.

"I should have said that. Please don't ask questions; it's not my story to tell. I shouldn't have said anything. Forget you heard that if you value our friendship," Kendall begged.

"So, I heard Emmett proposed?"

"Lily accepted, so his days as a single man are dwindling. She's a lucky woman, Emmett's a great guy. He proposed by telegram, but for some reason Lily didn't get it."

"Don't you think that's odd?" Alan asked.

"Yes, I mean who sends telegrams in this day and age?"

"That's not what I meant..." Alan replied then let it go. "Have you heard any more news about the murders of Emmett's sister and brother-in law and all those other people?"

"You haven't been snooping? Have you?"

Kendall searched Alan's face.

"You have... I told you to leave that to them," Kendall stated annoyed.

"I've been looking into the case, because it worried me from the start. It's obvious it was an inside job. Who killed all those people?" Alan began.

"That's not our case and not our information to find out. You stay out of it, Alan, or you'll embarrass the department," Kendall commanded.

"Too late, I think I may have found something. You see the mom, Dianna was shot before the father," Alan stated showing Kendall.

"Alan you have to keep this to yourself. Who is this going to hurt, but Emmett and those kids? If they find out their father killed their mother...," Kendall replied.

"I can see your point Kendall; but isn't our job to reveal the truth?" Alan demanded.

"The truth is I want to protect a fellow officer and so should you. His family has suffered enough you have no proof. Let it go Alan."

"I guess I could," Alan responded.

"Good then." Kendall stated, "Now let's work on the case at hand Sherry-Anne Jones and the carbon monoxide poisoning of Emmett, Carol and Amelia."

"We have to go interview Dafydd again. I'm glad you received permission from that O.P.P. cop we don't want to screw over our careers. Dafydd may know something that he does even comprehend he knows."

"I hope so; but this case always leads to dead ends."

"Maybe we should interview him about some more people from his past?"

"Sounds like a great idea to me Alan. Maybe that will give us some new leads because so far this case is deadlocked."

"Let's go, I'll follow you," Alan insisted.

~0~

Chapter 23 - Divide and Conquer

I'm getting so sick of that Lily Kelly-Brooksfield. Something more has to be done about her. The carbon monoxide has only succeeded in making Emmett sick, and Lily move in.

Damn her! Now she's pulling the damsel in distress, I'm pregnant with your baby card. Must she have all the men? Lily seemed to be getting along well with his nieces and nephew too. It was all poor Lily this, poor Lily that, just because she was having a baby and the doctor said she needed bed rest.

Really? Women had given birth for centuries and if she couldn't carry that baby to term, without lying around like a Victorian heroine, then she didn't deserve Emmett; now did she? I had to do

something; before Emmett was swayed
over by her. It wasn't a baby yet? Now
was it? If Lily was stressed, maybe she'd
lose it, then I could sweep in and Emmett
would meet and see me for his one true
love. I could dance like Snow White and
sing that song. You know the one! He
would see that I was sweet and kind, and
the one who could truly make him happy

Dafydd would like that too. I'd be off his
hands; for he didn't want me anymore.
Somehow, he knew what I had done. I
hadn't meant to harm his son, Daniel. I
would never harm a hair on his beautiful
little head, and ultimately Daniel lived,
didn't he?

Now Sherry-Anne, she was another thing
altogether. If she had just gone quietly
and hadn't made me push her...I'd try to
control my temper and be cold and
calculating, but she made it so difficult.

Dafydd would understand eventually and
if he didn't while then I'd have Emmett
anyway. That is, if I could get rid of that

simpering bitch, Lily. Maybe the baby
wasn't meant to be? I wouldn't do
anything overtly to harm the child, but as
I said if Lily got stressed and lost the
baby then it was Lily's fault, not mine.
How to achieve that end? Divide and
conquer? Yes, that was how.

Lily was already at odds with her adopted
daughter. Yes, I knew that, but she
seemed like she was more Lily's than her
real mother's. That little slut! I saw how
she went to a party with alcohol and sex.
Funny, what you could hear when you
listened in corners and Lily knew nothing
about that party. Maybe all I have to do
was to wait for the kid to reveal how she
lied to her mom? But wouldn't it be even
better if that sanctimonious cousin of
Lily's, Amelia happened to overhear?
Then they'd all be mad each other and act
like the idiots I knew they were. Families
didn't stick together they just fractured,
when stressed. I knew that… look at
mine.

Now how could I arrange all this? I could plant little seeds and then Lily would stress out lose the baby and Emmett would be so angry he'd dump her. It was a solid plan; it would work. I'd see to it.

But I am so scared. I know Emmett's going to find out all I've done. How could he not? I didn't want to do this, but I had to. I had no choice. There is much he doesn't know and much he cannot find out. I go on, as if nothing had happened; but I am a murderer. There is no doubt one day I will pay for my crime; but not yet. Not yet. I love him. Emmett's been so good to me. Emmett can't find out. He won't if I can help it.

But I'm dealing with Lily and she is evil. Pure evil, that wants to harm everyone she knows. She loves him and she hates him.... Emmett, I mean. She is so cruel; she makes me do her bidding. She probably did some mojo to make me kill Sherry-Anne; so, it's not really my fault...is it?

I'm surprised he doesn't see her schemes and lies. He is a police officer. He thinks he sees everything, but he doesn't. He so kind; that's probably what makes him blind to her. The children are what matters for now. I will not let her harm them. Whatever it takes, I will do it to protect them. The boy is troublesome though, and his twin sister is annoying they do vex me so.

They are almost like little adults. If they were adults, they wouldn't need my love, or protection. Now would they? I protect the ones I love; but it's hard to love those that refuse to love you back. The little one Deirdre is sweet... ***now she loves me***.

I have done all I can for that child; even if it means I go to jail if it comes to that. I will not fail her; but for now, I give into protect them and myself. I won't go to jail and I'll protect what is mine with all I am. This is my vow.

~0~

Chapter 24 – Opposite Forces

Lily entered Emmett's home and

started going down the hall to Emmett's bedroom. Laura grabbed her arm and proceeded to take her to a room past Emmett's.

"Emmett's room is next door. I'll just take my stuff there," Lily stated turning around.

"Now you know you wouldn't get any rest if you two shared a bed. I made you up a bed, in here," Laura insisted.

"That's very kind of you; but Emmett and I plan on sharing a bed."

"No, I insist. You wouldn't want to harm Emmett's health, would you?"

"No, of course, I wouldn't." Lily
answered.

"Now you just get into this bed. I put
fresh sheets on the bed and this is a nice
new comfortable pillow," Laura
concluded, helping Lily into the bed.

Lily wondered if she should be worried
about Laura's remarks about Emmett. Did
Laura have a crush on Emmett? Should
she be concerned? It was just she was
getting strange vibes from her. Lily would
just put up with her. They were both
recovering and once they did then they
would get rid of Laura (if she was a
problem.) They would give her good
recommendation and find her a new job
and Grandma Katha would help them find
a more capable nanny; who wasn't so
focused on Emmett.

She had a new life growing in her and
Emmett wanted to get married before the
baby was born, but that would have to
wait. The doctor told her she had to have

bed rest for awhile, to keep her blood pressure down.

Lily was scared and worried. If her blood pressure wasn't kept down; then the baby would be born, too soon and at six months more than likely it wouldn't survive like her first child. She would put up with the bed rest; but it was so hard that she wasn't allowed to work. The doctor had forbidden her to work. Would she lose her job? No, there was protection under Canadian law she knew that; but still she worried they'd find a way around it.

Didn't they know she could work from home? But no, they insisted that it would be too stressful with her high-profile cases. Lily still began to worry she be fired from her position and then she worried that she was being selfish. She had a child to think of nestled carefully under her ribs. This child would be cossetted and loved; but it needed Lily to incubate it and get it born healthy and safe into this world.

This Little Girl had a Little Curl
S. G. Lee

"Aunt Wily?" a little voice asked from the doorway.

"Hello," Lily stated.

"Wara said you wus here. She said I wasn't to disherb you," Deirdre said softly.

"Disherbs? Oh, you mean disturb," Lily stated.

"That is what I said, isn't it?" Deirdre replied slightly annoyed, "Uncle Emwettt is sleepin' and since he lubs you I want to make you feel better and sing and read to you. My mommy always said that made me better, when I was sick," Dee stated.

"Thank-you Deirdre, that's very kind," Lily replied amused.

Deirdre then stepped into the bedroom and crawled into the bed beside Lily, with a nursery rhyme book.

"My mommy always used to say this one to me, *There was a little girl who had a little curl right in the middle of her forehead, and when she was good, she was very, very good..."*

"But when she was bad, she was rotten*.*** Just like you,"** finished Joseph coming into the room and looking annoyed.

"I wasn't rotten; honest, I wasn't," protested Deirdre.

"Maybe, but you weren't supposed to come in here; were you Dee?" scolded Joseph.

"No, but Laura was busy. She stands by Unca Emwettt's door watching him all da time and Daniel is visiting da nursery school. I thought maybe Wily would be bored too and I read to her," Deirdre said defending herself.

"We need to get you a speech person," Joseph complained.

"Do you mean a speech therapist?" Lily asked interested.

"Ya, she doesn't talk so good." Joseph complained, "She calls Uncle Emmett,

Unca Emwettt and now she's calling you Wily."

"I don't want some stupid person telling me, I talk funny. Do you think I talk funny, Aunt Wily?"

"No,sweetheart, I just think you need some help with speaking clearly, so people understand you. I could get you some help with that; if it's okay with you." Lily stated, "I know a nice speech therapist who is kind to little girls and boys."

"I don't like peoples, I don't know," Deirdre complained.

"Would you like to meet my cousin Kieran? He actually likes to help little girls speak more clearly."

"He's your cousin? Like the babies that belong to Aunt Swoosie are my cousins?" Deirdre asked.

"He is my cousin, just like your cousins, Emma, and Abigail, who are your Aunt Suzy's daughter and your cousins, Greg and Austin who are Aunt Paula's sons," Lily replied.

"You won't give me to him; will you? Cause I like living with Unca Emwettt," Deirdre asked, fingers in her mouth looking scared.

"No never, we would never willingly give you away. We love you Deirdre." Lily answered.

"When would I see your cousin?" Deirdre asked bravely.

"I have to talk to him first; maybe he could come see you here, the first time."

"I think you should be talking to Mr. Rogers about this first." Laura retorted, disapprovingly as she came angrily marching into Lily's room; obviously having listened to the entire conversation.

"Would Unca Emwettt not like me to go see the man?" asked Deirdre scared.

"I'm sure that Uncle Emmett would be happy for you to meet my cousin. This is really none of Laura's business," Lily said firmly and gave Laura a look that said you'd better go along with this.

"Is this good Laura?"

"I'll mention it to your Uncle; but I don't know…," Laura replied.

Lily is feeling quite annoyed and cross. How dare Laura contradict her in front of Deirdre? She hated being confined to bed. Yet here she was alone in bed, because Emmett was listening to Laura and not joining her. Maybe some of Laura's reasons made sense to him. Laura insisting that not sleeping in the same bed would have kept them from jostling each other was at most ridiculous; but interfering in Lily's bonding with Dee was not acceptable. As for the separate beds this wasn't working out. Lily knew her best rest was safely beside Emmett. To heck with Laura! Lily was going to go to Emmett. She wanted to be beside him…close to him. Lily rose out of bed and meandered down the hall.

This Little Girl had a Little Curl
S. G. Lee

"Why are you here Lily?" Emmett asked as Lily came in his room.

"I decided I wanted to join you. It's foolish for us to be apart," Lily insisted.

"I don't think that's a good idea; maybe you shouldn't you go back to your room," Emmett claimed.

"Why?" Lily asked, hurt.

"You need your rest; you wouldn't get any with me. The after effects of the carbon monoxide poisoning have made me snore."

"I don't care about that."

"Well, I do; our baby needs his, or her rest," Emmett explained.

"Fine, then, see you later," Lily snarled, leaving the room.

Emmett breathed a sigh of relief. It was hard for him to do that. He wanted nothing more than Lily by his side; but Laura had explained to him that the

doctor had said that could be dangerous
for both Lily and the baby. He hoped that
Lily would understand, that he was doing
the best thing for the baby. He wished he
could remember the doctor telling them
all about the baby's condition; but since
the accident with the carbon monoxide his
memory was faulty and full of holes. The
doctor insisted this was normal; but it
truly scared Emmett. The clown was out
of the closet and being used as a
punching bag. It was the only thing
keeping his stress levels down.

Luckily Laura had come along with him
to the doctor and was able to tell him the
entirety of what the doctor had said.
Laura had explained to him that the
doctor thought for the next three months,
he should have as little close contact with
Lily as possible as the residual effects of
the carbon monoxide poisoning might
linger and hurt the growing foetus.
Emmett had the heart to tell Lily about his
memory problems; or the fact that
exposure to him might hurt the baby. She
needed him and even if he couldn't be

that close to her, he was nearby. Emmett was tired of the bed rest. He would have thought it odd that the doctor insisted on so much bed rest; if Laura hadn't told him what the doctor had said. Emmett closed his eyes and went to sleep.

Down the hall in her own room, Lily was feeling frustrated. Laura wasn't working out; she was too bossy and seemed possessive of the children. Lily wasn't even sure Dee liked Laura. Lily didn't know how to broach the subject with Emmett, especially since he had hired Laura. Technically Grandma Katha had, but Emmett was paying the woman and not sanctioning her for her bad behaviour.

Laura refused to let anyone else in the house, wasn't that strange? Almost like Laura was keeping them prisoner, or was that Lily's imagination? Laura had even turned away Grandma Katha and Amelia. Lily had expected Grandma Katha to say no and barge in; but she'd agreed with Laura and wandered off. Lily had phoned Grandma Katha and told her to come back and she had; but Lily didn't like how controlling Laura was being. Lily also didn't like the looks Laura was giving Emmett.

The kids seemed to like and obey Laura, more than Lily so maybe Lily was just reading things into this because she was jealous? No. Laura might have known the children longer; but Lily would be their Aunt; surely that should count for more? Would Emmett listen to her about her concerns about Laura? He seemed to be brainwashed. Lily regretted not replacing Laura sooner. Laura's crush on Emmett seemed to be stronger than ever.

Emmett had told her that Laura was crushing on him; but she thought it would pass, now that the woman realized he was taken. However now it seemed that Laura had taken completely over.

Laura held sway with the children and Emmett. Lily felt displaced and superfluous. They didn't seem to need her at all and Rose still hadn't come home to

Lily. Lily missed her daughter. She
wished Rose would forgive her.

Rose insisted on staying with her
Grandma Katha and Grandpa Terrence.
Rose had the right to be angry with her;
because Lily had kept the secret that
Cordelia was not in a regular jail; but in a
criminal mental facility. Lily had done
this because she'd made a promise to
Horace and because she knew it would
harm Rose; but that didn't matter Rose
was hurt and angry.

Something else was going on with Rose
though; Lily could feel it in her gut. Lily
was sure it wasn't just that Cordelia was
back in that fugues state again either.
Something major was going on in Rose's
life and instead of reaching out to Lily;
like she had done in the past; she was
shutting Lily out. Lily prayed that Rose
would let her in soon. Lily had to find out
what was going on. She couldn't lose her
daughter Rose. Lily wouldn't push the
issue, maybe she would give Rose a few
more days and then demand that she

come and see her mother Lily. After all,
no matter what, Lily was still Rose's
mother. Cordelia hadn't been there for
her, Lily had.

Something else had happened the night
Cordelia had killed her pimp. Something
Cordelia wouldn't even talk about;
frankly Lily hoped Rose would never
remember what that was. The child
psychologist had seemed to think it was a
traumatic thing that had happened to
Rose. Lily couldn't even think of the
word so how could Rose?

Rose didn't remember, maybe that was a
good thing, Lily didn't want Rose to have
to relieve any trauma and that's what the
psychologist had said was that cause of
Rose totally block out that night.

What of Caleb, what was going on with
him? He had been around when his father
had been hurt; but he seemed angry that
Lily was having his father's child; like
that child would come in between them.

Why everyone was so angry; she didn't know.

A baby was supposed to bring joy into the world? Damn this imposed bed rest, it was keeping her from all her loved ones. And it was so immensely boring. There wasn't a lot to choose from on daytime television. **General Hospital** was okay; but she missed **All My Children** and she wasn't about to watch cooking/ talk shows for hours on end. She watched everything on Netflix. Thank goodness for her Kobo; if she hadn't had those 101 books pre-programed when she bought it, she'd have gone out of her ever-loving mind.

She missed her job and she even missed her colleagues. At least they couldn't fire her for taking time off. She found out that thanks to the government's generous year maternity leave she could take some of that now, but she would have preferred to use it when the baby came.

This Little Girl had a Little Curl
S. G. Lee

No one seemed to need her and that didn't feel good. Lily liked being needed. Carol and Amelia were on a buying trip in New York City. Amelia had decided that Carol needed some musical theatre and a shopping trip to feel better. Regan and Edward Stewart had agreed. Regan had joined Amelia and Carol and they were all having a good time. Carol was attending regular grief therapy, but would miss a few sessions, while they were in New York.

Why had Rose refused to go? Was she that mad at the world? Amelia and Regan had invited her too. Had she figured out Amelia knew about her mother as well and was just as mad at her? All of this was making her head hurt.

Lily decided she was going to sleep; maybe she'd wake up to Emmett creeping inside beside her. A girl could dream, couldn't she?

~0~

Chapter 25 – A stage where everyone must play a part

Lily awoke sometime later with the baby pressing on her bladder. Now she understood why pregnant women were always in the bathroom. Men who complained about that, should try having something poking them and making them pee every five minutes and see how they liked that. She was cross and bored, she thought after she came out of the bathroom. She peeked in on Deirdre. Deirdre was playing with her Barbie dolls. As she listened, she heard Deirdre say "Shush you mustn't tell it's a secret."

This Little Girl had a Little Curl
S. G. Lee

"I know that but ...," Deirdre had the other Barbie say.

"No, buts, keep quiet, or else," the first Barbie responded.

What kind of game was this for a child to be playing? Shouldn't Lily be putting a stop to this kind of play? What had this poor child learned at her father's hands? Lily had to speak up.

"Deirdre is everything okay?"

"Will you play Barbies with me? Laura won't. She says it's boring," Deirdre answered, sidestepping the question.

"Sure, I'd love to play Barbies; but I'm supposed to be lying on my bed. Do you want to come and play on my bed? As long as you don't get too bouncy on it; we can play Barbie's there," Lily offered.

"That would be nice thanks Aunt Wily," Deirdre said "I mean Aunt Lil llee… Lily. There I said it."

"You did indeed say it correctly. Good for you, Deirdre," Lily praised as Deirdre beamed.

Lily climbed back in the double bed; followed by Deirdre who got up very carefully and then asked..., "I didn't hurt the baby did I?"

"No sweetie, the baby is fine."

"Mama's baby isn't fine." Deirdre said, "It died."

"What did you say?" Lily asked thinking she's misheard Deirdre.

"Mama's baby died." Deirdre said sadly then she asked, "What's Rape?"

"Rape? Where did you hear this Deirdre?" Lily demanded to know then softened her tone, "I'm not mad honey; I would like to know what you are talking about."

"You're not mad that I eased dropped it? Mommy always said that wasn't nice."

This Little Girl had a Little Curl
S. G. Lee

"Sometimes we can't help; but hear what people say when they say it when we are right there; and the word is eavesdropping Deirdre."

"I eavesdropped when I hid in my mama's closet and daddy climbed on top of her and she said, "Stop, this is rape." Daddy said, "Husbands don't rape.""

"I don't think you should repeat this to anyone; but your psychiatrist, Deirdre Some people might not understand."

"Oh, okay; I am sorry. I also eavesdropped at Grandma Kaffa's. Grandma Kaffa went to the bathroom and Grandma Kaffa and Grandpa Tewwence came in and started talking. They didn't see me."

Grandma Kaffa said, "Amelia is not doing well."

"Things will get better. She needs to talk about it though."

"I hate the way things are between Lily and Rose."

Rosy said, "I can't help that I feel that way right now, I feel so bad about what happened between us; but I don't know how to make it right, I kept secrets from mom; what if he had raped me?"

"You should file charges against that evil boy," Grandpa Tewwence said.

"I don't think I can ever tell Mom."

"Lily loves you. You can tell her anything."

"Not since I yelled at her and told her I hated her."

"She understands that you are angry about your mother Cordewia."

"How can I tell her that I more mad at me then her, when I found out about my mother, I was just so angry about everything that somehow I'm finding myself still angry with her. I should have told her I went to a party which she would never have let me go to I should have told mom that my so-called boyfriend tried to rape me there. I just knew Lily would be mad; because I didn't listen to her about dangerous parties. So, how could I tell her?"

"That's all I heard Wily. I tried to member exactly what she said; but some of the words are hard," Deirdre replied sticking her fingers in her mouth, because she was afraid of Lily's reaction "I is so sorry, that Rose had a bad boyfriend. She's so nice. Maybe Unca Emwettt can go punch that boy. Should I tell him?"

"Thank you, Deirdre, for telling me all this; but please don't tell anyone else this, especially not Laura. Okay?" Lily begged Deirdre.

"Don't worry I won't tell anyone. I can keep secrets. I gots lots of them." Deirdre reassured Lily then turning to go as she jumped off the bed she added, "I don't like Laura anyway. She's really not nice. I try to stay out of her way, so, she doesn't see me; kinda like I used to do with daddy's sister wife Ethel. Bye now, Aunt Lilee."

Good grief ,Lily felt like a bad parent.
Dee was unhappy with Laura and Rose
had been almost raped. Her daughter had
almost been raped and she hadn't known
anything about it. What kind of mother
did that make her? Lily felt so selfish, she
had been upset that Rose wanted to see
Cordelia. Of course, Rose had been in
turmoil about her mother. She had wanted
to see her mother Cordelia, because Lily
was pregnant.

None of her anger had been about Lily,
okay Rose was a little angry about
keeping the secret that her mother was in
a criminal mental facility but she was
more scared and angrier about that nasty
boy. Why hadn't Lily seen that? All the
time Rose had been eaten up by the
turmoil, she'd gone through and hadn't
been able to articulate it. Rose hadn't
been able to share this with Lily; because
Lily had been so absorbed in her own life,
she had neglected Rose. So Rose snuck
off to a party; poor Rose had paid for that
mistake, more than any girl should. Lily
just wanted to take her in her arms, hug

her, and tell her everything would be all
right. The trauma that poor child had been
through it was enough to twist Lily's
insides. She wouldn't push; she'd let
Rose tell her in her own good time. She
knew that when Rose saw how much Lily
loved her, then Rose would relax and
share with Lily her trauma, or maybe she
wouldn't. Either way Lily was going to be
there for Rose.

What did Deirdre mean that she had lots
of secrets? Obviously, the child was
exaggerating; because she wanted to feel
important. It had to be scary for the poor
little girl, what with Emmett injured and
also Lily. It seemed though that the little
girl didn't like Laura, maybe it was time
to get Emmett to replace Laura, so, they'd
all be happy.

"Lily, I want to talk to you," Amelia
demanded as she strode into Lily's room.

"What's up Amelia? I thought you were
in New York?" Lily asked worried about
the expression on Amelia's face.

"I came home early. The business is in trouble and my lease is up so, thought I'd drop in on you."

"Thank-you for coming Amelia. Is there anything I can do about your lease?"

"Like you care. It's all Grandma Katha's fault, if she had riled up the mayor, I wouldn't be losing my home and business. You could have helped me weeks ago but you're all about yourself and it shows. I snuck past the dragon, Laura so, I heard what Deirdre said. I'm worried about Rose turning into her mother."

"I beg your pardon?" asked Lily, not sure that she was hearing correctly.

"Rose has been sneaking out to parties and getting into adult situations. You're falling down on your job as a parent Lily."

"I can't believe you are saying this Amelia. What business would any of this be of yours? What is wrong with you?"

"I'm trying to help you," Amelia retorted.

What Rose did, or did not do, is frankly, none of your business."

"You have another child on the way and three other little ones, plus two teens to worry about; you'd better get your house in order," Amelia insisted.

"I'm warning you Amelia. I have supported you through thick and thin; but you will not speak of this to Rose. Do you understand me? I think you should leave now! We'll speak later about this when you've had time to think."

"How dare you Lily? I am just speaking the truth and you know it."

"We have nothing to talk about. Get out and don't you dare speak of this to my daughter. Cousin or no cousin, I will make you very sorry if you do.

"Someone has to speak to her."

"Mind your own business. I am your landlady; after all, and you don't even pay me rent."

"Not anymore, you're not. I'm moving out. I'll find my own place, by the end of the week."

"Does it have to come to this Amelia? Why can't you let this go? Rose has suffered enough in her short life and we're barely speaking. I'm breaking a confidence with Grandpa Terrence to tell you this…"

"Tell me what?"

"A boy tried to harm Rose. He probably drugged her and then tried to rape her."

"What was she doing in a place like that? You aren't raising her correctly Lily!"

"When did you get so ultra-religious?"

"I was a lapsed Catholic; but I returned to the fold recently and I am doing it everything possible to make it right with the Lord."

This Little Girl had a Little Curl
S. G. Lee

"Keep your religion to yourself and leave
my daughter out of this; because she is
my daughter, not yours, Amelia."

"We have nothing more to say Lily,"
Amelia retorted angrily slamming Lily's
door.

"Amelia, please come back here."

Lily then heard the front door slam. Lily
picked up the phone.

"Grandpa Terrence?"

"Lily, how are you dear?"

"The baby is well; but we have a bit a
situation developing. Deirdre overheard
you and Rose talking and she told me
about what happened to Rose."

"I'm sorry Lily. I couldn't tell you it was
Rose's secret to tell. Not mine,"
interrupted Terrence.

""I understand that and I love Rose, the
only thing; I'm worried about now is her
well-being. She did what she needed to do

I understand that Terrence. I wish I had been there for her though, and saw her through this. I'm her mother, I should have been there to comfort and help her through all of this."

"She knows you love her, Lily this is been traumatic for her. All of it."

"I do understand that; but I'm a mother and when our child suffers, we want to wrap them in cotton wool and make them all better. The problem as I see it now though, is Amelia overheard Deirdre telling me what she overheard and Amelia has now turned into a very religious person. We had a fight and she may go to Rose with something she overheard ."

"That is definitely not good. But don't worry I won't let Amelia bother Rose here."

"That will work; but what if she approaches Rose outside your home?" Lily asked.

This Little Girl had a Little Curl
S. G. Lee

"I'm going to have to tell Grandma Katha
and then maybe she can talk some sense
into Amelia. You know Grandma Katha
is Catholic. She took you to some church
services when you were younger; but
when you didn't want to go anymore, she
didn't force the issue. She even married
me without a Catholic priest."

"Amelia and I had words. I think she's
moving out of the carriage apartment,"
Lily retorted.

"So much for idea of having all our
family under one roof," Terrence replied.

"I'm sorry Grandpa Terrence. We've
really brought a lot of turmoil in your life,
since you married Grandma Katha."

"No worries, granddaughter. You've also
brought me great joy. We will sort this
out. We are all family after all."

"I hope so; but I will not allow Amelia to
hurt my daughter. My daughter comes
before her, or anyone," Lily said.

"Mom?" a voice interrupted on the line.

"Rosy?"

"Yes, mom it's me. I'm sorry I was listening in; but I'm glad I did. I should have told you, but I was so ashamed about the ...the near rape. I thought you had lied to me about my mother for spite and to marry my Dad. Then when I saw her, she was so fragile and got mad all over again."

"It's okay Rose, I understand and I love you forever, no matter what," Lily began before Rose interrupted.

"I don't understand. Why did my mother go crazy? What happened that night? I don't remember it all. Why doesn't she want me anymore, enough to come out of it?"

"Oh darling, she is ill, mentally ill. She was traumatized that night. Mothers would do anything for their child and she proved that by saving you," Lily insisted.

"Yes, she did. Didn't she?" Rose agreed softly, "You are my mother too. You want to protect me from Aunt Amelia and her foolish ideas. Does that mean you still love me; despite what I did?"

"Rose I have always loved you, I loved you since before I married your father. Nothing has changed, except that love has grown even stronger. Nothing you could do could make me not love you. You really did nothing wrong; accept trust the wrong person. We all do that."

"I'm coming over to see you, right now. Oh, but I can't. I forgot. I have an appointment with my shrink. I'll skip it."

"Honey, I'm coming over to see you after the appointment. We can talk then." Lily insisted.

"No, you have to take care of yourself and the baby." Rose insisted, "I'll come over after my appointment. I promise. I love you Mom."

"I love you too Rose."

"Bye, Mom."

Lily was happy that she and Rose had finally made up. It was a good start. They had lots to talk about. Lily was sure that she and Rose were back on the right track and that made her happy. Maybe now Rose would forgive her for keeping the information about her mother Cordelia from her. She certainly hoped so. She was worried though, that Amelia was off on this rant; that she wouldn't come around.

Lily had always known that Amelia had been raised in the Catholic faith like her father, but it had never pulled them apart like this. Hopefully, Grandma Katha could make her see that her opinion could harm a fragile Rose and that Lily wasn't going to stand for her enforcing her opinion on Rose. Either way she was just going to hope that it all worked out; she couldn't afford to let herself get all stressed out. It wouldn't be good for the baby.

This Little Girl had a Little Curl
S. G. Lee

Lily took some big breaths and chanted "Oom" to calm herself. She then closed her eyes and fell into a deep, restful sleep.

~0~

Chapter 26 – This Little Girl had a Little Curl

"There was a little girl,

Who had a little curl,

Right in the middle of her forehead.

When she was good

She was very, very good,

And when she was bad, she was horrid."

BY HENRY WADSWORTH
LONGFELLOW

Lily stirred and awoke slowly. Her

head was killing her. Wait a minute; this
didn't feel like her bed, this felt like the

floor. Where was she and how did she get here? She opened her right eye to double vision. Was her blood pressure up? The baby was due in about month; she just had to make it a little further. Had she fallen and didn't recall? She felt around and felt the stairs. What was she doing at the bottom of the stairs? Good grief, her head hurt. Someone was chanting the same thing that Deirdre had said her mother said to her, ***"There was a little girl who had a little curl right in the middle of her forehead, and when she was good, she was very, very good. But when she was bad, she was rotten."***

"Lily, come on let me help you up. You fell down the stairs," Laura said suddenly at her elbow and she realized that it had been Laura chanting.

Through her one good eye she noticed, Laura now had a curl right in the middle of her forehead. This was obviously, the foolish thoughts of a head injury. Yes, she must have a head injury, Lily convinced herself.

"Maybe, I shouldn't move for the sake of the baby and my head. You should call for some help," Lily protested.

"I think I should help you into the kitchen and get you a drink. Then I'll call the doctor for you."

"I guess that wouldn't hurt," Lily replied still not able to think straight, let alone see straight.

Laura led her into the kitchen.

"Sit here, Lily." she commanded.

Lily complied, what choice did she have? Laura set her down like a sack of potatoes. She was barely sitting, when Laura grabbed her arms twisting them behind her back.

"What are you doing Laura?"

"What does it look like I've done Lily? I've tied your hands and now, I'm tying your feet."

Laura wiped the curl from her forehead.

"Everything is falling apart and it's all the fault of you Lily Kelly. Damn you."

"I don't understand Laura."

"Boy, lucky for me, you took a good one to the head. I pushed you down the stairs; unfortunately. that didn't kill you. I'm going to have to resort to other actions. Now how am I going to kill you all?"

"Kill? Why would you kill me? Wait a minute, kill us all? Who are you planning to kill?"

Laura looked puzzled for a moment then she started ranting, "Let see first you played games with my brother and then ditched him for Emmett. But I can kind of understand that Emmett is cute and a terrific catch. But you know if you weren't around, he could fall for me. I know he could learn to love me. I'm a better person then you and I'm far more beautiful."

"Your brother? You think I wronged your brother. Who is your brother?" asked Lily trying to make sense of this all.

"You are so stupid. All this time, you had no idea, did you?"

"You are talking in circles. I don't understand why you are doing any of this. Please think of my baby."

"The baby is the problem; don't you get it? Through it he'll always be tied to you. I can't have that. Why did you have to go out of town? You should have died in that gas leak, or at least be hurt, not dear Emmett."

"You were responsible for the gas leak? You hurt Emmett, Amelia and Carol? But why?"

"For a university graduate, you really are dense, aren't you?"

"Please explain this to me in terms, I can understand then," begged Lily

This Little Girl had a Little Curl
S. G. Lee

"Okay, I'm going to start at the
beginning. I was born when my parents
were in their late forties. My mom died
shortly after I was born, okay so I was six
(but still too early)and my father raised
me. My brother was in med school when I
was born. He's forty now, you know."

"Who is your brother?"

"You are stupid, aren't you? How did you
capture his interest when you are so
stupid?"

"Whose interest?"

"Why my brother's and Emmett's of
course."

"Please explain this to me more, you owe
that much to me," Lily begged stalling for
time ,while trying to get her hands and
feet free.

"Okay, I'll play; since you're not going
anywhere and neither are, they," Laura
said, pointing to Joseph and Rebecca.
whom Lily noticed were tied and hidden

behind the door in the kitchen which
Laura now opened."

"What have you done to them? Let them
go! And where is Deirdre?"

"Deirdre is probably playing in her room.
I like that little girl. She can stay and be
mine and Emmett's little girl of course;
but they rest have to go. They're too old
and really not manageable at all."

"You are going to kill us?"

"Of course, I am. How else can I get my
true love Emmett; when you hold onto
him with your clawing fingers?"

"I still don't understand why you are
doing this? I'm sure you could make
Emmett love you, easily. You're much
younger and prettier than I am."

"Well of course that's true, but a baby? A
baby ties a man to a woman and we just
can't have that."

"Kill me then and take my baby. You can raise it with Emmett." Lily pleaded trying to sway Laura, not to kill her baby.

"I could do that. Couldn't I? I've heard of that happening, people cutting babies out of the womb and raising the baby for their own."

Lily tried to hide a grimace of pain as she felt the start of contractions. She was scared. Laura was a nutcase and she held Lily, Rebecca and Joseph, too as they lay prone on the floor hogtied and now the baby was coming way too early. What could Lily do?

"Lookee here, I won't have to kill the baby. It's already happening. It's coming way, too soon. Now to plan yours, Joseph, and Rebecca's death," Laura laughed.

"No, I won't let you kill the baby, or any of dem. Youse evil Laura and you need to pay by going to jail. You untie my sister and brudder right now. Or I'll shoot you," Deirdre snarled.

Lily looked on in horror spotting Deirdre holding Emmett's service revolver. How had she gotten the gun? It was under lock and key.

"Where did you get that gun Deirdre?" Laura demanded "Give it to me right now."

Where was Emmett? His appointment with his doctor had been at 2 p.m. and it was 8 p.m. now. Where was he when they needed him most? Oh no, Rose would be here soon. Her appointment was at 7:30 and it was almost 8:30 p.m...

How could she prevent Deirdre from shooting Laura? Lily had to save them all. Rose would be here soon and walk in on this as well. This was her family and she'd be damned if that evil murderess would win.

This Little Girl had a Little Curl
S. G. Lee

Lily suddenly felt light headed as her blood pressure dropped. She fought to stay awake; but she felt herself slipping into blackness as her embryonic fluid flowed down her leg pooling on the floor along with blood.

~0~

Chapter 27 – Life is a masquerade
Later that night

Dafydd stared at the picture as he

took out of his wallet. It was her birthday today and he knew it was late; but he really wanted to see her. She was now twenty-two. The doctors had told him she had been sexually assaulted by his father at a young age warping her personality. Of course, his father had denied it and so, had she; but there was evidence. Why hadn't he seen what his father was doing to her? Was he that absorbed in his own life in medical school studies that he hadn't see anything? She was a little girl and she should have been safe. Instead, she had become obsessed with his father because of his assaults.

This Little Girl had a Little Curl
S. G. Lee

Then she had felt betrayed when his
father had said he was going to take a
new wife; so, she had tried to kill them
both. Thank goodness ,she hadn't
succeeded. Father had paid Peri a lot of
money for her silence and she lived in
Europe somewhere now. His father didn't
pay with his life. The bastard managed to
live for a few months, then had died of
heart attack; but not before making
Dafydd promise to see to her care.

He was glad he was going to see her
today. She'd like that; after all it was her
birthday. He was bringing her a cupcake.
The doctors had allowed him to do so
other years. He had thought about what to
bring a twenty- two-year-old for her
birthday and had decided on a new dress.
A red dress, very tasteful and something
she could move around in; maybe even
twirl in. Eileen loved to dance. She would
adore it. He knew she would. The doctors
wouldn't allow her to have an I-pod, since
she had hit a patient with the one. He had
given her that same I-pod for her
eighteenth birthday. He felt so bad that

she was unwell but a dress was the best present. She couldn't harm herself or anyone with that and she loved clothes. Dafydd entered the facility, the door clanging behind him and the lock clicking in place.

"Doctor Dafydd Jones, to see Eileen Jemima Jones," Dafydd announced to the guard, at the desk.

"Just a moment," The guard said picking up the phone.

The guard took a few minutes but then said, "Doctor Buttons will speak with you now." The guard said motioning him to Dr. Buttons' office.

"Good evening, Dr. Buttons. I know it's late; but since it is Eileen's birthday, I thought you might make an exception and let me see my sister."

"Doctor. Jones? Didn't you receive my letter seven months ago?" asked Dr. Buttons.

This Little Girl had a Little Curl
S. G. Lee

"No, I didn't receive your letter has something happened to Eileen?"

"Eileen was here voluntarily and she decided she wanted to leave. Since, we couldn't prove she was a danger to herself, or others any longer, she was free to leave."

"Oh my God, did you say seven months ago?" asked Dafydd incredulously.

"Yes, we sent out a letter to you as a courtesy, simply, because you are family and a doctor yourself. See here is the discharge date."

"You let here out of here? I wouldn't even let her hold my son."

"What? That makes no sense Doctor Jones, when Eileen came back for her follow-up appointments, she said that she had held Daniel. She said he was a darling baby, that you let her rock to sleep."

"She's never even heard of my son!! Let me see those discharge papers?" Dafydd demanded then with horror and realization he yelled, "Do you have any idea what you've done?"

"Really Doctor Jones there is no need to get angry with us. Should I call back the guard and have you ejected?"

"You don't understand what you've done. Seven months ago, my wife was murdered."

"Are you saying that you think Eileen killed her?" Dr. Buttons demanded disbelievingly.

"Yes, didn't my father ever tell you the real reason he committed her here? She tried to kill him and his girlfriend."

"She what? Your father never told us this. We knew she had attacked one of the residents with her I-Pod (when she was eighteen); but she's been a model patient since then."

"She's very convincing; she always has been at hiding her misdeeds. I don't know why I didn't see it sooner. I thought that she loved me, simply because I was her brother, Why, didn't I see that she was obsessed with me? I took the psyche courses. I told her I had married Sherry-Anne and that we were going to have a baby. She knew. Oh my God, what did I do? It's my fault Sherry-Anne was murdered. Where could Eileen be? We have to find her before she harms anyone else."

"Don't you think you are jumping to conclusions, Dr. Jones?"

"Tell me Dr. Buttons; what happened when she hit the patient with the I-pod?"

"That was an isolated incident. That patient had been flirting with her and then ignored her for another patient...Oh, I see what you mean, Dr. Jones; but really to go from there to killing?

"Do you really want to take that a chance Doc? Because I believe she has killed and therefore is a danger to all those around her."

"The director arranged for an interview
for nanny position at an agency her in
Vancouver; but she wanted to work in
Happy Valley Ontario to be nearer to you,
and we thought that was progress; so, we
arranged for a rooming house to house
her in Happy Valley and a psychiatrist
she could see there. Here is the address."

"A nanny position? But Eileen has no
experience."

"She was really good with the little ones
here; so, the director wrote a reference for
her given that experience."

"Did you follow up with her or check
with the agency?"

"No, we don't like to interfere in our
former patient's lives; unless it's
indicated."

"Unbelievable. I hope that she hasn't
been placed with a family yet, because
Doctor Buttons, you've got to know she's
really sick. As I said I wouldn't want her
around my son. I'm calling the police."

"Really Dr. Jones, let's not be hasty. I think this maybe a matter for our lawyers."

"And I think as much as I promised my Dad, this is matter for the police," Dafydd said taking out his cell phone and calling Kendall and getting no answer.

"Please Dr. Jones ;you'll ruin our reputation." pleaded Dr. Button.

"Better your reputation ,then someone else's life," Dafydd replied picking up the phone again to call Caleb.

"Caleb this Dafydd. How's Daniel?"

"Everything is fine here. Daniel is cooing at me as we speak. When are you coming home from the coroner's conference?"

"Caleb, I need you to take Daniel and go to Suzy's until I get home. Don't answer the door to anyone, but me," Dafydd insisted not answering the question.

"Why? "Caleb asked.

"I think I know who killed your mom; but I haven't been able to alert the police so she's on the loose. Someone told me she's held Daniel."

"You are saying that the person who killed my mother, held my brother? Who is it who killed my mother? Is Daniel in danger?"

"I think Daniel is in danger and you maybe you too. I'm sorry Caleb. I had no idea she would do this. She was supposed to be locked away where she couldn't hurt anyone. It's entirely my fault," Dafydd confessed.

"How can it be your fault? And who did this?"

"Eileen Jemima Jones," Dafydd said in a whisper.

"Who is she?"

"Open the top drawer of my desk with the keys I left. It's the smallest key on the ring."

Dafydd heard rustling then the sound of a door being opened.

"Okay, it's open; so, what do you want me to get?"

"The picture that is in the frame in the drawer, please pick it up and look at it. That is my little sister, Eileen."

Caleb picked up the picture and stared hard at the young woman in the picture. She appeared petite, almost bird like, and her long dark curly hair hung right down to her shoulders. In the middle of her forehead, one small curl lay. Caleb stared at her eyes and then Caleb gasped in surprise. He only seen her a couple of times; but he knew this woman.

"That isn't Eileen. That's Laura, the nanny who is looking after Emmett's nephew Joseph and his nieces Rebecca and Deirdre."

"What did you say?"

"If she murdered my Mom; then Lily is in danger. I think the carbon monoxide poisoning at Lily's house was meant to kill Lily."

"Carbon monoxide poisoning? When did this happen? Why didn't you tell me?"

"I didn't want to worry you and make you come back. My Dad, Amelia, and Carol, were poisoned in Lily's house. Emmett, Amelia and Carol are still recovering and Lily? Lily is expecting a baby, but she's on bed rest. She's completely at that woman's mercy, so is my Dad and the kids. I have to go save them."

"Caleb, think about this, who will look after your brother and keep him safe? I promise, I will call the police and get help immediately," Dafydd stated.

"Daniel needs me; but you have to save Lily and my dad and the kids. She killed my mother; you know she could kill again."

"I'll save Lily and the children. I'll send someone from the police department to your Dad's house right away. Now go get your brother to safety, Take him to Chief Stewart's house. You'll both be safe there," Dafydd reassured then hung-up.

Dialling Kendall's number again Dafydd heard her answering message and left a message.

"Kendall it is Dafydd Jones. If you are getting this message, then I have to tell you I know who my wife's killer is. It's my sister, Eileen; once more Caleb has positively identified her as Laura Lynwood, the nanny who works for Emmett and Lily. I believe Emmett, Lily and the kids are in danger. Please send someone there immediately," then he hung up and proceeded to dial the operator.

"Directory assistance, how may I direct you?"

"I'd like the police department in Happy Valley, Ontario please."

"Just a moment please."

"Happy Valley police department, Patrolwoman Violet Garden speaking. How may I help you?"

"Violet this is Dr. Dafydd Jones, the coroner speaking."

"Yes, and what can we do for you this evening?"

"I am in Vancouver, British Columbia; but I believe I have discovered who killed my wife. Once more she is masquerading as Laura Lynnwood, the nanny that Emmett Rogers hired. So, you see Emmett, Lily and the children are in grave danger. You need to send someone there immediately and apprehend her," Dafydd explained.

"We can't just arrest someone on your say so Dr. Jones. We have to follow the evidence and really I'm sorry; but your wife's case is a cold case now."

"Listen Violet, I would have explained all of this to Kendall Evans; but I was only able to leave a message on her cell phone.

Do you want me to call the chief directly or are you going to do your job?"

"No don't do that. Did you know the Chief is her dad? I found out today. I'm sure she's not answering; because she was shot today."

"Kendall was shot?"

"Some perp was trying to rob a variety store and Kendall walked in on it. He winged her; but she shot and killed him. She's getting stitched up at the hospital as we speak. She'll be off for a couple of weeks."

"What about Constable Barnes is he available?"

"He's here. He's writing up the paperwork on the shooting since Kendall's at the hospital." Violet volunteered then she started in on her previous conversation, "So did you know her Dad's Chief Stewart? It's all over the station. Her Dad went tearing out of her earlier this evening, after the call come in.

He was shouting *"Oh my God, my daughter's been shot."* Kendall sure hid that good."

"As nice as it is talking to you Violet, time is of the essence put me through to Alan now, people are in danger! Didn't you hear anything I said?"

"Sure thing, Dr. Jones," Violet said finally transferring him.

"Alan, I need you." began Dafydd explaining it all to him.

"I'll send out some patrol cars right away. We'll apprehend your sister quickly and safely," Alan promised after hearing him out.

"Thank-you, Alan. I've got the next flight out of Vancouver; but it could take a while."

"Not to worry Dafydd. I'll handle this personally. We will stop your sister from harming anyone else."

"I hope so Alan. But please handle her gently. She can't help it you know. She's mentally ill."

"We'll do our best, but no promises. She's a murderess at best, an attempted murderess of a cop and she may have harmed Lily, for all we know." Alan stated.

Dafydd hung up. He should have been relieved Alan was going to go get Eileen and she wouldn't be able to harm anyone again; but somehow, he was filled with dread. He hoped that this wasn't an omen of things to come.

~0~

Chapter 28 – When was she ever good?

Rose entered the house and felt instinctively that something was very wrong, just like when she had entered her Mom's house and Brad Owens and Silas Rentford had been holding her family hostage. Her heart kicked up a notch and her limbs felt heavy. She shouldn't have lied to her mother about going to see her shrink. She'd gone to see Carol instead. If she hadn't, she would have been her sooner. She then heard raised voices and silently crept to the kitchen and heard…,

"What did you do to my Wily?" Deirdre asked.

"Shut-up and give me that gun right now, Deirdre. I thought I liked you; but I was wrong, you're a brat."

*"No, you shut-up you nasty lady and you
untie dem, all of dem now, or I'm going
to shoot you like Joseph shot my
daddy!!"*

"You knew you little brat? You knew he
shot your dad and you didn't tell
anyone?"

"Mommy said, don't tell. Tell everyone a
bad man came and shot everybody. Don't
tell anyone daddy shot her either. I can
protect my family with this gun; just like
Joseph. You know I can; cause he's my
brudder. I love him and Rebecca. Lily's
my family too. You're not family! You're
really mean and I won't let you hurt them
anymore. I know you hurt my Unca
Emmett, too."

"Your dad killed everyone there, didn't
he?" Laura asked.

"I'm not supposed to tell," Deirdre said
the gun quivering.

"Doesn't matter, you're good at keeping secrets. You and I would make a good family with Emmett."

"No! I'm not listening to you anymore. My Unca Emwettt loves Wily, not you. My mommy told me you can never make someone love you. They either do, or they don't. You are so wicked. If you don't let dem all go, I'm going to hafta shoot you. I don't want to hurt or kill you; but my Wily is bleeding. She needs help now and I'm going to get her to the hospital and save her and da baby. I need to call an ambulance and the police."

All of this was unbelievable had she heard correctly? Laura had hurt Rose's mom, Lily and Joseph had shot his father, after his Dad had shot his mother? What the heck was going on? Why was Laura behaving this way and who shot all the other people where Joseph lived? Had Joseph's father shot the whole village as well? Where did little Deirdre get a gun? Could it be Emmett's gun?

And what had Laura done to her mother?
Why was mom bleeding? What could
Rose do?"

Rose worried, "How could she stop all
this? Obviously, she had to step in and get
the gun from Deirdre and stop Laura.
Maybe Lily was wrong and they were
cursed. They kept stumbling on either
murders, murderers, or crazy people, or
both. Why was it always up to Rose?"

"You are not going to shoot me. You
probably don't even have any bullets in
that gun."

"Do too. This is Emmett's gun. I found
the key on the ring and opened the locked
box; then I opened the drawer with dem
bullets. I opened the gun, just like I saw
daddy do and put them all in. I'm smart. I
can do it easily. I'm a good shot, my
daddy taught me. You'd better start
listening to me, or I'll make you really
sorry Wara."

"Give that gun to me, now," Laura said
striding towards Deirdre.

"No!!"

Rose however reached Deirdre, before Laura and took the gun from Deirdre's hands aiming it squarely at Laura's chest.

"I'm sure if you are so obsessed with Emmett; that you know about the shooting he and I were involved about last year. It's where we really got to know each other," Rose said calmly.

"What are you talking about you're just a high-school student!" Laura laughed.

"Two cops were obsessed with my Aunt Amelia. It didn't end well for one of them when I fired Emmett's gun. Emmett nicknamed me Annie Oakley after that. I'm sure you've heard of her. She was a crack shot from the old west. Funny thing though, it's not just a nickname, I'm a crack shot too, my dad taught me well."

"I don't believe you, and I'm not going to let you ruin my plans. Sadly, you all have to die. Emmett will be miserable at first; but he'll have me to comfort him."

"You are out of your freakin' mind,"
Rose commented, "Shall I prove it to you,
that I am a crack shot? I'll fire right
between your shoes."

Rose then shot the gun the bullet hitting
the target as she had predicted, it caused a
graze on Laura's big toe.

"Now since I still have the gun and I'm
not happy with you, sit yourself down
there; before I just decide to dispense
with you."

"You're as crazy as your real mother,
Cordelia."

"You bet your crazy ass I am. You'd
better listen to me now. Sit in that chair,
before I change my mind and plug you,"
Rose cried menacingly.

 Rose pointed to a chair across the table
from where Lily lay on the floor in a
heap.

"Deirdre, go untie Joseph and Rebecca
now."

"Kay."

"Don't you dare, "Laura protested.

"I have the gun! Must I show you again I mean business? I'm going to shoot near your feet again and miss; will that prove it to you?" Rose said firing at Laura's feet with the gun and missing.

Laura blanched and sat in the chair Rose had directed her to. Deirdre untied and ungagged Joseph, but at this point he strode over to Laura and slapped her hard across the face.

"I didn't want to help you harm them. Uncle Emmett loves us," Joseph cried.

"But you did help me? Didn't you? You just didn't want to go to jail."

"I wouldn't let you kill them, though."

"No, you lost your nerve. Didn't you kid?"

"Shut up." replied Joseph.

"Just tie her up Joseph and ignore her."

"Don't listen she spews evil," Rebecca shouted.

"I'm not going to let *him* tie me up," Laura protested.

"Look we can make this the easy way, or the hard way. You're going to let Joseph tie you up, or I'm going to shoot you in a knee and continuing shooting you. Joseph will then still tie you up and we'll move you into a back bedroom and not tell the EMT's right away that you've been shot."

"You're a stone-cold bitch," Laura cried as Joseph began to tie her feet.

"Takes one to know one; at least I don't hurt people on purpose."

"My brother is going to make you very sorry you did this to me, Rose Brookfield."

"We need duct tape for her mouth. I think there's some in the kitchen junk drawer Rebecca. We then need to call an ambulance for my mom," Rose stated.

"I'll call for the ambulance and make Lily comfortable. You keep that gun focused on her, she's tricky, Then Joseph or Dee can find the duct tape," Rebecca offered after Deirdre untied and ungagged her.

Dee ran out of the room followed by Joseph and Rebecca as Rose continued holding the gun on the now tied Laura.

"You're wasting your time your adoptive mom will die, but it's no great loss," Laura insisted.

"Shut-up!!"

"Don't listen to her Rosey. She's sinful and mean as a hornet. You know that's what Daddy would have said. I got the tape and Rebecca called for an ambulance. It should come soon that's what Becky said. We'll save our Wily," Dee replied entering the room carrying duct tape followed by Joseph.

"How's my Mom?"

This Little Girl had a Little Curl
S. G. Lee

"She's breathing and Rebecca is tending her she took a first aid course so she knows what to do," Joseph reassured.

"She and the baby better be all right, or you won't be, and that's a promise!" Rose said pointedly to Laura.

"Like I freakin' care!" Laura said straining against the ropes that grew tighter as she struggled.

"I have the gun, submit to being kept still with the ropes and tell me who your brother is!! Who do you think will protect you?" Rose demanded.

"None of you know who I am? How utterly delicious. I guess since I want you to be nice to me, I'd better tell you that my brother is Dafydd Jones. He's a doctor you know."

"But your last name is Lynwood."

"No, it's not Lily, she lies as easily as she breathes. I don't think her first name is even Laura. You can't believe anything she says, just focus on your mom. I'll watch her and make sure she doesn't escape," Joseph exclaimed.

"Lily, Lily, Lily! Good grief the world doesn't revolve around your mother. Don't you want to know who the mastermind was that perpetrated all this? It wasn't *Laura*, she's too nice. What a dreary insipid name that is," the fake Laura snarled trying to get the focus back on herself.

"So, your name isn't Laura?" Rose asked.

"No, it's not Laura Lynwood. She was my roommate; but she died poor thing."

"Did you kill her?"

"Really what do you take me for? I liked Laura; even if she was too nice. No, my name is Eileen Jemima Jones. Eileen means bright, shining one or beautiful bird."

"Your brother is a doctor? You're Dafydd's sister? But he never mentioned you and he's so kind," Rose cried shocked.

This Little Girl had a Little Curl
S. G. Lee

"Of course, he didn't know I was here. He was just a teensy bit angry with me."

"Why was he angry with you?"

"I don't want to talk about that right now. I know stuff about you too, Rose Brooksfield. I heard that you were almost raped."

"That's none of your business."

"Oooh touched a nerve, did I? We girls have to stick together. I had an abortion or rather two; my first when I was let's see thirteen; or was it fourteen? Daddy made me. He was so mean. He said people shouldn't know about me and my problems. I asked him if he was worried, they'd think it was his? The baby wasn't daddy's ,of course, it was Hercules Kane's, my boyfriend. The second abortion was when I was sixteen it was one of my guards at the sanitarium. Silly daddy, that he didn't know sex is a power just like any other. Johnny slept with me one night after I drugged him. Of course, I told daddy he took advantage of me.

This Little Girl had a Little Curl
S. G. Lee

They fired him and I felt bad at first but
then I remembered how he touched me
and the other girls and I thought he
deserved it."

"At first daddy paid attention to me; but
right after that he took up with Peri. She
was twenty-eight; but I swear she looked
twelve and Daddy would pay attention to
me anymore. I was so mad. The doctor
said I would never have babies after the
second one and here he was taking up
with the likes of her. The doctor said I'd
be in a hospital for a long time. Daddy
didn't love me anymore; he just wanted
me gone; because I'd could never give
him grandchildren. You'll be our baby
though won't you Deirdre, mine and
Emmett's? Then Emmett will love me."

"No. Laura, I mean Eileens. I feel sorry
that you won't have no babies; but I can't
be your baby. I'm sorry your daddy
stopped loving you. He was a very bad
man, just like my daddy. My Daddy was
going to hurt Rebecca fore he died,"
Deirdre volunteered, then realizing she

said something she wasn't supposed to
tell she looked aghast at Joseph.

"It's okay Dee; it's time I told the truth to
Rose. My Father was going to give
Rebecca away in marriage to Rupert
Hines. Mr. Hines had five wives and he
was seventy years old. Mother stood up to
my Father and said no, she was going to
allow it. She hid Rebecca in the woods
the day of the wedding and Father was so
mad. Mr. Hines had given Father a dowry
for her and he wanted it back. Father and
Mr. Hines got into a fist fight and Mr.
Hines won. Father came back with his
gun and started shooting. First, he shot
Mr. Hines. Then when others tried to go
to Mr. Hine's aid, he shot them too. He
just went crazy shooting everyone. I went
home and got daddy's other gun, a pistol.
I was so scared. My daddy was a crazy
wild man. He was so out there, you
know? I ran back, but by that time he shot
most everyone. They were dead or dying
and I couldn't do anything. Then I
realized he was going back to the house to
kill Dee and Mom. He probably had

planned on killing me and Rebecca too; but we were hiding. I ran as fast as I could and found I was too late; he'd just shot my mom three times. Dee was hiding in the closet all ready. I'd carved that space secretly when daddy and I built the house so I'd have a place to hide. Mommy guessed that there was a secret space and she set up a phone in there. Mom said don't tell daddy; but if me or my siblings ever need a place to hide, that is where we needed to go."

"That sounds so scary I'm sorry Joseph," Rose commented.

"When I met up with daddy, he laughed at me as I pointed the gun, he pointed his pistol back at me. He said I wouldn't shoot him I didn't have the guts. He aimed and cocked the gun and I did the same, but I shot him first, right between the eyes. I killed my Father. Are you going to tell anyone, Rose?"

"No not right away. This is your story to tell Joseph."

This Little Girl had a Little Curl
S. G. Lee

"I'm going to trust you with the rest of the story because Laura, or whoever she is, will tell anyway. She guessed what had happened and used it blackmail me in to doing what ever she asked; but I promise you I would never harm you, or your family No matter what she said."

"I know that; just tell me what happened with your mother, Emmett's sister. Dianna."

"Mom knew she was dying, she told me and Deirdre, to lie and say someone else did it. She also told Dee to call Uncle Emmett; then she sent me into the woods where Rebecca was. I convinced Rebecca to give me an alibi. There you have it, the truth now, I killed my father in cold blood," Joseph finished with tears in his eyes.

"You couldn't help it Joseph," Rose exclaimed.

"He could have helped it. He could have let his Dad kill him. Of course, that would have been stupid. Great story kid, but you murdered your father. Own it! Now that you have that off your chest; go sit down and shut up. Let me tell you my story. At least I didn't make that mistake of killing my Dad. I admit I lost my head. I really did. I tried to kill Daddy and that bitch Peri, but I didn't succeed, so I don't know why Dafydd was so mad at me. Daddy was so mean too. I was so sad when Daddy died from a heart attack, a couple of months later. I didn't even get to go to the funeral. Daddy with Dafydd's help had me locked up in that place by then. I forgave Dafydd though, he was just being a good son and brother."

"What place?" Rose asked.

"A rest home in British Columbia. It's so far away, but Dafydd still came to visit me. He loves me you see."

"A rest home, don't you mean a mental institution?"

"Now you aren't being very nice Rose. I heard your real mother was in one. Killed her pimp, didn't she?" laughed Eileen.

"Did you kill someone?" Rose asked, convinced that Eileen may have killed Emmett, because where was he when all this was going on? Rose looked around as if to see Emmett's dead body.

"You think I killed Emmett?" Eileen laughed, "You silly girl, I'm not like the infant there. I love Emmett. I wouldn't harm a hair on his princely head. Besides you don't kill relatives. I learned my lesson. After all Emmett is going to be my husband."

"Then where is Emmett?"

"He's not coming for awhile… you see his doctor was called into emergency surgery and his doctor asked him to wait and wait and wait. When I called pretending to be Lily, they said his appointment would probably be at 8 p.m."

"He's not dead. Thank God. But you were in a mental institution for trying to kill your own father... Wait a minute, you killed Sherry-Anne, didn't you? You caused the gas leak, didn't you?"

This Little Girl had a Little Curl
S. G. Lee

"Why thank you, you clever girl. You recognized my work. I'm very proud of it you know. Sherry-Anne was such a frivolous bitch. She had her eye on the main prize, any rich, kind man stupid enough to take her on. I almost admired her, except she went after Dafydd.

Then look how she treated Emmett tricking him. What does my fool-hearted brother do? He gets mixed up with the likes of that sleazy bitch and she pulls the oldest trick in the book. I'm pregnant, she tells him and he marries her. Poor Daffy. He needed me to rescue him. I thought maybe I could reason with Sherry-Anne. I behaved myself to trick them into letting me permanently out of the hospital, only to meet her you know. I had to make sure she was right for Dafydd. But she wouldn't listen. I knew as soon as I saw her what she was made of. She couldn't be reasoned with. She wasn't worth even talking to. I snuck in the window and when she stood at the top of the stairs, I pushed her. Then I called the ambulance. I didn't want the baby, poor little Daniel to die. I'm not heartless. I didn't even know Sherry-Anne was pregnant until then. I wouldn't have pushed her if I'd known. Don't look at me that way. I would have waited until the baby was born. Daniel was okay; so, it all turned out. Such a sweet baby, such beautiful smiles he had when I sang and told him stories."

"You've held Daniel?" Rose asked horrified.

"Well of course I did. He's my flesh and blood. I'm a proud auntie. I had to make sure he was okay, didn't I?"

"And the gas leak how did that happen?"

"It was your fault that it didn't work. You were supposed to die too; but you had to run off and find your biological mom. That made me kind of glad, you see I admire you Rose. I guess I understood that. I didn't have a mom you see. Not really, she died shortly after I was born. Kind of silly though, she fell down some stairs. Daddy said it was my fault she wouldn't have wanted a nasty child like me. She was mean to me calling me a brat before she slipped down the stairs tripping over my doll. At least that's what they thought. Ha, ha!!

As for daddy he was always saying *'There was a little girl that had little curl right in the middle of her forehead and when she was good, she was very, very good, and when she was bad, she was rotten."* My middle name even came from that little girl; so really you can lay all my bad behaviour at my dad's feet. He encouraged it; you see. It was my little rebellion, at least that's what my shrink says."

"My mommy said that poem too and I'm not evil. I'm a good girl. I don't do really bad things." protested Deirdre.

"You are good, Dee," Rebecca agreed.

"Thank-you Rebecca. You're good too."

"Your shrink is an idiot. You have to take responsibility for what you do, Eileen," replied Rose.

"Rosey's right. Mommy used to say admit you made a mistake and make it right."

"What a ridiculous sentiment! I am what they all made me."

"Nonsense my biological mother killed someone you don't see me killing people," Rose admitted.

"You said you shot someone and now you are holding a gun on me. How are we so different?"

"We're different; because if I were to kill anyone it would be to protect someone; unlike you, who would kill and did kill for your own personal gain."

"I don't agree and you know when the police arrive, I won't really be punished, they'll take me to the same place as your mother Cordelia."

"That's too good for you."

"I'm crazy you see. They know that and so, off to hospital I go. Speaking of crazy, did you know your grandmother, Lily's dead mother, isn't so dead?"

"You are not making any sense."

"Okay, let's try that again. Lily's mom who supposedly died when she was nine? She ain't dead."

"What a crazy lie. Do you really hope to make me believe that? And what do you get out of telling me this lie? Do you think I'll let you hurt my mother anymore?"

"Okay, so don't believe me. Don't come whining to me when it bites you on the ass. I'm an expert in information seeking. I can get information on everyone. It's my stock and trade. So just so you know Heather aka Lily's mom has been skulking around for weeks now. I saw her on your Grandma Katha's doorstep. Your Grandma Katha's a tough old bird. I kind of admire her. She sent Heather packing and she yelled at her to stay the hell away from Lily."

"You are a nasty witch to make up a story like this. It isn't bad enough you tried to kill her; you have to make up a horrendous lie that you know will hurt her? I hope they drug you out of your mind and keep you drooling to the end of your days."

"I didn't lie. You'll find out and then you'll be sorry. They'll all just feel sorry for me. I'm very good at making people feel sorry for me. I had one doctor that figured me out, but I got rid of him. I told Dafydd tearfully that he had made advances against me and Dafydd got me a new doctor. He threatened him with professional misconduct. Dafydd always believes me you see. I'll tell him I don't remember doing all this and he will make it all go away. He's good that way. He'll get me sympathetic lawyer who will convince a judge and I'll have a short stay, get out and make you sorry. You'll be so sorry you treated me like this Rose Brooksfield," Eileen threatened.

"Then it's a good thing I taped all of what you are saying isn't it?" Rose said, pulling her left hand out of her pocket to reveal her cell phone and playing some of Eileen's tirade.

"You are just twisting my words with that thing. No one will believe it. I'm good. They'll believe me. Dafydd believes in me. When she was good, she was very, very good. I'm a good girl. Right daddy?" Eileen said staring at a point past Rose.

"That won't work you know. They'll never believe you are that crazy," Rose commented.

Eileen just continued to speak to a spot on the wall and Rose was soon convinced she wasn't faking it. Eileen was bat shit crazy, Rose thought; I'm not taking my gun off of her.

Alan arrived just then his gun out. Seeing
Rose with her gun pointed at Eileen, he
said "I'll take that gun Rose. We're here
now. We can handle her. Rebecca told us
your mother is injured. You go see to
your mother and let the EMTS in."

"But she'll fight you. She seems crazy
now but she can flip on a dime."

"There's more than just me, Rose. She's
not getting away with this."

"Alan? Do I know you? No, I don't; but
you're cute. Run along Rose, Alluring
Alan and I have lots to talk about."

"You have the right to remain silent and
refuse to answer questions. Do you
understand?' "Rose heard him say as she
stepped back into the kitchen.

She heard Alan finish mirandizing Eileen
and she felt sick when she heard Eileen's
comments.

"This is so deadly dull Alan. And you are
so smart. You guessed everything. I did;

didn't you? I'm very good, but when I'm bad I'm rotten," she ranted.

Rose continued to listen from the other room while kneeling beside her mother. She couldn't believe this woman, Eileen. Did she actually think that all that flattery would work and she'd get off from her crimes?

"Where's my brother. I want my brother before you take me away," Eileen pleaded, when she realized her wiles weren't working.

"Your brother's in British Columbia. Happy Birthday, by the way."

"So Daffy told you? He didn't forget my birthday? He does love me. Where's my cake?" Rose heard Eileen say as they dragged her off.

The EMT'S stabilized Lily the best they could and placed her on a gurney.

"Is my mom going to be okay?" asked Rose.

"Not sure kid. She has a very serious head injury, multiple contusions, from a fall the little girl said. And she's in labour and bleeding excessively. We'll do all we can but we have to get her to the hospital now."

"I'm going with you. Joseph, you and Rebecca look after Deirdre, until Emmett gets back."

"No problem, as long as I'm not arrested." Joseph answered.

"Why would you be arrested son," asked another cop."

Rose gave him a look and he answered, "I was just joking."

Rose jumped into the ambulance and it tore away from the curb with sirens blazing. All Rose could do was to repeat as if a prayer, "Mom, please don't die on me. I'm so sorry. I've been such a bad daughter. I love you. Live for me. I'll make it up to you. I love you."

~0~

Chapter 29 - Heather

Lily lay on the hospital stretcher. She had a lead going to her finger; obviously to check her oxygen output and oxygen coming from a tube in her nose. Lily's head hurt; but the doctor had said he was waiting on a consultation from a neurosurgeon and an obstetrician, before making a decision on whether she needed surgery. The children were all right. Rebecca and Joseph would babysat Deirdre; until Suzy got there and she had to be there by now and there were police officers there; they were safe. Emmett had arrived there too, by now. They were fine she had to remain calm and concentrate on this baby.

This Little Girl had a Little Curl
S. G. Lee

The emergency room was in an uproar, because of a forty-car pileup on the highway. The doctor didn't feel she was in grave danger any time soon and had given her medicine to stop contractions, before rushing off to help the critically injured, as they came in.

"So far so good," she thought as she didn't feel any contractions; but she bit back that reply as a strong contraction possessed her. It felt like something was cracking her in two. A few minutes later she felt another and reached to find the call bell; but it slipped on to the floor.

Rose waiting outside in a waiting room; spotted a woman with long blonde hair. As she noted the gray strands shimmering throughout the woman's head; something about the woman struck her as familiar. Rose dismissed the thought as one of those tricks your brain plays on you. After all she had been through trauma yet again, of course she was seeing things.

This Little Girl had a Little Curl
S. G. Lee

The woman moved quickly, as she
entered the hospital. The woman then
entered the emergency, went into what
Rose assumed was the employee's
entrance. Soon the woman came out
dressed in scrubs, which had the name
Candice on them. The woman looked
both ways out of the locker room door,
then exited. She walked slowly down the
hall; as if she didn't want to be seen. This
was ridiculous. Rose was seeing actions
that just weren't occurring. She had to get
herself under control; mom needed Rose
to be in tip-top shape as Grandma Katha
would say.

Rose looked away, concentrating on the
task at hand, arguing with the nurse to let
her in. Ignoring them both, Candice crept
by them entering the room, without either
of Rose, or the other nurses noticing.

"Mom?" Lily asked.

"Hush baby, yes it's Mommy. I'm here
and I love you. The baby is coming; but

it's going to be okay," Heather stated softly.

"I don't why I'm imagining you Mom; but I have to admit I'm so glad you're here. I'm so scared Mommy."

"I know baby; but I'm really here and they are going to help you and my grandchild. I promise," Heather reassured.

"Ooh, Mommy, it hurts," Lily complained.

"I know sweetie; but that's just nature saying hello. You'll soon forget all of this when your baby is in your arms."

"I missed you so much Mommy," Lily began holding her stomach as another pain racked her.

"I missed you too, Lily, but it wasn't safe. I couldn't be with you. Lily, I have something I have to say."

"You want to tell me something Mom? That's okay. So, that's why I'm seeing

you. You obviously want to tell me
something important."

Heather then suddenly hid behind a wall
of equipment, puzzling Lily.

The nurse came in for a second then and
said, "Well that medicine didn't work; but
you are not dilated enough yet. So that's
good. You've got a couple of hours yet.
We are overrun with patients. I have to go
for a couple of minutes; but I'll be right
back."

"Do you see her?"

"You sure you are okay, honey? There's
no one else here. We will get the doctor to
take a look at that head of yours again
when he comes back from triage and the
patients from that 40-car pileup. Or
maybe you were talking to the baby? Of
course, you were," the nurse reassured
herself.

This Little Girl had a Little Curl
S. G. Lee

"Mom, are you still here with me?" Lily asked wearily after the nurse once again left.

"Yes, baby. I need to tell you some things, one of them is be kind to Amelia. I know she's been mean; but you don't know what happened to her."

"What happened to Amelia?"

She is in danger of losing her business to bankruptcy, and lost her lease then Amelia also lost a baby. She may never have another, then she found out you were having one and she turned to religion for comfort.

"Oh no, poor Amelia! Thank-you for telling me this, mom."

"There's more, I need you to sign this paper."

"What is this? I can't just sign something; that I don't know what it is," Lily protested.

"You have to sign this to protect your baby, Clover."

"How did you know I was calling her Clover? I don't understand. Why I'm imagining this."

"You are not imagining this; now sign the paper dear and protect Clover."

"You are dead. What is wrong with me?" Lily pleaded struggling to understand why she was seeing her dead mother.

"Please listen to me, Lily. It's important you sign this," Heather asked putting a pen in Lily's hand and producing the document.

Lily was dazed confused from the pain and from her head injury; but she signed it anyway. Her mother wasn't real, none of this was real, so it didn't matter.

"I'm sure I'll see you soon."

"You are leaving me? Please, Mom; don't leave me again," begged Lily tears forming in her eyes.

This Little Girl had a Little Curl
S. G. Lee

"I'm sorry, honey. Sorrier, than I can say; but I'll be back soon, I promise. I just want to protect you and your little girl."

Lily closed her eyes and when she opened them her mother was gone. She had imagined her, of course she had. But why did she envision her with hospital scrubs wearing a nameplate that said Candice? Her mother was dead. Lily knew that. The authorities had searched for a long time; but had not found her mother. They had only found blood after the kidnapping; but Lily knew that if her mother was alive, she would have come back to them a long time ago. It was obvious the head injury and the stress had conjured up her mother in her time of need.

"Finally, I snuck in, the nurses are so busy they didn't notice me. Do you know they tried not to let me come into you? They wouldn't believe I was sixteen. Do I look fourteen or something?" Rose complained.

"I'm glad you are here." Lily commented.

This Little Girl had a Little Curl
S. G. Lee

"Sorry, mom! Here you are in pain from your head...I thought they stopped the labour ...it's way, too soon. You're only eight months pregnant. I hope the baby doctor gets here, soon."

"Hello, I'm Doctor Kenworth," a man in scrubs said coming in the room.

Rose stared at him in disbelief. He was tall and very skinny; but he looked way too young to be a doctor.

"You've got to be kidding me. What are you sixteen years old?"

"I am a second year OBGYN student," Doctor Kenworth answered sounding offended.

"We'll wait for the next doctor," Rose replied.

"You'll be waiting a long time. It's a holiday weekend, Thanksgiving you know. I rather be eating turkey, but here I am. There is a baby boom going on, we have a forty-car pileup and your sibling is on its way," Dr. Kenworth said crossing his arms.

"I'm the patient and I have all the say. Rose, he stays." Lily replied forcefully, "Oh, I think I have to push, now."

"Let me have a look," Doctor Kenworth replied going to the foot of the bed to check on the status of the labour, "Yes, I believe you're correct this baby is coming right now."

"Rose is it? You need to go out in the hall and grab a nurse now," Doctor Kenworth ordered.

Rose went into the hall and spotted a woman in scrubs. On her name plate it said Candice.

"You have to come now my mother's having the baby now and it's too early," Rose demanded.

"Me? But I'm off shift," Heather covered.

"I need you now, nurse."

"Okay, fine; but I better get a neonatal
unit if the baby is early."

"Be fast."

Rose went back into Lily's room.

"That's good, Lily. I see the head
crowning. One more push and you'll be
able to see your baby too."

Rose thought all of this was a little gross.
Her mom clearly was in pain. Why did
woman have babies anyway when it hurt
so much? If men had to go through any of
this there would be none. Rose glanced
over at Lily who was perspiring heavily
in her effort. Her hair clung to her face.

"Okay Lily, this it. Push!" Doctor
Kenworth ordered as Nurse Candice came
back with the neonatal unit for the baby.

A loud crying was heard as the baby
breathed in the cool air and the doctor cut
the umbilical cord. Rose noticed
something odd though as the nurse
stepped in; she took the umbilical cord.
She then turned her back to do something

with it. It was all quite weird; but what did Rose know, she hadn't had a baby before, maybe that was normal?

"It's a girl and a very healthy one. Let me clean up your daughter weigh her and measure her length, then we can let you hold her," Doctor Kenworth explained.

"They were right. She's a little girl? Oh, Rose, you have a little sister," Lily cried tears of joy spilling from her eyes.

"Mom, she's beautiful. She looks like those pictures of you when you were little that Grandma Katha showed me."

"She does have my curly blonde hair that I had when I was born," Lily said, as the doctor placed the baby in Lily's arms.

"She's early Lily. but the shot that we gave you will speed up her lung development. She looks fairly healthy for being so early; I would estimate that she is about five pounds," Doctor Kenworth explained.

"She'll be okay?" Lily replied.

"We'd like to keep an eye on her for a little while and make sure her lungs and other parts are working well."

"You don't think she was harmed by Laura… I mean Eileen as well?" asked Lily worried.

"No, as I said I believe she's very hardy for a preemie. Have you and your husband picked out a name for a girl?"

"I don't have a husband …yet. Emmett and I were thinking of calling a girl, Clover." Lily replied then turning to Rose she said, "Oh no, I forgot to get you to call your Grandma Katha, so she could find Emmett. He hasn't come home or he would have called here."

"I love the name, mom. I'm going to call her Clover." Rose responded, "I'll go call Grandma Katha now. I'll be right back."

"Can I hold her just for moment?"

"I shouldn't let you; but if you don't dislodge the leads, then you can hold her for a few minutes. Remember though, baby needs to immediately go to the Neo-natal Intensive Care after that."

Lily breathed a sigh of relief everything would be okay now. Her little girl, Clover had five fingers and toes she noted. She was starring happily at her little girl when her vision began blurring and she worried she would drop Clover.

"Doctor Kenworth, please take the baby. My head...," Lily cried.

Someone took the baby from her arms. Lily's eye rolled back in her head and her eyes, head and body turned in one direction without her volition. Her body then became stiff followed by jerking of her muscles. Another doctor entered the room right about this time and began examining her.

"Nurse take the baby to the neonatal intensive care nursery," Doctor Kenworth ordered.

Heather hid outside the door torn; should she go with the baby, or stay with Lily?

This Little Girl had a Little Curl
S. G. Lee

She'd taken precautions by having Lily
sign the papers. If anything happened, she
could help Clover; but what if something
happened to Lily? She may have watched
Lily from afar; but she loved her
daughter. Heather wanted her to raise
Clover; even if she did it with that sad
excuse for a man Emmett Rogers who
hadn't protected Lily.

"How is she doing Doctor Shutworth?"
Doctor Kenworth asked the
neurosurgeon.

"She's got a nasty brain bleed, according
to her scan. If the X-Ray department
hadn't been so busy with other patients
from that forty-car pileup, I would have
got the scan sooner. We would have had
her in the OR already."

"I'm stabilizing her and then taking her
up to the emergency OR 7. Can you call
ahead Paul?"

"Will do. I know I'm on OBGYN
rotation; but is there any way I could

scrub in and watch? I'm almost off shift anyway," Doctor Kenworth begged.

"If you feel you are up to it; but you won't get any surgical time;" Doctor Shutworth answered.

Lily was taken to the elevator and rushed to the operating room, where Doctor Shutworth began the long eventful surgery.

Heather followed, but lost them in the elevator. She went to a phone and asked where she could find Lily Kelly. She put on Grandma Katha's Scottish burr and upper crust accent and told them she was Katha Stewart. They told her Lily was in surgery. Heather went to the floor; but was refused entry. They told her to wait in the alcove for patient's relatives; soon a representative came in and told her in hushed tones that Lily Kelly had died.

"And my grandchild?" Heather asked.

"She's in the nursery and very healthy," they answered.

"Oh thank –you the board will hear of your diligence," Heather said in Grandma Katha's tones.

Heather took a big breath; then asked to see the baby and was directed to Clover. Lily had always said she would call her baby Clover. Of course, Lily was only nine years when she decided that but Heather knew that Lily would have followed through.

Heather cradled Clover close to her body and told Clover how so sorry she was that Clover had lost her mommy; but that everything would be okay. Talking to the baby, she told her Grandma would take care of her and keep her safe forever; because she loved her.

Now Heather had to fake Clover's death so Emmett wouldn't keep looking; it wouldn't do to have a copper on her tail. Clover deserved the best life Heather could give her. Emmett wasn't an incompetent police officer, or he would never have let that woman near Lily and

This Little Girl had a Little Curl
S. G. Lee

Clover. Heather would never give him the chance to let Clover down again. She would protect Clover with her life. No one would be near Clover, without Heather's full surveillance.

~0~

Chapter 30 – Bad News Comes in Threes

Rose was angry with herself. Why hadn't she checked her cell battery? Her cell phone was dead and she couldn't seem to find a phone in this hospital. She had thought of asking someone; but everyone seemed so busy. Maybe she could find an old pay phone near the coffee shop? She was starving anyway and thirsty. She would get something to eat and drink and someone could tell her where a pay phone was. A coke and a chocolate bar would be her meal for today; that should keep her calories down and keep her skinny.

Rose had grabbed her purse at home before getting in the ambulance as a reflex and she had lots of change and bills, so no worries there. Where the heck was that coffee shop? Rose thought, as she walked back down the corridor for the second time. Did she turn right here? No left, that is that where she had gone wrong. Rose turned right; yes, there it was a coffee shop. She went in grabbed a chocolate bar, a bag of Doritos and a coke and went to the cashier to pay. The Doritos would be okay it was not like they had a lot of calories and she'd used up some just finding this shop she reasoned.

"Excuse me do you know where I can find a pay phone?" Rose asked the woman at the counter.

"Follow the yellow line turn right and then left then right again and there are banks of phones on the wall. I hope you have a Looney; because it costs a dollar to use them." the woman said dismissing her, "Next."

Rose took her sandwich and her drink and went to a table to look through her change purse for a Looney. Finding one, she walked down the hall following the directions the woman gave her. Just when she was about to give up, she found the phones. Setting her chocolate bar, can of coke and chips in her big purse, she picked up the receiver and dialled her Grandma Katha's number by heart.

"Hello?"

"Grandma Katha? It's me Rose."

"Oh, thank goodness Rose. I was getting worried you told me you were visiting your Mom after your appointment; but it so late now and we hadn't heard from you. I tried calling your cell phone and your Mom's; but there was no answer I was just about to go over there," Grandma Katha rambled sounding relieved.

"Grandma, are you sitting down?"

"What has happened that you want me to sit down? Land sakes child just tell me."

This Little Girl had a Little Curl
S. G. Lee

"It's long story, but first of all I'll start with the good news. Mom gave birth to my little sister tonight her name is Clover Claire; but Mom said it was okay to call her Clover..."

"But it's too soon; she wasn't due for another month," Grandma Katha protested worried.

"It is okay, Grandma Katha the doctor said though she was a preemie she seemed healthy. They took Clover to the Neo-Natal Intensive Care."

"Oh, thank heavens; but you said that was the good news. Give me the bad."

"The nanny you hired for Emmett was a fraud. Her name wasn't Laura. Her name is actually Eileen Jones, Dafydd's sister; she's a mental case and she killed Sherry-Anne."

"She what? Are you saying not only is she Dafydd's sister; but she was the one who murdered Sherry-Anne? The carbon monoxide poisoning... it was her wasn't it?"

"She was trying to kill Mom, but she blew it. She is fixated on Emmett; but it gets worse Grandma Katha."

"Worse how could it be any worse? I hired a killer to be a nanny!"

"No one knows this yet; but Eileen will shout it from the rooftops. Joseph needs a lawyer. He was trying to protect his sister and his mother when he killed his father. His father killed everyone in their compound; then he was going to kill his family. He shot his mother and Joseph killed him. His mother told him how to cover everything up before she died. Deirdre knew, so did Rebecca; neither told. Apparently 'Laura' overheard them talking and she blackmailed Joseph so he would help her get away with her dirty tricks. He threatened to tell Emmett and that is when she decided it was time to kill Mom, Joseph and Rebecca."

"Oh my. I'll hire someone right away."

This Little Girl had a Little Curl
S. G. Lee

"When I got to the house, she had shoved mom down the stairs; trying to kill her and when that didn't work, she marched her into the kitchen tied her up with Joseph and Rebecca and was going to take Deirdre and set the house on fire. What she didn't count on though was Dee. Deirdre went to Emmett's lock box with the key, took out his service revolver, load it with the bullets he keeps in the other locked drawer and then held the gun on 'Laura'. That's when I got there; took the gun from Dee and held it on her until the police got there. Rebecca looked after Mom after Dee untied her."

"Your mother's okay?"

"She said she had a headache and she just had a baby; but yes, she seemed okay." Rose answered, "She does want you and Emmett though."

"It is late, why wasn't Emmett home?"

"I don't know his appointment was changed to 8 p. m. , according to 'Laura'".

You don't think 'Laura' did something to him, too?" Rose asked.

"I'll find him and be there soon meanwhile go back and be with your Mom, until I get there. Okay?"

"Okay, Grandma Katha, see you soon." Rose replied hanging up the phone.

Rose sauntered down the hall, following the lines back to the cafeteria. From there she could find her way back to the emergency room and her mother. She got lost at one point again; but a quick retrace of her steps until she found the emergency rooms. She was just about to go in her mother's room; when a nurse stopped her.

"You can't go in there, honey," the nurse said

"Why not?" asked Rose.

"We just lost a patient and they haven't come to take them to the morgue yet."

This Little Girl had a Little Curl
S. G. Lee

"What was the patient's name?" asked Rose scared.

"Lily Kelly." The nurse answered, then seeing Rose's paleness she asked, "Were you a relative?"

Rose didn't answer as the blood rushed to her head and she fell into a dead faint on the floor.

~0~

Chapter 31 – Heartbreak is not just a word

Rose awoke to a tube in her arm and a pounding headache, throbbing behind her eyes. As her eyes adjusted, she saw a woman she recognized, sitting beside the bed adjusting a blood pressure cuff.

"Good, you are awake; aren't you, Rose? How do you feel?" asked Doctor Hana Abrahams.

"Like a ten-ton truck hit me. Is this your intern rotation in the ER? What happened? Oh no, I remember Mom...Mom's DEAD!" screamed Rose in anguish.

This Little Girl had a Little Curl
S. G. Lee

"No, Rose the person that told you thought you were asking about a different Lily Kelly. We had a Lily Kelly who was fifty-five years old, who died as the result of a car accident this evening."

"Then where's my mother?"

"Cousin Lily is in surgery. She is having surgery to remove a blood clot on her brain."

"Then she's still in danger?'

"While it is difficult surgery, I've been assured that Dr. Pope is the best neurosurgeon on staff and she has personally taken over the surgery."

"Then mom will be okay?"

"Hopefully; but you may not be able to talk to her for a few days. They will have to place her in a medically induced coma to bring down the swelling in her brain.

"But what about my little sister Clover, she needs her mother."

Dr. Abrahams grimaced then tried to hide what she was thinking.

"What wrong is there something wrong with Clover?"

"Emmett would like to speak with you," Hana continued.

"There's something wrong; tell me what it is."

"First, we should talk about you. You've lost a lot of weight and your electrolytes are out of balance."

"So?"

"A lot of people are worried about you. Grandma Katha thought you were seeing your psychiatrist; before you went to your mother's home, but you didn't go did you?"

"How do you know that?"

"I spoke to your psychiatrist, Dr. Georgia Jeffries."

This Little Girl had a Little Curl
S. G. Lee

"How did you know Dr. Frobisher wasn't my shrink anymore?"

"I have my sources. A lot of people are very concerned about you."

"I'm fine. Now tell me what you are hiding." Rose demanded.

"You are not fine. You are eight- eight pounds and five-feet six inches."

"So?"

"Your weight should be much higher. Tell me what is going on. I can help Rose."

"It's none of your business."

"It is when you wind up my patient."

"Fine then...my real mother is a mental case; my adopted mother has replaced me with some other kids and now she's got my sister she won't need me at all. I went to the mall and window shopped."

"Do you still love your birth mother?"

"Yes."

"Then how can you think Lily could love you any less?"

"I went to party she wouldn't have let me go to; I didn't share any information about what happened at that party with her for days; then I ran off to find my real mom and dismissed her as nothing," Rose explained.

"Did she yell at you when she found out?"

"No."

"Did she judge you?" Hana asked.

"No."

"Then Lily loves you," Hana commented.

"Were you raped?" Hana enquired calmly.

"No, someone tried; but Caleb saved me. How did you know that?" Rose exclaimed.

"I guessed by your reaction when you first came to."

"I should have told the police; but I had no proof. I hate him; but it's not mom's fault. I've blamed everything on her and I almost lost her."

"You'll talk to your shrink about all these bottled-up feelings and start eating and taking care of yourself better?"

"Yes."

"Promise, me, that no matter what happens you'll talk? And if you can't handle your problems, you will see your psychiatrist more often?"

"Okay. Now can I see Emmett? He probably wants me to explain what happened with Laura... I mean Eileen."

"Yes, I still can't believe how she fooled us all. You can come in now Emmett," Hana said opening the door.

"Hello Rose. How are you?"

"I'm good."

"That's not what I heard. I heard you collapsed."

"They told me Mom was dead. I should have been there to protect her all the time from Eileen."

"Yes, that would have upset me too; but it wasn't your fault Laura... no, Eileen fooled us all."

"Mom told me she didn't like Eileen. I just thought she was jealous."

"As I said she fooled us all." Emmett stated looking sad, "I need to tell you something and ask you some questions."

"Questions? Where were you Emmett, when Mom needed you? You're a cop you should have realized she was a criminal. Mom and Clover almost lost their lives."

"Clover?"

This Little Girl had a Little Curl
S. G. Lee

"Clover. She was born. Didn't Grandma Katha tell you Emmett? She's a beautiful girl, don't you think? I know I'm not her blood sister; but she looks a little like me. Isn't that strange?" babbled Rose happily.

"You saw her? Can you describe her for me?"

"I have her on my cell phone. I took a picture before it died."

"Can I see it?" pleaded Emmett tears coming to his eyes.

"Why are you crying? Why would I need to describe her?"

"I don't know how to say this…"

"Just spit it out is she sick? Is Clover sick because of something Eileen did?"

"Eileen's actions killed my baby girl," Emmett exclaimed.

"But that's not possible," Rose replied with disbelief, "Clover was cooing. she was fine.

"The nurse took her back to the unit; but she died on the way and they can't find the body."

"Nonsense! That's impossible she's in the nursery. She has to be there. If there's nobody then someone's lying."

"She's not. The nurse says she died and was taken to the morgue; where someone disposed of the remains, because of that huge car pile-up where people died."

"Then why aren't you out there finding my little sister? She's not dead; it's obvious, someone kidnapped her. You are a useless human being. First, you let that bitch psycho stalker move in with you and my mom, then you abandon her to her manipulations, not backing up my mom. Where were you when she tried to kill my mom and your baby?"

"I'm sorry Rose, she fooled us all."

"Really? You are a useless sack of shit!! I thought I could trust you to make my mom happy but all you've brought her is misery. Clover was the only good thing you gave her. Where were you when they stole my sister?"

"I'm sorry. I'm so sorry," Emmett cried.

"Don't you dare cry crocodile tears! Those tears are for yourself! Mom is fighting for her life. Why aren't you with her?"

"Your mother is in surgery and you needed me."

"I don't need you. Clover needs you. Clover's your daughter; why aren't you moving heaven and earth to find her? My mother would do that! I hate you Emmett Rogers! Get out of here and find Clover! What am I saying? I'm going to find her myself," Rose screamed?

Rose then proceeded to pull out the intravenous line out of her hand and step down onto the floor off the bed. As her feet touched the floor she fainted again and Doctor Abrahams put her back in the bed stuck in the intravenous line with a sedative and approached her supervisor to admit her patient to the hospital.

~0~

The End or is it? Look for the further adventures of the Kellys in *London Bridge Is Broken Down-Book 7 of the Kelly Murder Mysteries* coming soon; an excerpt appears on the next page.

If you enjoyed *This Little Girl Had A Little Curl* please leave a comment where you purchased this book.

Sincerely S. G. Lee

Excerpt from London Is Broken Down-Book 7 of the Kelly Murder Mysteries

Preface:

L ondon Bridge is Falling Down are

the usually remembered lyrics, but the original lyrics to this song/ poem used in a game were (as printed in Tommy Thumb's Pretty Song Book (c.1744) actually as the listed below. What most people don't know is that the lyrics actually refer to the numerous repairs to the bridge and how they watched Anne Boleyn in her imprisonment. I thought this rhyme appropriate for the title; as we delve into Heather's background and why she took Clover.

London Bridge Is Broken Down

London Bridge is broken down,

Dance over my Lady Lee.

London Bridge is Broken down

With a gay Lady

How shall we build

It up again,

Dance over my Lady Lee, and company

Build it up with Gravel and Stone,

Dance over my Lady Lee and company

Gravel and Stone, Will wash away

Dance over my Lady Lee, and company

Build it up with Iron and Steel,

Dance over my Lady Lee and company

This Little Girl had a Little Curl
S. G. Lee

Iron and Steel, Will bend and Bow

Dance over my Lady Lee and company

Build it up with, Silver and Gold,

Dance over my Lady Lee and company

Silver and Gold, will be stolen away

Dance over my Lady Lee and company

Then we'll set, a man to Watch

Dance over my Lady Lee

Then we'll set, a man to Watch

With a gay Lady.

~0~

Excerpt from London Bridge Is Broken Down ~ Chapter 1 - No Never Again

A week ago

Heather adjusted the blanket on the baby, tears streaming from her eyes. How could her baby be dead? Lily was so young... much too young to die. Eileen Jones would pay for what she did to Lily. She would hire someone she knew to take care of that evil, little bitch. She would drop dead, unexpectedly, in her cushy mental health cell. She would hire someone she knew to take care of that evil, little bitch. Heather was due a few favours, and she still had loyal contacts no matter, what the agency might think. Eileen Jones would be dead. She wouldn't live a normal life, while Lily

This Little Girl had a Little Curl
S. G. Lee

had none. Because of Eileen Jones,
Clover would never know her mother.
The best of Lily. Her sweet Lily, who was
kind, generous, and sweet, and never saw
bad in anyone. How that girl became a
prosecuting attorney Heather could not
understand. Lily had a hard time seeing
that anyone could be bad; when she was
young and she hadn't changed that much
even though Grandma Katha had raised
her. Grandma Katha had poured all the
love; that she hadn't given her own
daughter, Florence, or her granddaughter,
Heather, into Lily and Amelia. Did they
know how lucky they were? Amelia must.
If Lily hadn't known; she never know,
now. She had to make that damn Eileen
pay for taking Lily's life. She couldn't
leave Clover with Emmett Rogers; the
damn man hadn't even married Lily
knowing that she was having his baby and
he brought havoc in his wake. How many
murders had he exposed Lily and Rose
to? Okay, so a few had been nut jobs; but
being crazy in Heather's book, did not
excuse murder of innocents.

This Little Girl had a Little Curl
S. G. Lee

Gerhard Brandt was on Heather's tail.
How had he discovered that she was
Lily's mother? Had she had exposed
Clover and Lily to him? Heather should
have spirited Lily away to safety with the
baby and Rose. She'd allowed Katha to
take Lily away out of the country and be
raised without her mother to protect her;
hadn't that proved love? Instead, Katha
considered that desertion. Would Lily
have thought her mother abandoned her if
she'd known? No, put those thoughts
behind her. Heather had to deal with the
here and now. If only her mind was so
foggy at times; but if she took her
medicine it would be okay. She could
protect hem both. Though Clover would
never be safe as long as Gerhard was
alive. Gerhard wanted to make her pay for
killing his wife and daughter. They
weren't supposed to die; but he was. He
wanted Heather's blood.

Heather remembered how she'd been
under orders at the time; to tell them
where Gerhard would be and at what
time. Heather had hesitated; but she knew

it was her job and Gerhard was a
dangerous man to the world. His plans for
terrorism in the U.K. could have killed
the monarchy and thousands more.
Heather was loyal to Queen and country.
She couldn't let the fact, that a man could
die, enter her work. She knew when she
joined that people could die; as long as it
wasn't her family member; she could live
with it; or so she thought.

She had heard on the news, that Gerhard's
wife and daughter had arrived
unexpectedly. Gerhard had gone to the
market to collect food; when the bomb
went off killing his wife and daughter.
Lily not been directly involved with their
demise. She had consoled herself; that
maybe some other agency had placed the
bomb; but she had questioned her own
role in it. She had reasoned; that she was
a low-level spy and she had no control
over agency business. So, why was
Gerhard blaming her? It was irrational;
but grief often was. This was a cold-
blooded business and so was being a
terrorist. Did he think there would be no

after-effects, or collateral damage because of his actions? Yet, Gerhard was so arrogant; he probably thought there was no consequences to himself for his actions and all he wanted was vengeance.

All hell broke loose, Lily's mother, Florence who was living with them when Gerhard's wife and daughter were killed; Gerhard targeted Florence and when she walked a across a street; then Lily and Heather were snatched out of Lily's car. Heather blamed herself for not thinking about how they would retaliate against her and grab Lily and herself. After all actions have consequences.

That fateful day she had been driving Lily to school. Lily happily chatted about the play she would be in; when a car came out of nowhere and started banging her bumper. Heather speeded up and so did the car. Heather drove defensively trying to lose them. Until they drove her into a lamp post. Suddenly Heather was fenced in.

This Little Girl had a Little Curl
S. G. Lee

Two cars were in front of her and the car
behind her, became two as well. Four cars
against one; boxed in, so. Heather
couldn't move. Men at all the escape
routes; they couldn't escape. Guns trained
on her and Lily, what else could she do…
to protect Lily she surrendered.

At first, she thought it was Gerhard
Brandt coming for his revenge; but before
she surrendered it occurred to her that she
and Lily would already be dead if it was
Gerhard. These were other people who
had turned their sights on Heather and her
spying that she had been doing for the
English crown. Paperwork that's all she
really been doing recently, so why target
her? Okay, so she freelanced a little
business with Gerhard for them; but
nothing else. Heather had racked her
brains; but had not come up with a
reason, except perhaps leverage. or
mistaken identity.

She begged them to leave Lily, but that
was her mistake. That made Lily her
weakness. She should have remembered

her training, but with Lily at risk
everything had gone out the window. The
agency had promised her family would
never be at risk that they would be
protected foolishly Heather took them at
their word.

The villains took them both in the back of
an unmarked van. Heather and Lily were
driven to an unknown location, hustled
into what looked like an abandoned
building. It was there the torture began on
Heather. Heather held strong; but when
they hit Lily and blackened her eyes, then
threatened to do more evil things to Lily,
Heather started to bend. She offered up
some information; none of it was good
enough for them they wanted what she
couldn't divulge; or didn't know.

A week had passed and still they were
prisoners; something had to give. Heather
knew if she gave in, they still kill them;
both she started planning their escape.
Unfortunately, things got worse, one of
the kidnappers started getting over
familiar with Lily. Heather found one of

them stripping her to her underwear. Only
intervention from another kidnapper
saved Lily from his tendencies.

Heather waited for two of them to leave,
leaving only the abuser. She hit the abuser
over the head and wanted to kill him; but
then another kidnaper came back and the
job wasn't finished. Heather knew there
would be no escape...unless...she offered
up herself. The kidnapper locked Lily in a
room and then he had taken Heather to
another bedroom. Heather had offered
herself willingly anything for Lily's
safety. Heather had endured it all with a
smile pretending she liked it. The
kidnapper told Heather his name was
Jake. It probably wasn't his real name;
but it felt like they were bonding. She got
him to agree to help Lily escape and get
her daughter to safety. Heather didn't care
what happened to herself as long as Lily
was safe.

 The man had stabbed the abuser spilling
blood everywhere. He then took bags of
stored blood out of the fridge and poured

it on the floor. Blood didn't come from nowhere. What had he been planning and for how long? Would he take Heather and Lily somewhere they didn't want to go? He'd promised to help Lily escape; Heather would do anything to make that happen.

"What was that for?" Heather had asked.

"You haven't been a spy, long have you?" he answered.

"I'm a low-level spy. I've been a spy for ten years. I married Peter, he's an attaché about eight and half years ago. He has no idea what I do."

"You've only been married for eight years? But the child is nine! How long did you know him?"

Heather was appalled; how she could have revealed so much to this kidnapper, she didn't know. No one was supposed to know about Lily's father, that she'd never reveal, not only for Lily's sake; but her Peter's. Heather could say that Peter and she knew each other longer that was the story, they'd told everyone.

"Peter adopted her," she admitted and she didn't quite no why.

"You have shown such trust with me, I will help the little girl escape. They should never have taken my child."

"Thank you, Jake. Wait a minute, my child, why are you calling Lily your child?"

"Do you sleep with every Peter, Tom, or Harry, my Scottish flower?"

Heather had remembered how Jacob had called her that and how he'd vowed to protect her and they'd said he was dead.

"Jacob? They said you were dead."

"My darling, I've looked high and low for you. I couldn't find you. We can get away from these criminals; but for now; we have to spirit our daughter away to safety for Lily is my daughter correct?'

The man then helped Lily out the basement window and told her where the police station was.

"We need to be away, before the police come. Meet me at the Prague Astronomical Clock in one week's time. If you're not there I'll understand that you can't, or won't meet me. If I'm discovered I'll tell the others, or the police that you are dead, "Jake insisted.

Heather had agreed thinking she be safe and so would Lily. She'd be reunited with her daughter. Heather had done what she could to save Lily and hoped that her daughter wouldn't be traumatized; but she had heard that Lily didn't remember what had happened to her after her stay in the hospital. Heather knew Lily's psyche was fragile and it was therefore better if she thought Heather was dead. Katha had spirited Lily away to Canada believing that Heather was dead. Heather had hoped to come to Canada a retired agent and be reunited with Jake and her daughter (Peter would understand and give her a

This Little Girl had a Little Curl
S. G. Lee

divorce);but Heather had been grabbed
again and taken to Russia. Instead. the
two other kidnappers and some others
from the Soviet government had grabbed
her and she'd languished in Siberian
prison. At first, they had tried to break her
and take all the secrets she knew. She
hadn't given in after a year and they had
then sent her remote prison camp, Petus,
in the Siberian region of Russia.

Breaking rocks and doing menial labor,
with little food, Heather slept on the floor
and longed to be free. She waited her
chance and had succeeded too late to be
with Lily, as by then Lily was an adult.
Grandma Katha probably thought she'd
abandoned her daughter, but she hadn't.

Heather saw here was no place in Lily's
life; that her presence could harm Lily at
least that's what Lily's shrink had told
Heather. She felt guilty how she had held
that shrink at gunpoint and yet the
psychiatrist had held her ground and
actually told Heather the truth about Lily.
Lily had been scarred by all the traumas

she had suffered; but she had pulled
herself together to become a good mom to
a little girl that needed one simply
because she too was scarred.

The psychiatrist felt though that if she
were to see Heather alive that would be
too much and that Lily would recall her
ordeal and might not be able to handle
what had happened to her when she was
nine. So, Heather hadn't come forward
but; she kept an eye on Lily through her
network. She felt like she knew her
daughter that way; but it wasn't enough,
especially now that Lily was gone. She'd
never get back that time with her little
girl, or see her daughter in person again.

Heather had given up all rights and ties to
Lily to protect her; but no one knew that.
Grandma Katha just thought she was
selfish. Who cared what that old bat
thought! She didn't still care, did she?
Poor little Rose, but she had Grandma
Katha, Rose would be okay. She couldn't
take the kid away from everyone she
knew. That would traumatize the child.

This Little Girl had a Little Curl
S. G. Lee

Rose had bonded with Grandma Katha
the woman wasn't all bad, even if she
irrationally hated Heather. Okay, the truth
was Heather hated Grandma Katha too.
She hated her for judging her; without
talking to her. Grandma Katha had been
responsible for some of the troubles in
Heather's life by abandoning her to her
mother, Florence and her terrible choice
of a husband… the man that called
himself Heather's father. He wasn't
though, was he? And Grandma Katha and
Florence knew that. Her father was her
grandfather!! Talk about family secrets
admit that Grandma Katha!!

Rose wasn't Heather's flesh and blood,
either, but Clover was. She wasn't about
to try and raise an almost full-grown
teenager like Rose. Rose was a kind sweet
girl; but Grandma Katha would do a
much better job of that. Grandma Katha
had to be better the second, or third time
around. She done an okay job with Lily
and Amelia.

This Little Girl had a Little Curl
S. G. Lee

As for Emmett Rogers, the father of the baby; men were nothing, but trouble. It was his fault, his and Grandma Katha's that this cretin Eileen Jones had come into Lily's life.

So, Emmett had served in Afghanistan and got a medal... Who the heck cared? That didn't make him father material! Clover needed lots of love and affection. She needed her mother Lily, but she'd never have her, so Heather would give her the next best thing her grandmother's love and affection. Heather would be the best mother to this baby girl she could be, a better mom then she'd been to Lily. She'd be a wonderful mother to her granddaughter. She would make up for all the love she should have given Lily.

She'd get to raise a little girl. That alone made her smile through her tears. Lily had been taken away from Heather when she was only nine years old.

Lily had a wonderful childhood (with Grandma Katha), unlike Heather. Heather

This Little Girl had a Little Curl
S. G. Lee

hadn't seen Grandma Katha for years not until she was an adult and she had suffered living with her mother and the man she called Heather's father.

Heather's mother Florence had suffered as the broken battered wife. Heather had felt sorry for her. Heather's childhood was traumatic and filled with only bruises and broken bones from her father. Heather had retreated into books. Her eidetic memory made her memorize all sorts of useless facts and situations. Unfortunately, with her synaesthesia, everything, even bad situations; became remembered in vivid colours. Sometimes Heather could use this to her advantage; barely even glancing at the books to remember and score A pluses in all her courses. The intelligence tests they gave her showed her scores off the charts. These scores were sent on and someone finally noticed Heather. Sixteen years old and they recruited her for government work in England where she lived. Heather left her home and didn't see her mother again; until she found herself pregnant with Lily.

Heather had been devastated at first, to find out she was expecting. How could she raise a child? She was a spy, and a spy needed no encumbrances; that and the fact that the father (the love of her life) had disappeared. Heather couldn't believe that all she had left of Jacob MacAulay was a note that said he was sorry but he had to say goodbye.

How could the man she'd given her heart (against all her brain power) telling her this was wrong disappear without a trace? She tried all channels to find him and had ended up with nothing. Then she'd taken an over-the-counter test to find out she was pregnant. How could she raise a baby? She'd thought about abortion; but she couldn't bring herself to do it. Days when by and it was too late for an abortion and she'd been told she was being transferred to Paris. She should have been happy; but the agency didn't know about the pregnancy and she feared what they would do to her. Heather decided she only had one choice. On a cold snowy April morning at 2 a. m., she decided to take action.

Heather climbed the span of the Pont Neuf (the oldest standing bridge across the river Seine in Paris, France) This was the heart of Paris in medieval times and in her mind the right place to jump into the Seine. As she was about to put her foot forward and leap when she heard a voice.

"Nothing is that unsurmountable. Talk to me tell me how I can help?"

Heather had turned around and she'd seen an older man; somewhere between about thirty-two and thirty-five years old. He was dressed in a double-breasted suit, that she recognized as from St. Jacob of London. This man had money she categorized and then wondered, why she did. He had red hair, graying at the sides and warm blue eyes and as he talked, his smile met his eyes. He was charming and compassionate. He listened as she found

herself revealing how Jacob had left her
and she was alone. She told him she was
working a clerical job and that she didn't
know how she could do it and raise a
child alone.

Peter was a marvel a hero in suit, He told
her. he too had a problem that he couldn't
quite solve. He needed a wife in name
only; because the rumours about him
were getting too intense.

"You have a mistress? Is that the
rumour?"

"No, I've never said this aloud. It's very
hard and if anyone found out, I'd lose my
job."

"You're gay," Heather stated.

"I am," Peter had admitted.

Peter had talked Heather off her perch
and they talked in his car. Peter had come
up with a solution to both their problems
that made sense. Heather could have
financial stability, a loving father for her
baby (and although he didn't know) a

cover for her spying. Peter after all worked as an attaché for the government of Canada in Paris. Later they moved to Prague. Peter had no idea, that he was harbouring a spy; but then Peter needed a wife and family so he asked no questions and Heather needed not tell any lies.

Heather could even provide a home for her mother who had been released from prison after spending a year in it for killing Heather's father. For nine years long years Heather had looked after her mother seeing that she had what she needed and then just like that, Florence was killed in an accident. At least it looked like an accident… at first; until her contacts told her they were really looking for Heather and had killed Florence thinking she was Heather. All that plastic surgery Heather had paid for to reconstruct her mother's damaged face (from her abusive husband) hadn't helped anyone; but Heather.

Heather felt guilty and devastated to realize that the surgery had made her mother look so much younger that they had mistaken Florence for Heather. Her mother had seemed a different person though, very confident and happy, so maybe Heather should stop blaming herself for her mother's death. No, it was her fault they killed her mother because Heather was a spy.

Then of course Heather and Lily had been kidnapped and her life had spiralled once again, into sadness and bleakness. She had continued with her career spying, after she escaped from the Russian prison. She thought about coming back to Peter and Lily; but it was too late, they had moved on with their lives. Peter had continued with his career and to Heather's surprise (in Heather's absence) had long ago abandoned his daughter to Katha and a country far away.

Heather had watched Lily from a distance, watched her grow into the attorney she became. Heather had met Horace once and threatened him if he ever harmed Lily, or took Rose away.

This Little Girl had a Little Curl
S. G. Lee

Heather had believed Horace had been
frightened, he hadn't revealed that
Heather was alive; but he obviously
hadn't believed her because at the time of
his death he'd plan to take Rose and
divorce her. That cop Brad Owens had
fixed that problem. Heather hadn't even
had to lift a finger to get him to do that
either. Luckily for her the agency
although they heard about the murders;
they knew Heather wasn't involved.

The agency however seemed to recently
think Heather was a little unstable and
that would have convinced them for sure.
Heather worried that they would either
imprison her in a mental facility or
sanction her. She knew she was a little
off; but if she stayed on her secret
medications she could function. She
convinced them she was stable and they
were off her back for now; but when they
found out about Clover, all bets were off.
They'd try to take Clover and give her
back to Emmett. No, she wouldn't let that
bastard have Clover; he couldn't protect

her not like Heather. Look how little he'd
protected my Lily.

Heather could never get back that time
with Lily, thanks to Grandma Katha.
Grandma Katha had threatened to inform
those same Siberian people; where she
was if she didn't stay away from Lily.
How had Grandma Katha known about
them had she known all along… no it was
probably her husband, Terrence. The man
was a former judge and busybody.
Grandma Katha and Terrence hadn't even
told Lily. Lily hadn't even known; her
mother was alive.

But Heather hadn't been able to stay
away. Lily was her little girl, even grown
up and Grandma Katha had no right to
keep her from her. Grandma Katha would
have seized the baby and tried to raise her
like she raised Amelia and Lily, but that
cow was too old now and that damn
Gerhard had found Heather and Heather's
family and was threatening them Gerhard
had found Heather and Heather's family
and was threatening them. The rest of

them were safe; even though, she had revealed too much, with a recent lover who had drugged her. He had been sent to find out information about her; she realized too late that she had told him of her attitude about the others. Gerhard who had probably sent him knew she only cared about Lily.

If she ran, he'd know she didn't care about Rose and Katha and he'd leave them alone. They'd be safe, but Clover? Clover was at risk because of her connection to Lily.

This was Heather second chance; she could raise Clover in one of her secret London flat. Her flats all had different names. the one she was living in with now. was for Sarah Crouse. She had another that was sold to Amanda Lee. No one would find Clover and Heather. Heather would do what she needed to do to protect the two of them.

Rose would be happy with Grandma Katha; after all she was only two years away from adulthood. Grandma Katha was old now and probably wouldn't live too much longer then that she reasoned.

Clover deserved a mother who was young enough to raise her. Heather could be that mother; she knew she had the tools. Clover's father had put her in danger, as had Grandma Katha picking that fake nanny, Eileen Jones. That evil bitch, Heather was reminded of how she wanted to make her pay for killing Lily. Her time was coming; Eileen better enjoy her time now because sometime in the future when Eileen least expects it, karma would bite her on the butt. Heather would see she suffered as much as Lily had. As for that Emmett Rogers; he didn't deserve to raise Clover, so Heather would step in. She wouldn't let Lily down. Not again …no never again. "This is my promise Clover. I will protect you," Heather vowed;

~0~

This book will be available early 2022

Excerpt from Love's Labour's Won

Preface:

Love's Labour's Won

*S*arah sought a job,

Biting back a sob,

Her love and life,

All constant strife,

And filled with unbroken sorrow,

Like there was no tomorrow.

This Little Girl had a Little Curl

S. G. Lee

She thought her future,

Safely to be assured,

Instead of that Sarah found,

Many wonders to astound,

The world changed forever,

Yet the pull of a tether,

For the prize she sought,

And the joy and pain it wrought,

And all that she had done,

Was "Love's Labour's Won"

By S.G. Lee

S. G. Lee

Except From Love's Labour's Won ~ Chapter 1 - Want Ads

Life was getting Sarah down. She

was twenty-one years old and what did she have to show for it? Did she have a career? No, she didn't. Did life produce a boyfriend, husband or children? Another no! Or even a significant other? She had no one, no one to care if she lived or died. She had worked so many dead-end jobs; too many to count.

She had once been a Wal-Mart Greeter and even spent a winter as a telemarketer selling lawn services for the upcoming spring. She failed miserably not making

S. G. Lee

that job a success either. Numerous hang-ups ensued and no sales.

They kept her for a month and then said… "I'm sorry you're not working out."

Like, duh. She didn't complete any sales. She had to make a living somehow.

She scanned the want ads. There remained lots of jobs for coffee servers, but she was so tired of smiling and serving food to people. Then she spotted the ad, the ad which made her sit up and take notice.

Companion wanted.

Must be young presentable and personable.

Apply by phone at 555-5555 only serious inquires need apply.

This Little Girl had a Little Curl

S. G. Lee

Must have two references

What was this some kind of weird scam
luring young woman to their peril?
Really, how dramatic was she being?

Sarah normally ignored such an ad, but
she was getting short on cash and the rent
was due next week.

She didn't have the eight hundred and
fifty dollars the landlord wanted for this
dump…err…wonderful furnished
apartment. She'd be out on the street if
she didn't earn some money. It wasn't
like she had a lot of friends, which she
could ask to crash on their sofas. Melanie
would have let her, but she was off on a
modeling job in France. Melanie had
sublet her apartment to a yuppie couple
that obviously didn't know Sarah.

Should I or shouldn't I call? Sarah
thought. I mean was it safe? What if the
employers subsisted as white slavers? The
people Gran were always warning her

S. G. Lee

about growing up? Gran's notions bordered on the ridiculous, of course. So, I should just seize the opportunity. Sarah thought. Gran was gone and so were her worrisome and outdated ideas. Sarah looked at the ads again.

Barista wanted must have previous experience and two references.

Must be prepared to clean and carry up to 40 pounds of product.

The ad's specifications were a new take on the job. They were warning people that they would be heavy lifting. Hmm, generally they told you this when you started the job. But forty pounds, what the heck?

Were they having the baristas carry coffee beans? There had to be another job offer somewhere in these online sites. She scanned the ads once again.

This Little Girl had a Little Curl

S. G. Lee

No nothing in the ads but a companion
job. A companion job didn't sound so
bad. Did it? She needed a job and jobs
were scarce that she qualified for right
now. She had to at least try to get the job,
didn't she? She took a huge breath and
dialled the number.

"Hello," the voice said on the other end of
the line.

A real live person answered instead of the
answering machine Sarah expected. Sarah
took another deep breath.

"Uh I'd like to apply for the job; you
placed in the Free Press." She replied
with all the enthusiasm she could muster.

"I see… and what makes you believe
you're the person we are looking for?"

This Little Girl had a Little Curl

S. G. Lee

Asked the voice on the other end of the line

"I like people and people like me. I am often stopped by strangers and they always seem compelled to tell me their complete life histories," Sarah replied.

"Uh huh, and how do you respond to these indignities to your peace and quiet?" asked the voice.

"Well I am aware not everyone would listen; I find it fascinating to hear the stories people tell and to just listen if that's what they need. In some way I feel I can help them. It's not an intrusion," Sarah answered without even thinking.

"I comprehend one such as you, may have led a very difficult life. People do not always return the kindness to that you seem to offer so freely. You are an old soul," replied the voice sounding distinctively male, and little too familiar.

"Well...I don't know if this is odd or what but a long time ago, I decided I liked

me. If others find me a Pollyanna; a
person who is too kind, too naive for the
world, that's their problem. I like being
different even if others think me odd, I
can only be me. Oh, I can't believe I'm
telling you this, in a job interview no less.
Now you'll never hire me and I'm sorry
I've wasted your time, sir." Sarah
responded embarrassed and about to hang
up.

"Miss, please don't hang up. I think you
are an excellent potential candidate for
this rather unique job."

"You think I might be the person you
want?" asked Sarah incredulously.

"Well clearly my employer would have
the final say, but you sound as if you
might make my short list of candidates."

"Not to make you mad or anything and
lose my chance at this job; but don't you
think you should know more about me?"

This Little Girl had a Little Curl

S. G. Lee

"I am a very good judge of character. That's why my employer trusts me in this manner," stated the man with an almost mesmerizing voice. Sarah felt herself believing every word he said.

"Wow, you must be in a prestigious job," replied Sarah without thinking again.

"The only possible drawback to your employment might be your tendency to forthcoming with your thoughts. Do you do this often Miss?"

"Miss Sarah Dexler, and no I don't usually blurt out everything. There is simply something about you."

Sarah realized her blunder. "Sorry I'm doing it again I don't know what has come over me. I promise I'm not typically like this and would guard myself with your employer."

"Never fear Miss Dexler. I'm a good judge of character and you seem to be

S. G. Lee

nice and kind. My employer needs kindness, and someone who will listen most of all. You said you do that with strangers. You listen and help others, so that makes you a candidate we simply must see."

The man suddenly sounded very interested and in the next second, he surprised Sarah with, "So would you be available for an interview tomorrow at 3 PM?"

"Yes, of course," Sarah became tentative. "I guess I could."

"Obviously given the generalities of our ad some applicants have been taken back and would like assurances of our trust worthiness. My employer, though he wishes to remain anonymous until the candidates are found, will be quite happy to provide references for himself.

Confidentiality agreements are signed as well. These, of course, will be provided at

S. G. Lee

the interview stage. Interviews will be conducted at our temporary office at 1000 Park Street. We look forward to seeing you their Miss Dexler. Goodbye," the man ended the call abruptly.

Sarah closed her cell phone and thought... how strange this man appeared so mesmerizing on the phone He even seemed to snatch thoughts from her head. It was all a bit odd. Then as she thought some more, she realized even stranger he had forgotten to share his name. Had she distracted the poor man? Why had he forgotten to share his name? His English upper crust accent sounded so prim, proper and professional it seemed even peculiar to her now that he did not reveal his name. Still, she hoped this job would pan out or in a few days she'd be begging on the street corner.

~0~

S. G. Lee

Chapter 2 - Venimus, Vidimus, Vicimus

Sarah was in a hurry. She tried on

every outfit she owned for this interview.
Most of her wardrobe now lay strewn
across her bed or floor. She finally settled
on this black pantsuit. The tailored jacket
was flattering and her pants that went
with the jacket sculpted her rear end. Not
that was necessary in an interview but it
gave her a lift. She felt like a model in
this outfit. A tall shapely model, because
of these four-inch heels on her black
sandals. They had cost her quite a fortune
when she was pulling in a pay cheque, but
they were worth every penny. Sarah felt
beautiful and hope her confidence would
translate into a job. She really needed this
job.

This Little Girl had a Little Curl

S. G. Lee

She entered the door at one thousand Park
Street. The building was one of those
non-descript glass buildings without
about forty floors. She entered the
building and realized the man on the
phone had not given her the office
number only the building number address.
Without the office number she was lost.
She could take the elevator but to where?

Sarah was in near tears thinking maybe
the whole conversation with that man was
a joke, a terrible joke on her. She spent
her last five dollars to take a cab, so she
wouldn't be late. She was lost…. the job
was lost. Oh no even worse she'd be out
on the street in a few days.

No, she couldn't let that happen. She had
told the man on the phone she was good
with people. That she could charm total
strangers into telling their stories, so here
was the time to prove it. She'd find the
office. It might take a little talking; asking
people questions that would lead to the
office number. But surely being late
would be excused when he realized he

This Little Girl had a Little Curl

S. G. Lee

forgot to tell her the office number. Sarah began by talking to the receptionist at the desk in the hallway. She approached the young woman and she was almost taken aback. The receptionist appeared gorgeous her hair a beautiful honey blonde and cascading down in corkscrew ringlets. The receptionist's bright blue eyes were like diamonds and red lipstick finished the face that could launch a thousand ships. She was dressed in a very tight red dress. It didn't seem quite appropriate for the office, but who was Sarah to judge? Sarah couldn't help but wonder if this was the type of beauty that they hired here if so, she was in trouble. She couldn't compete with someone so incredibly lovely, or wear those oh so revealing clothes.

"Hi, my name is Sarah. I have a little problem I'm hoping that someone as knowledgeable and as intelligent as you are, could help me with," Sarah began.

"That's so flattering you think I can help you. People tend to treat me like a bit of

an airhead because I'm a receptionist it's
my job to assist people. I guess my
parents didn't do me any favours by
naming me Brandy," babbled Brandy
breathlessly while snapping her gum.

"Oh, your name is Brandy? You know,
some say Brandy is better than fine
wine," Sarah piled on the charm.

"I'm not... you know.... so, if ...you
know if that's what this is all about you
can stop right there. Nothing against your
preferences, but I'm seeing a guy,"
replied Brandy awkwardly
misunderstanding.

"Oh no....no .... Really, there's nothing
to worry about. I am straight too. I'm here
trying to get a job. You see, I applied for
this job, but the man on the phone forgot
to tell me the office number where the
interview is," explained Sarah.

"That's difficult because there's tons of
offices in this building. Do you know
what the guy looks like?" asked Brandy

This Little Girl had a Little Curl

S. G. Lee

looking at her red painted fingernails and sliding a nail file over them.

"Sadly no, you see I talked to the man on the phone. He had an upper crust British accent though. Does that help you identify him for me?" begged Sarah.

"Oh, you are so in luck today." Brandy replied, "We have only one guy who talks like that here. Mr. Poundstone. He's conducting interviews today too so he is probably your man."

"Oh, thank you so much Brandy, you don't know how much this means to me. Oh, wait a minute I have a coupon for a free coffee, here this for you," answered Sarah digging the coupon out of her purse.

"But if you're looking for a job you must need the coupon."

"I wanted to let you know how much I truly appreciated your help," Sarah insisted sincerely.

This Little Girl had a Little Curl

S. G. Lee

"You are a really nice person Sarah; I hope you get the job. Maybe we can share a coffee break when you do. You know... if you end up working in this building. Now the office number for Mr. Poundstone is 304. And just because I want you to get the job, if anyone asks for the number because he forgot to tell them I won't tell them," Brandy insisted winking.

"Oh no, that wouldn't be right," asserted Sarah, although delighted. "If they ask please tell them. If this job is meant to be, I'll get the position."

"Did anyone ever tell you Sarah, you're too nice for your own good?" asked Brandy, as Sarah walked towards the elevator.

"Yes, people do say I'm too nice. But I can't be any different than I am," Sarah answered turning back to Brandy. Sarah then entered the elevator waving goodbye to Brandy.

This Little Girl had a Little Curl

S. G. Lee

The elevator reached the third floor and
Sarah glanced at her watch, she realized
she wasn't late at all; it was only 2:55
p.m. She was early, how amazing. She
stepped off the elevator to find a room
full of women of varying ages, shapes,
sizes and colours. Sarah couldn't help but
noticing the other women appeared all
extremely attractive.

Oh, so I'm not the only one up for the job,
Sarah thought as she entered into room. If
she had it her way when she left today,
she'd have the job despite all these
beauties. No second interviews, or third
interview. This wasn't a beauty contest
after all. She would win this job. She was
as sure of it as she was that her name was
Sarah Dexler; Sarah thought proudly as
she remembered the family Dexler motto,
"Venimus, Vidimus, Vicimus". It meant
"We came. We saw. We conquered!

This Little Girl had a Little Curl

S. G. Lee

Sure, her ancestors had blatantly borrowed the saying from Caesar, but it was a good motto to live by and inspired confidence. Of course, if you could use your God-given charm and win the day why shouldn't you? She didn't think you had to use your attitude violently or cruelly, like a sword. A charming disposition worked as well or better than the sword and without drawing blood.

Sarah steeled herself marched up to the receptionist and confidently said… "Sarah Dexler, I have an appointment at 3 p.m."

"Yes, Miss Dexler, your name is here. Please, take a seat. Mr. Poundstone will be with you momentarily," the receptionist said hardly looking up from her desk.

The office door opened and a congenial looking man came out. If Sarah were to describe him, she would describe a dignified Santa, maybe an Edmund Gwenn style from Miracle on 34th Street.

This Little Girl had a Little Curl

S. G. Lee

His appearance was stylish and dignified,
like an upper crust Englishman, suiting
his voice on the phone. His suit was a
gray Burbury throughout. His hair
trimmed short and he had a tiny white
moustache. He seemed to be in his sixties.

"Miss Dexler, I presume?" Mr.
Poundstone looked straight into her eyes.

"Yes, I am Sarah Dexler," Sarah stood
tall and threw her shoulders back, holding
out her right hand which he clasped
firmly with both his hands.

"I am Harry Poundstone. What a great
pleasure to meet you in person. I worried
I had steered you wrong as I remembered
not giving you my office number. But I
can see you are as good as your word and
you obviously found me. Please do come
into my office so we can discuss the
particulars of this job and your
qualifications for the position," said Mr.
Poundstone, while still smiling.

This Little Girl had a Little Curl

S. G. Lee

"Certainly, I would be happy to Mr. Poundstone," replied Sarah while stepping into his office.

Mr. Poundstone continued to smile even more broadly, almost unnerving Sarah.

"Miss Dexler, I didn't want to tell you in front of all those job applicants, but we decided to give the job to you," Mr. Poundstone declared with great flourish.

"Me? But you didn't even interview me? Are you sure?" Sarah was shocked but rambled on, "Well, of course if you are sure or you wouldn't have said so. Oh, I'm doing it again. There's just something about you that makes me do that. Oh, did I just say that aloud. Sorry," Sarah, blurted, and then blanching, asked… "Do you still want me for this job?"

Mr. Poundstone couldn't help but be amused.

"Miss Dexler. Or may I call you Sarah?" asked Mr. Poundstone.

This Little Girl had a Little Curl

S. G. Lee

"Please do, Mr. Poundstone," Sarah replied

"Please, would you care for some of this freshly steeped tea? Or, would you prefer coffee?"

"Yes, I would love some tea, two sugars and a little cream please," answered Sarah

"Huh, exactly how I made your tea. Most people prefer milk rather than cream. It's Harry actually. Please call me Harry. Mr. Poundstone is so formal," expressed Mr. Poundstone, and then followed quickly with, "Where do you see yourself in five years Sarah?"

"Well I could lie and say I see myself in an executive position but the truth is I want it all. I want a career that fulfills me and I want children and a husband."

What a weird start to the interview, Sarah thought. Why, oh why, had she mentioned she desired a husband and children? Was she sharing things that were too personal? Were there bounds

S. G. Lee

that were being overstepped? There had to be something in the tea, a truth serum perhaps? What was it about this man? What caused her to blurt out exactly what she was thinking? What possessed her? He would think she didn't want this job and would leave at the first opportunity.

Sarah continued thinking knowing she needed to reassure Mr. Poundstone her priority was this job. "Oh, but I can tell you I see this position as a real opportunity to gain experience…"

Sarah wanted to continue but could not. She could not hide her suspicion and was suddenly compelled to ask "Did you put something in my tea to make me tell you only the truth and in fact say everything I am thinking?"

"No, but I'm finding this conversation absolutely amazing," Mr. Poundstone replied smiling and Sarah suddenly found his constant smile slightly creepy.

This Little Girl had a Little Curl

S. G. Lee

"What's amazing?" asked Sarah bravely, "That for some unknown reason, I believe that you have the power to mesmerize and draw words from people?"

Mr. Poundstone just grinned even wider like he knew a secret, a secret that Sarah didn't know but needed to uncover.

"Holy cow, I can't believe it. That's it isn't it? You have some unusual power and I can feel it. You can get people to tell you what they are really thinking," Sarah exclaimed while truly surprised by her own words.

Mr. Poundstone reached into his jacket and pulled out a pocket watch which he proceeded to open. The watch was gold and attached to a long chain.

"This is truly amazing. I have never encountered anyone with such acuity. Two minutes, that's all it took for you to perceive the unusualness of our conversation. Most people who have any ability require days to detect my power,

S. G. Lee

but you became aware it within less than two minutes."

Mr. Poundstone's next words shook Sarah to her core.

"He said you would be the one. I heard glimmers of your abilities in our phone conversation, but he was absolutely right. This is so truly, truly astonishing." His voice became high pitched with excitement, almost maniacal, and belied the dignified image he had shown earlier.

"Uh...Ok... I'm going to leave now." Sarah had become slightly frightened of the nature of Mr. Poundstone's behaviour, "But no harm, no foul."

"Oh, please my dear lady, do not be frightened of me or my employer. I know I am not explaining this well but we've looked so long for one like you..."

Sarah found this last statement even more disturbing.

This Little Girl had a Little Curl

S. G. Lee

"That's okay but I think I'm going,"
Sarah replied reaching for the door
handle.

"Please Sarah, I beg of you, give myself
and my employer another chance.
Wouldn't you like to find out the real
reason why we chose you? Don't you
want to be aware of the untapped power
that you alone hold?" Mr. Poundstone
begged again with his voice once again
deep and compelling.

"No! If you have some deep dark plan for
me you can just forget it," Sarah turned
the doorknob and continued to try to
make her escape. "Quit trying to compel
me. I know you're doing it. I don't
understand how you're doing it but I can
grasp you are doing it."

"I apologize but it is sometimes hard to
turn off one's gift," Mr. Poundstone
stated calmly. "Did you ever wonder
where you came from? Who your parents

S. G. Lee

were? Who were your other relatives? Sarah, we know you started life in Foster Care."

Sarah retorted, her fear changing to anger, "How dare you? That…has nothing to do with a job interview. How did you access those records? You didn't even have my social security number?"

"I know a lot about you Sarah Marie Dexler. For instance, I know your real last name is Maidenstone. The Dexler's adopted you when you were four years old, and isn't the truth, before they adopted you, you did not speak."

Tears formed in Sarah's eyes and her anger grew. "I'm going to report you and your agency to the Better Business Bureau, the police, and a lawyer; in that order. You have absolutely no right to snoop into my life."

"I've hurt you and that was not my intention. I know your grandfather and if

This Little Girl had a Little Curl

S. G. Lee

he could have found you, believe me, he would have. He would have taken you from that foster home. It really wasn't his fault. Your parents disappeared without a trace in America. They were British citizens, born in Coventry, England. Your grandfather was not even aware of your existence. He found out six years after they had perished, that his beloved daughter and her husband had died. He went crazy with grief, and we despaired that we would never get him back again. But he did recover over time, albeit never to the same contented state. But he discovered by searching through numerous records that she had a given birth to daughter; that daughter was you. And he asked me to find you."

"So, this was all a ruse? There is no job? Of course, there is no job! Why…why am I still here? Did you hypnotize me? All this because you say my so-called grandfather wants to meet me?"

Sarah was going to tell Mr. Poundstone, he was a very bad man, but he cut her off.

This Little Girl had a Little Curl

S. G. Lee

"Needless to say, your grandfather waits anxiously to meet you in person. Moreover, he is well aware of your current predicament and has an exciting job…mmm…opportunity, he wants to discuss with you. But I'm afraid, I have been forbidden to share the particulars with you at this time."

"I don't know about this. None of this seems right. A strange man tells me I possess a grandfather, a grandfather who didn't come forward to me when I was young? And now he wants to meet me? And then he expects me to just take a job from him?" Sarah composed herself. "I just don't know. This is a lot to take in."

"Think about meeting him. Please," begged Mr. Poundstone. "You won't be sorry if you agree to this meeting. Your grandfather is a wonderful and wise man."

Mr. Poundstone couldn't help but smile slightly at the corners of his mouth but he

kept his eyes penetratingly fixed on
Sarah's own deep gaze.

Mr. Poundstone mused out loud, "What if
I go tell the other applicants to come back
another day for an interview for the actual
job, I brought them here for?"

"Please don't keep them waiting. If
there's an honest job for them at least
interview them. I can wait in the lobby,"
Sarah replied, relieved the other women
were not being duped. And, she realized,
she was not surprised Mr. Poundstone
sensed her concern for those who
unwittingly helped him in his duplicity.

"No, please, I have another office here,
I'll interview them there. Just please…
take your time. Have a cup from the
freshly steeped pot of tea and I hope
you'll make the decision you will see your
grandfather," begged Mr. Poundstone
while leaving the room.

This Little Girl had a Little Curl

S. G. Lee

"Fine… I'll wait…but I'm still not sure," Sarah exclaimed with exasperation to Mr. Poundstone's departing back.

In a room next to the one where Sarah waited, a man watched through a two-way mirror. From his side he could see her seated in the chair in front of Mr. Poundstone's desk. The man was mature, his hair greyed at the temples and sides but with a shock of black hair that ran through the middle of his thick mane. He was tall and stood over six feet, possibly as tall as six feet six inches. He was broad shouldered and lean looking while surprisingly well muscled.

He looked to be about sixty, or maybe sixty-five years of age, but he moved with the ease of a much younger man; as he paced back and forth with his focus on the mirror. Dressed in a suit tailored perfectly for him, he exuded confidence. He seemed mesmerized as he intently surveyed Sarah though the glass. He appeared somewhat amused, that he knew

This Little Girl had a Little Curl

S. G. Lee

Sarah was unaware that she was being watched.

The door opened to the chamber, where the tall man stood watching. Mr. Poundstone walked into this room with a much different demeanour, than the one he displayed when he had earlier greeted Sarah. Mr. Poundstone lowered his head and seemed hesitant to approach. He moved forward cautiously as if any misstep could trigger an explosion like bomb in a minefield.

"This is the one? This is she? No mistakes this time?" the man demanded harshly while taking a seat.

"Yes, my lord, this is the one. I promise there has been no mistake this time. As promised, I supervised this one myself," replied Harry Poundstone, his voice very subservient.

"Good. What did you tell her?" asked the tall man.

This Little Girl had a Little Curl

S. G. Lee

"I told her you were her grandfather and you kept looking for her, just as we rehearsed. I told her you grieved for her mother and searched for her as soon as you knew she existed."

"Marvellous Harry, a falsehood that is so close to the truth is always so much more believable," said the tall man pleased.

"I hope this makes up for the failure of my operatives last year?" asked Mr. Poundstone meekly, obviously seeking approval.

"It does if this is truly her!" replied the tall man, Sarah's grandfather. "Does she show any essence of her mother? Or is she only tainted by him?"

"The taint is there my lord. I am sorry my lord…but if there is any of you in her I see none of it." Mr. Poundstone cowered as he said this, expecting to be castigated. He was all too familiar with the consequences of failing to please his master, through words or deeds.

This Little Girl had a Little Curl

S. G. Lee

"I'm sure you are mistaken. She is of my line after all. I think I have seen glimmers of myself. If not, while then it is decided," pronounced the tall man, dismissing the matter.

"Must we, Lord Eccklestone?" Mr. Poundstone dared to ask.

"Are you questioning me? You dare to question me?" demanded Lord Eccklestone.

The tall man's face turned purple and his rage consumed the entire room. To Mr. Poundstone it seemed as if darkness surrounded him, only broken by the fierce glower of his lord's penetrating eyes.

"No sir, of course I am not questioning you. I would never dare," replied Mr. Poundstone submissively, mollifying him.

The pair continued to observe Sarah unbeknownst as she waited anxiously in the adjoining office. Sarah found herself consumed by many thoughts that raged incessantly through her mind. A

This Little Girl had a Little Curl

S. G. Lee

grandfather searched for her? She had family, but a family that took this long to come forward? Could the story really be true, that he just couldn't find her until now? What an incredible story, much like a fairy tale. Those usually didn't end well.

What of Mr. Poundstone? He was to say, a very unusual man. True. Still there was something not quite right about him. At times she felt he seemed a jovial Santa Claus, but could it just be a false persona? If Mr. Poundstone wasn't who he pretended to be, then how could she trust that this man would put her in touch with her real grandfather?

Maybe she should just leave. But if he did know her grandfather and he could put them in touch maybe she should give him a chance? Mr. Poundstone was distinctly odd, almost chilling with this strange power he had. He actually eluded she might have one as well, a power. That, of course, was ludicrous stuff and definitely nonsense. Then there was the fact that he had snooped in her personal business.

This Little Girl had a Little Curl

S. G. Lee

He had found out facts that she had never told anyone. It was like stripping her bare. She wasn't happy about that. What did she really know about these people? Only what he, Mr. Poundstone, had told her? She had already found out he had a power that made people believe and do what he wanted them to do; so why was she sitting here waiting for Mr. Poundstone? Or waiting for this man that claimed to be her grandfather?

How trustworthy was a man who manipulated people with some spellbinding ability and made them do what he wanted? She suddenly became afraid again. There was something definitely not quite right about this and she felt it down to her very bones. If her grandfather had truly wanted to meet her there was no need for this deception. And why were so many people interested in a companion job? And why were they all attractive young women? These thoughts had just entered her mind. What had prevented these thoughts before? There

This Little Girl had a Little Curl

S. G. Lee

were just too many things that didn't add up here.

So, what was wrong with her that she hadn't bolted all ready? Mr. Poundstone had used some of his power on her; that was the only explanation. The power that she was starting to believe he really possessed. Was it some kind of hypnotism? She was leaving now, this very minute, before something bad happened.

Just then the door opened to Mr. Poundstone's office and Sarah watched a man enter. He was tall, dark haired and mysterious looking. His hair was raven coloured, his eyes blue and piercing and his gaze centered on her. He was muscular and dynamic looking and he just seemed to be one of those people that drew upon all eyes upon them. Simply put, this man radiated power and one could not help but put all focus on his presence.

This Little Girl had a Little Curl

S. G. Lee

It was odd though when he came in the room it was like time stopped. She looked at the clock on Mr. Poundstone's desk and realized that it wasn't as if time had stopped, it actually had. The circumstances were getting more bizarre for Sarah the more she went along today. Had she really gotten up this morning, or was this all a dream?

As she gazed upon the man, he spoke…, "Come on then, we have to leave now," he requested of her.

"We…we have to leave now? I don't think so. I have had enough with your weird people. I don't understand what is going on but I'm not going anywhere with you," Sarah reacted, annoyed.

"I don't have time to explain this to you. You deserve explanations, but we definitely don't have time. This only lasts so long. It takes so much power and energy, that it's very draining. We have to go now. We have to be away from here before I lose my power, which could be at any moment," said the man urgently.

"Again, with the power? I'm getting out of here but not with you. I don't want to see any of you weirdoes ever again," replied a disgusted Sarah.

"Fine, just come with me now. Let us leave and get away now!" pleaded the man.

"I don't even know your name. I'm not going anywhere with you. I'm going home," Sarah's anger grew and she was very determined to get away.

"They know where you live. They want something from that you don't even know you have," The man then said cryptically, "They are not nice people. You don't understand the lengths they will go to or the things they have done."

"Enlighten me then," Sarah demanded.

"I told you there isn't time. Please I beg of you, come with me now."

This Little Girl had a Little Curl

S. G. Lee

"And you are? And I should come with you because? I'm tired of this. You and all these other people just come into my life making impossible demands."

"You can do things that aren't possible or real. Oh…just go away and leave me be"

"My name is Demetrious Blackstone and we are sort of related. I promise I'll tell you more once we are away from here." Then seeing her face, he added, "I know all of this is difficult for you to understand and I will explain when we get away from here but we must get away now."

He then took Sarah's hands and pulled her to her feet. Moments later they are out the door. Sarah wasn't sure how they got to the waiting room so fast. Or even why she didn't fight back and resist but here they were. In this room Sarah saw all the people she had before, but there was still not a ripple of movement. Time was stood

This Little Girl had a Little Curl

S. G. Lee

still and it seemed as if only they moved through it. It was all so unreal and peculiar. Demetrious opened the front door of the building and they passed out into the street. Cars were stilled, not moving at all as time and space stood still. Not even a breeze blowing. Sarah was amazed and frightened all at once. What was going on?

"How long will this last?" asked Sarah.

"Not much longer. We must be long away when it stops. He will know it was I and come after us," warned Demetrious ominously.

"I'm going home," insisted Sarah, afraid but determined.

"Do you not understand their fierce abilities? Don't you understand the danger you are in?" Demetrious asked, staring at Sarah. Then slowly searching her face he sighed and said... "No, of course you don't. How could you know that there is a great peril to you here? This

This Little Girl had a Little Curl

S. G. Lee

man, who is your grandfather, is kin to a vampire. He finds power from innocents, from those who are not aware of their power. He then takes their power from them and not in a pleasant way, I assure you. What he leaves of these people is a nothing but a zombie like creature; a creature that only exists to obey their lord and master; your grandfather. Or, if he chooses, they are left a broken soul whose mind is completely stripped, so they function only on a basic primitive level."

Sarah did not believe her ears and denied everything the man was saying.

"This is all so utterly ridiculous. I'm starting to think that Mr. Poundstone drugged me, so I'm very glad you got me out of there Mr. Blackstone. I thank you for everything you have done so far but I'm going home. Now!"

"I am sorry I have to do this to you. I wouldn't if it wasn't necessary to protect you. But you don't even realize the great power you hold and how and what could

S. G. Lee

happen if someone as unscrupulous as your Grandfather got a hold of that power."

Demetrious gripped the back of her neck gently with the fullness of his hand and Sarah began to feel light headed. Slowly the world seemed to fade away and she fell into a deep unconsciousness.

~0~

S. G. Lee

Excerpt from Dreams Can Kill~ Chapter 1- Survival

T he rain pelted down on me, as I struggled to come to my senses. My head felt like it had split in two, as if little lumberjacks had taken up residence. I opened one eye. The world spun sideways like a ride at the fair. I tried shutting one eye, then the other. I nearly fell back to sleep. I opened my eyes again, fighting the sleep which wanted to overtake me. I shuttered my eyes again, as my stomach protested. My whole body manipulated, bruised, bent and broken like some old rag doll discarded.

This Little Girl Had A Little Curl
S. G. Lee

Sleep...sleep would solve my problems, my brain protested. No! I had a reason I needed to stay awake and alert...A little sleep, a part of me protested again. No, I must stay conscious. But I remained so tired. I dragged myself across the pebbled ground. My right leg stuck out at an impossible angle, obviously broken. I saw by lifting my head slightly and turning it that there appeared to be a road up ahead. I had to get to the road. If I dragged myself that far, surely, I would be rescued?

But it was oh so hard, to drag yourself backwards, when you couldn't perceive where you were going. Oh no, what if he came back. He would finish me off...finish what he had started.

He who? Who was this person, who left me to die? Why couldn't I remember? Don't panic... the thing to do is right now is to reach help; then and only then would I be safe. I caressed large pieces of gravel which cut into the back of my head. I sensed I was close to the road. I reached

out with my good hand and touched a
paved surface.

I knew I didn't have much strength left. I
experienced the energy drain quickly
leaving my body. I tried to fight the drain,
but the world faded to black.

~0~

Chapter 2- Time Flies When You're Having Fun

I opened my eyes slowly. A tube appeared to have been inserted in my arm, feeding me intravenously, another tube down my throat as well. The lumberjacks in my head had been replaced by a dull achy sensation, as if I wasn't quite there. I suffered from weakness all over, but my body didn't have the same sensation, as when I had blacked out on the road. My leg felt whole again and yet my leg didn't appear to be in a cast, or slung up on a tripod. How much time had passed? This definitely looked like a hospital room. The walls were pale white and I lay in a single bed. I rested in a private room how about that?

A nurse in a white cap entered the room. She grabbed my wrist and she proceeded to take my pulse. Alarmed, she stared straight into my face, "Well! Look who is awake. Welcome back to the real world," she proclaimed.

I tried to speak and realized the tube in my throat prevented that. Why was a tube in my throat I wondered? How long I been here? I assumed I looked scared because the nurse explained in a soft voice, "There, there honey, you take deep breaths, easy now."

"Why don't I go get the doctor? He can come and have a look at you and remove the tube from your throat."

I tried to nod my head in agreement but my head moved like lead. It seemed like eons before a man in a white doctor's coat appeared at my bedside. He appeared tall and lanky; with dark curly brown hair and warm deep blue eyes. Without any preamble he announced, "We will now remove this tube. Take a big breath now."

The tube came out as I gagged. Now I could ask the questions which plagued me.

"How did I get here? And, where am I?" I tried to ask, croaking out the words, as if my voice hadn't been used in a while.

"Speak slowly. Here, have sips of water," answered the doctor.

"How did I get here?" I repeated, sure that I had been speaking clearer because I had taken a sip of water.

"I don't know who found you, but an ambulance brought you here in critical condition. You had a broken leg, some broken ribs, and a fractured skull."

"I came here in critical condition? So, I've been here awhile?" I asked shocked.

"Yes, you've been here awhile. You were at a different hospital first. You are in Andrews' clinic now."

"Your condition appeared to be perilous there for some time. They lost you twice. We had placed you in a coma to let your brain swelling go away. Then we didn't know if you would ever come out of the coma."

He continued to explain like he couldn't quite find the words. But why would a doctor have trouble explaining a medical condition?

"I guess time flies when you have fun," I stated flippantly, hiding fear I didn't quite understand and becoming puzzled.

Why did he say first they then we? Hadn't he been there?

"I would like to examine you to see how you're doing now and get an update on your condition."

"I'm good. As you can see," I answered in response.

"I don't know if you even realize, but your speech isn't as clear as you think. You're slurring your words," he stated, "I'm sure the words will come easier in time, but I'd like to check your reaction time and some other physical reactions."

What could he be talking about? I wasn't slurring my words. Was I?

The doctor began his examination. A flashlight flashed deep into my eyes. I blinked in response, as the light, so bright, made my eyes hurt. His response seemed to be to write down something on the chart, and pick up my wrist to take my pulse and blood pressure. He then listened to my chest with his stethoscope.

I moved my head and tried to sit up, but the effort zapped all my remaining strength. I surprised myself at how I felt like a newborn baby. He continued his examination. I grew tired but fought the sensation. If I closed my eyes for a moment, would the feeling would go away? I closed my eyelids and fell fast asleep.

I ran over hills. The night appeared so dark, and ink black; I could barely view two feet in front of me. My feet stumbled, as I tried to see the uneven ground in front of me. My palms clenched with sweat, as my heart pounded like the organ would jump out of my chest. I turned around, my eyes darting from side to side searching for my pursuer. No sign, but I knew he wasn't far behind.

My hair in a high ponytail, whipped at my face, as I picked up the pace in my flight. He seemed close enough, that I had the sensation of his breath on my neck… so close he might reach out and touch me. I turned again to see if I could glimpse him near, and I saw a man. But what puzzled me was what materialized in the man's face. Where his face should be, a gaping black hole yawned.

How could this be? The thought plagued me only for moment, as fear gripped me and survival instinct kicked in. Realizing if he caught me, I would be killed, I ran stumbling over rock and uneven ground. When the inevitable happened, I tripped falling to my knees. He had me. There was no escape from my fate. I would die now. I struggled as he grabbed my left wrist twisting my arm.

This appeared no dream, I might awake from; he had me now and he would kill me. I twisted slightly trying to free my wrist but he grabbed my other wrist and shook me slightly saying…, "Quite a dream you were having, but a dream none the less. Nothing can harm you now."

I stared into his face and slowly his look changed, from the faceless man, to another face entirely. This wasn't the man in my visions; the demon in my nightmare. I knew in my heart this remained an altogether different kind of man.

This face with smiling blue eyes radiated warmth, and kindness. His face stayed gentle, not violent. I had been dreaming and had mistaken his touch for the man in my dreams. I flushed with embarrassment.

"You are quite awake now? I won't harm you. Now, do remember me?"

I stared at him, slowly waking up, and realizing where I was.

"I'm your Doctor, Doctor Andrews, at your service, my lady. We met before when you awoke from your coma," he continued speaking softly, and gently, bowing at the waist and smiling.

Shouldn't I have recognized him immediately? Heat rushed to my cheeks, as I turned red in embarrassment.

This Little Girl Had A Little Curl
S. G. Lee

I was a fish out of water. I didn't like the way I reacted; like something had happened and all was a secret to me. I liked to be in charge of my life every aspect, and right now it seemed like I appeared in charge of nothing.

"How long have I been here?" I whispered, trying to speak louder.

"I would have said it's a lot longer, than you think," he replied cryptically.

"Do you always answer a question with a question? I want an answer for my query," I demanded angrily.

"What do you remember?"

"I believe I asked you to stop making this an interrogation. If you must know, I remember waking up a little while ago the nurse came in and then you came a little later," I answered exasperated, wondering what could be wrong with me. I didn't get angry so easily. Did I? Why did I behave this way? Everything he said seemed to make me angry.

This Little Girl Had A Little Curl
S. G. Lee

"Your little while ago was two days
ago...," he explained, breaking off as if
afraid to say more.

"But that's impossible..."

"You fell into a restorative sleep. It is not
uncommon for patients who have been in
a coma to do so."

"Two days? I slept for two days?" I
commented incredulously.

"Yes," Doctor. Andrews stated.

"How long was I in a coma?" I asked
worried to hear what he might say.

"What month do you remember?"

"You have to be in charge, don't you?
Questions! Questions!" I replied, delaying
the answer. I was suddenly afraid that I'd
been in this coma far longer than I
realized, and grew angrier.

"I know you're scared. Are you sure you
want to know? The information can
wait," he insisted.

This Little Girl Had A Little Curl
S. G. Lee

"I'm not scared," I lied with false bravado, "I remember quite clearly the month is March."

"It is the eleventh of September nineteen hundred and seventy-one. Do you remember what happened the day of the accident?" he asked.

"That's not possible. I can't have been in a coma for six months. Why do you lie to me?" I spat at him.

"I know it's hard to assimilate but time has passed and it is September," he insisted softly, but firmly.

"Why do you persist in a lie? What do you have to gain with this preposterous story?" I demanded; still not ready to believe this.

"Exactly what do I have to gain? Sharron, I'm not lying to you," he stated sadly.

Until that moment I hadn't given any thought to my name, but as Doctor

This Little Girl Had A Little Curl
S. G. Lee

Andrews called me Sharron, I realized I
wasn't even sure if that was my name. I
didn't have a clue what my name was.
My name might be Sharron, but I didn't
recall the name. My name could be Mary,
or Angela, or any other name in the
world. If I had a surname, I couldn't
remember it either. A huge blank spot
stood where any recollection should be.

How could my last memory be of March,
but I still had no recollection of my name,
er names? This was normal after a long
coma. I decided.

Perhaps my memory had been so
underused, and only had temporary gaps?
Or I was hungry? Yes, it had to be one of
those things. A temporary aberration of
the mind... No need for me to worry. No,
need to share any such information.

My memory was only hiatus. That had to
be the answer. Give it a few days and my
memory would all come back. There was
no need to tell the doctor, especially since

my recollections would all come back. Absolutely not, I reasoned.

After all what good would it do to tell him? He'd look at me either with sympathy, or call in a shrink. I wanted none of the sympathy, and whispered glances which would follow. So, I had a few memory gaps, nothing to worry about. It was perfectly normal after a coma, I reassured myself.

"What will you do with all this information Sharron?" asked Doctor Andrews suddenly concerned.

"I must admit the information was a bit of a shock to find the month was September and not March, but I'm over the surprise. "I'm hungry what does it take to get food around here?'' I demanded, quickly changing the subject. Besides I was ravenous.

"I think you can start some light foods, some soft foods, Jell-O soup etc.," Doctor

Andrews spouted. Turning to the nurse he commanded, "Nurse get a light meal for my patient."

"Certainly Doctor," the nurse replied, coming into the room rather quickly, at his summons.

Just when I thought I had successfully gotten rid of the doctor, he turned around and said... "I know you are rather tired and hungry right now, but I'm sure you to want to discuss these revelations later today."

How could I get him to change his track? I didn't want to discuss my memory loss with anyone. I wasn't ready for anyone to find out I didn't know who I was. If I told him, would he treat me like a mental patient?

No, I wasn't going to tell him, or anyone. I needed to fake what I remembered. They'd never know, I couldn't remember.

I would then have the time to accept this myself, and hopefully everything would come back. No one would ever have to know.

Wait a minute, did he know, I didn't remember? He talked about the fact I'd been in a coma, but had he given me any knowing glances? I gave him a sideways glance. Deciding he didn't have a clue about my memory problem. I plotted to keep it that way.

"There is not a lot to talk about; but if you want to, we can discuss my medical condition we can get to that later," I replied, hoping he would take my response as an agreement and leave.

Luckily for me he took the hint. Maybe he would even forget to come back and discuss this later? No, I hoped for too much, but he did look convinced that I'd talk to him later. Good then he'd go away.

This Little Girl Had A Little Curl
S. G. Lee

"I will return later, Sharron."

He then left taking his questions with
him. I breathed a sigh of relief. Now
alone with my thoughts, surely, I'd
conjure up a memory or two. First, I
would eat and refuel. That would help the
memories, as well as my stomach.

I stared at the food the nurse had brought
in. I'm starving to death and the nurse
gave me not enough food to feed a rabbit?
I tried to pick up the spoon and found my
hand wouldn't cooperate.

"Would you like some help?" the nurse
asked kindly.

"I can do it myself," I responded
stubbornly.

Although I had found it difficult to raise my hand to my mouth, that soon became easier. I found by clamping my hand around the spoon I could manage to feed myself. It was then I realized how much work I had ahead of me. The nurse watched, so I smiled at her like everything was fine. She smiled back and left.

I soon made short work of the food and wanted to move on to the therapy I recognized I needed. I would set the memories, or lack of them aside, and working on building up the muscle tone and abilities I'd lost. When the body restored itself, I would begin to remember. I understood without being told, that I had to begin like a baby to exercise my limbs and I wanted to start immediately. Let's be honest. I realized I could remember something. I grasped now that I was an impatient person, at least when it came to doing things I had to be doing. I called the nurse on the call bell to ask about therapy and exercises.

This Little Girl Had A Little Curl
S. G. Lee

"Yes?" I heard a disembodied voice
somewhere over my head say.
Momentarily puzzled, I then realized the
voice came from an intercom.

"Sorry to bother you but when can I start
therapy? I need to get my limbs moving,"
I explained.

"Dear, you are barely out of coma. I'm
sure your doctor would want you to build
up your energy first. Or wait at least until
you started solid foods."

She sounded surprised and had a hint of
censor in her voice. No support there. I
wanted those six months back, but clearly
that wasn't going to happen. Move on, I
told myself. I'd wasted six months
sleeping, time to fight back and get back
into fighting form as they said. But who
had said that?

I somehow knew I was a fighter. I'd have
to do everything myself; something I
knew I always did. But how did I know
that?

This Little Girl Had A Little Curl
S. G. Lee

I thought about what would work, and
what limbs need to work. My hands
needed to a work out. Okay, they need to
grip. How do you make hands stronger?

You give them something to grip.
Squeezing something soft, medium soft,
would work. Where to get something to
work my grasp? I couldn't even get out of
bed. My limbs were useless, absolutely
useless.

My hand shook in weakness, from forcing
the stupid thing, to do its job and feed me.

All of this began to feel hopeless. No, I
wasn't some stupid helpless female. I had
to figure out a plan. You're on your own,
I told myself, nothing new. You can
overcome any odds. Think, Sharron,
think!

How about some finger exercises? Slowly
working each finger, and then in tandem,
I would get back movement. I began the
exercise I devised. It sounded so simple
when I had thought of how to exercise the
hand, but painful and tiring. Work

through the pain, I told myself. Isn't that what you've always heard?

I forced myself to do the exercises for what seemed like hours, until I couldn't take the pain any more. Then I decided to exercise my arms. Gripping well enough to pull myself up to the bar over my bed, I reached I'm with my right hand to grab the pole. My fingers won't cooperate. My fingers are weakened and my grip slipped. Damn it! Even simple exercise was impossible.

"Nothing is impossible," a voice spoke loudly in my head. But whose voice did I hear? My memory had fled, if it was ever there. I only comprehended the voice had been someone I loved, and respected. Was this a father, or a father figure? I knew I was bone weary, and a great sea of lethargy stole over me. It would be counterproductive not to take a nap, I reasoned. Surely a short nap would restore my energy and I would begin again.

I closed my eyes soon I began dreaming. At first the dream appeared happy. I viewed myself in a beautiful home and grinning at someone I couldn't see.

I smiled and felt great joy, but the sky grew dark and I found myself outside on a field. The moon overhead slowly covered by clouds, and I grew terrified. Something was wrong. The faceless man chased me once more. I ran over rocks and streams and more rocks. He kept coming and coming. I knew he'd soon be on me. He nearly had me when I willed myself to wake up saying… This is a dream and I want to wake up now.

I awoke gasping for air like I had been running a marathon. A strange man sat by my bed. His hair appeared dark, practically black, greasy, and slicked back. He had black thick glasses that he peered over like they were a prop.

An oversized suit coat in plaid and matching pants completed the picture. Despite his harmless appearance, he struck terror to my heart. What gave me the idea he put on this persona, like a piece of new clothing? I think it was his face which seemed to give it all away, like he tried too hard to portray someone he wasn't.

As I gazed at him, he jumped from the chair he sat and exclaimed… "About damn time you woke up out of the coma Sharron. I thought you laze there forever."

He then continued, as if choosing his words carefully, "Oh Sharron, this is the most wonderful day of my life." Then he pulled me to him, fiercely.

"Let go of me, this instance. Who do you think you are? I said don't touch me! And quit acting and looking around there's no audience for your play," I blurted out, before I stop myself.

This Little Girl Had A Little Curl
S. G. Lee

"Sharron that's not funny. Quit joking. You always had a wicked sense of humour, but I'm not laughing." the man stated, sounding annoyed and grabbing my wrist.

"I said let me go, and I meant every word. Now kindly take your hands off me," I demanded at the top of my lungs, struggling unsuccessfully to free myself of the grip, he now had on my wrist.

Taken back by my yelling, he let me go, but he still continued to treat me, like a bug under a microscope. Suddenly switching gears, his face changed. It was if a curtain went down over his face. He took on a concerned look and then a hurt look. I admit he nearly had me fooled.

I started thinking I had forgotten a boyfriend, but surely, I wouldn't suffer from such bad taste.

He wasn't my type. He seemed quite violent too. I wouldn't have been so foolish to get mixed up with a weirdo like him! Would I?

This Little Girl Had A Little Curl
S. G. Lee

"Sharron quit staring at me that way you're making me uncomfortable. I'm not amused here...Wait a minute you're not kidding. You don't recognize me at all. You don't recognize your fiancé?"

I recognized somehow that he was put on an act. No, I wasn't engaged to him. If I had been it would boggle my mind. He had to be lying, I decided. Why I didn't know, but I knew he lied.

I had no sparks with him. In fact, something about him gave me the creeps. He repulsed me and made my stomach hurt. He certainly didn't sound sincere. He put on an act ... but why? He grabbed my wrists again, once again in a vice grip. I struggled valiantly, but his grip tightened and I couldn't handle his fierce clutch in my weakened stated.

"Let me go you, caveman. I don't know you and what is more, I don't ever want to know you," screamed at him fighting frantically.

This Little Girl Had A Little Curl
S. G. Lee

"Sharron you cut me to the quick. Why do you say such things to me?" he whined, letting go of my wrist, but gripping my arms even tighter.

Maybe it was because of my dream, but suddenly I was terrified. Why did they leave me all alone with this crazy man? Where was everyone else? Couldn't they hear me shouting?

"Let me go. Let me go.... Don't touch me," I yelled at the top of my lungs, and then screamed, hysterically "Help me someone help me."

As I started to pull harder frantically to be free, he stilled held fast. What kind of evil demon had me in his grasp? I tried to bite him, but that was impossible; finally, in the answer to my screams were footsteps running. Seconds later a nurse and Doctor Andrews entered.

This Little Girl Had A Little Curl
S. G. Lee

"Let my patient go immediately. I said let
her go," Doctor Andrews growled,
pulling the man's arms behind his back.

I breathed a sigh of relief. I was safe.
Doctor Andrews had saved me.

"I wasn't hurting her! What kind of a man
do you think I am? Gee, I have more
bruises than her. She acted crazy, so I
grabbed both her arms to calm her," the
man explained, sounding plausible.

Surely Doctor Andrews and the nurse
who followed him in, didn't believe his
act?

"Your technique doesn't seem to have
calmed her, but it certainly frightened
her," Doctor Andrews said, checking my
blood pressure and heart rate.

"You can't tell me what to do. She's my
fiancée I can speak to her anyway I
want," complained the man, loudly.

This Little Girl Had A Little Curl
S. G. Lee

"You've upset my patient. Her blood pressure and heart rate are elevated as well. This is not good for my patient, so I can tell you what to do. What is your name?" demanded Doctor Andrews.

"Titus Brown is my name and Sharron is my fiancée," the man replied a little too quickly.

Doctor Andrews consulted his clipboard. He pointed to it and then announced, "This is the approved register and you're not on the list. Leave now, Mr. Brown, or I'll have security escort you out of the facility."

"I'm not going anywhere. Who do you think you are?"

Mr. Brown showed his true colours, I thought. They would trounce him faster than you could say Jack Robinson.

"Mr. Brown, so far I've been pleasant. The nurse has already called for a security guard. I suggest you leave now and don't come back, or you will find yourself with

a trespassing charge and jail time,"
Doctor Andrews said through his teeth.

"I'll be back with my lawyer and you'll
be sorry," Mr. Brown menaced.

Two security guards entered and
forcefully removed Mr. Brown from my
room. I began to shake like a leaf. I tried
to stop, but I grew frightened. Someone
had tried to kill me and that is why I was
in the hospital. What if it was Him, Mr.
Brown?

They wouldn't let him take me when he
talked to his lawyer? Would they? Words
I hadn't wanted to share, spilled out of
my mouth, first in torments, and then at a
screeching level.

"I don't know who the heck he is, but I do
know I don't know him. I'm not his
fiancée. Don't let him come back lawyer,
or no lawyer. I don't want to see him.
Someone did this to me! I wouldn't be
surprised if the person was him!" I guess I
appeared a little too hysterically and
forcefully, because the next thing that

occurred was Doctor Andrews plunged a needle into me.

"Please, please don't. It's not necessary, really. I'll be good," I pleaded too late.

"It's a little sedative. I don't like your colour, your blood pressure, or your heart rate. You've had a nasty scare and your body isn't able to cope with this right now. Calm down now," he said comforting "Go to sleep."

"I think I hate you," I replied vehemently.

"That's okay, you can hate me if you need to," he answered, smiling.

Damn him and his handsome smile! Something about the grin, made me want to smile back and tell him all my secrets.

"Don't leave me alone. He might come back," I pleaded as I drifted into a deep drugged sleep.

~0~

If you enjoyed *This Little Girl Had a Little Curl* please consider leaving me a few words at your favourite retailer and if you liked the excerpts and would like to read more of my books please check out one of my other books listed on the next page at Amazon

Sincerely S. G. Lee.

~0~

List of Books by S. G. Lee

Murder Mysteries:

The Kelly Murder Mysteries

Book 1-A Penny Saved A Murder Earned

Book 2- A Diller A Dollar A Really Dead Scholar

Book 3- Betty Blue Lost Her Holiday Shoe

Book 4- What Will Poor Robin Do?

Book 5- This Little Piggy Had None

Book 6- This Little Girl Had A Little Curl

Coming next year ~Book 7~ London Bridge Is Broken Down

The Kelly Murder Mysteries-Book 1-3

A Stitch in Time ~ prequel

The Stone Chronicles

Book1 -Love's Labour's Won

Book 2- A Tiger's Heart Wrapped in a Player's Hide

Coming Soon book 3 ~Hazard of the Die

Reborn – a novella~ prequel

Dreams Can Kill

The Sheriff Bullet Series

Book1- Stray Bullet

Book 2- Untraceable

Coming next year ~Book 3- Dead Center

Short Story Books

Murder Most Fowl

Jack be Nimble

Day of the Dead

Legends, Folktales and other Stories

The Stuff of Nightmares

ObsessionX2

Christmas Stories

Christmas is Calling

The Christmas Card

The Christmas Angel

Visions of Sugarplums

Poetry

A Poetic Touch - The Human Condition

Poetry in Motion ~ A Forest of Feelings

Children's Books

Mare the Hare

Henrietta and the Donor Egg

The Magical Life of Me

~0~

580
This Little Girl Had A Little Curl
S. G. Lee

www.ingramcontent.com/pod-product-compliance
Lightning Source LLC
Chambersburg PA
CBHW061520050726
47503CB00015B/2223